PRAIS
EKATERINA SI

The Secret History of Moscow

"Sedia's beautifully nuanced prose delivers both a uniquely enchanting fantasy and a thoughtful allegory that probes the Russian national psyche."

—*Booklist*

"A lovely, disconcerting book that does for Moscow what I hope my own *Neverwhere* may have done to London . . . "

—Neil Gaiman

"*The Secret History of Moscow* really feels like a secret: an alternative world a half-dimension removed from ours, a place woven out of whisper and shadow, populated with forgotten creatures and even less-remembered thoughts."

—*LA Times*

"A truly remarkable performance, written in a consistently graceful and focused prose, and it succeeds both as a coherent fantasy novel and a meditation on the anxieties of history."

—*Locus*

"Modern blue-collar Moscow is pitch-perfect . . . bustling yet seedy, disorganized and none too respectable."

—*Publishers Weekly*

The Alchemy of Stone

"Sedia's novel captures the surreal strangeness of a city whose power structure is about to be toppled, and her focus on Mattie's relationship with her creator allows her to grapple with the tiny power struggles inherent in all human relationships."

—io9

"Sedia's evocative third novel, a steampunk fable about the price of industrial development, deliberately skewers familiar ideas, leaving readers to reach their own conclusions about the proper balance of tradition and progress and what it means to be alive."

—*Publishers Weekly*, starred review

The House of Discarded Dreams

"Sedia's prose is a pleasure, her story a lovely place to have spent time, even with the horrors her characters face."

—*Booklist*

"A quirky, joyous fantasy, Sedia shows how competing natural and supernatural worldviews can enrich each other."

—*Publishers Weekly*

Heart of Iron

"Sedia superbly blends novel of manners, alternate history, and le Carré-style espionage with a dash of superheroes and steampunk."

—*Publishers Weekly*, starred review

MOSCOW BUT DREAMING

OTHER BOOKS BY EKATERINA SEDIA

Novels

The Secret History of Moscow
The Alchemy of Stone
The House of Discarded Dreams
Heart of Iron

Anthologies

Paper Cities
Running with the Pack
Bewere the Night
Circus: Fantasy Under the Big Top
Bloody Fabulous
Wilful Impropiety

MOSCOW BUT DREAMING

EKATERINA SEDIA

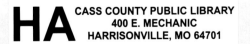
PRIME BOOKS

MOSCOW BUT DREAMING

Prime Books
www.prime-books.com

For more information, contact Prime Books:
prime@prime-books.com

ISBN: 978-1-60701-362-4

To everyone who was ever lost or found home.

CONTENTS

INTRODUCTION

The first piece of fiction I ever read by my fellow South Jerseyan, Ekaterina Sedia, was a story she sent me on the e-mail maybe a year or so before *The Secret History of Moscow* came out. I don't think it had the title it has now and I'm not sure that it hasn't been rewritten, but you can find its finished version in these pages, going by the title, "Zombie Lenin." I remember the ease with which I slid into this fiction—the writing was a joy, clear and flowing, and the story-line was dream-like and always potentially threatening. There's a scene where Sedia describes her zombie Lenin, and one of the attributes she gives him is that his flesh is "yellow." The use of that color in that instance really struck me, and I never forgot it. In fact, I "borrowed" it for a story I wrote years later. Since that first piece I read, I've followed her writing career, reading her fiction when I could find it and then eventually seeking it out.

Many of you will have read or at least heard of her novels, *The Secret History of Moscow* (ghosts of the Soviet Union, mythologies of old Russia, in a mosaic plot that gives a nod to Dante), *The Alchemy of Stone* (a dark, feminist, steampunk fairy tale with a sharp edge, every bit as good as Bacigalupi's *The Windup Girl*), *The House of Discarded Dreams* (the supernatural meets New Jersey reality in a lyrical and compelling fiction with my favorite female character of recent years—Vimbai). Each of these books is unique in style and structure, each brilliant in conception and brilliantly written. Don't take my word for it. You can read the accolades on-line from *The Guardian*, *Publishers Weekly*, *LA Times*, etc. Sedia is a major voice in novel-length speculative literature. It's my conjecture, though, that her short fiction is equally as important.

Sedia is part of a new wave of writers that have come to the fore since the onset of the 21st century. To generalize, they are incredible stylists, savvy craftsmen, and have a vision that exceeds the boundaries of the U.S. or U.K. (a side of the street worked for a long time by only Lucius Shepard and a handful of others). Along with Sedia, I'm thinking of Lavie Tidhar, Nnedi Okorafor, Hiromi Goto, Aliette de Bodard, etc. This is a welcome development for English language readers of the fantastic. In the stories in this collection, we get to experience the influence of Russia and the old Soviet Union, their realities and mythologies, their dreams and nightmares, and even in those stories that take place in the U.S., the pieces are informed by an outsider's sensibility that uncovers truths we natives had somewhere along the line willfully chosen to ignore.

As much as Sedia is part of this new wave, she is also part of a tradition in speculative fiction, that of remarkable female short story writers. This tradition has, in the last decade, really blossomed with the work of writers like Kelly Link, M. Rickert, Theodora Goss, Catherynne M. Valente, etc. (the list is long and growing). In trying to place Sedia in the current scene, it would be a mistake, though, to miss her idiosyncratic attributes, those things her stories do that the fiction of others does not.

A weak term to describe Sedia's short fiction would be "magical realism." At times, in order to submerge us into the story, she will use realism, but the magical parts of the stories aren't mere nods to the fantastic and the presence of the supernatural is usually not ambiguous. Her work is informed by a palpable sense of world mythology and specifically Russian folklore, often seen darkly, like nightmares in the light of day (shades of her countryman, Gogol). Sedia's fictional worlds many times are alive, almost anthropomorphic. I get a similar feel from them as I get in reaction to the old Fleischer Brothers cartoons from the 1930's. It's not that her houses have faces or that the clock has actual hands with gloves as the Brothers' did, but a sense that the world of the story has a certain sentience to it, more times malevolent than charmed. As in "The Bank of Burkina Faso," the darkness "*coagulates*" or this line from later in the piece—*And in his mind, another dance, entirely imaginary, unfolded slowly, like a paper fan in the hands of a young girl . . .* Although her writing is clear and unfettered, there is a richness of metaphor and simile that engenders this effect.

Another inimitable talent of Sedia's is that her stories defy you to figure out where they are headed, what the outcome will eventually be. She has a deftness with plots that turn, lyrically, like dreams, on a dime and take you far from their starting points. When you reach the end, though, there's a feeling that the journey, no matter how surreal, has made sense. There are no pat interpretations, but one is left with a field of possibility, and the contemplation of these stories, after you've finished reading them, will offer as much enjoyment and thought as the initial journey. I get the feeling that in the creation of her short fiction, she takes her hands off the wheel and lets her subconscious do the driving. There are no road maps. The story takes her where it needs to go and not the opposite.

For all of the dream-like, dark fairy tale nature of her stories, Sedia is capable of dealing with important contemporary themes in her work—child abuse, feminism, the futile nature of war, etc. The lyrical aspect of the fiction never blinds one to the real world, but instead is like some magical stereopticon that allows one to see with the help of the fantastic through to the heart of these issues.

All of this and more in a single volume that will delight readers of the fantastic and inspire story writers, who, like me, will be unable to refrain from "borrowing."

—Jeffrey Ford
author of *The Shadow Year*
and World Fantasy Award winner

A SHORT ENCYCLOPEDIA
OF LUNAR SEAS

1. *The Moscow Sea (Mare Moscoviense)*

Moscow is one of the most landlocked cities on Earth, but whatever disappears from it ends up in the Moscow Sea. The local inhabitants see a certain irony in that, and celebrate every new arrival. They cheered when the churches burned by Napoleon appeared and stood over the shallow waters of the sea, reflecting there along with the sparrows and the immigrants. They greeted the dead priests with coppers on their eyes, the hockey teams, the horse-drawn buggies. They are still waiting for the jackdaws, but the jackdaws are resilient, and they stay in their city.

Nowadays, if one looks into this shallow pool, one can still see the marching Red Armies, Belka and Strelka, and the Great October Revolution.

2. *The Sea of Rains (Mare Imbrium)*

The inhabitants of this sea are used to rain. It is a sea in name only, an empty basin long ago abandoned by water. But it rains every day. Sometimes, instead of water, flower petals fall from the sky; sometimes, it rains wooden horses and rubber duckies.

One rain everyone still remembers occurred a few years ago, when words fell from the sky. It did not stem for weeks, and the words filled the empty basin to overflowing. The inhabitants groaned and suffocated under the weight of accumulated regrets, promises, lies, report cards, great literature, pop songs, and shopping lists. They would surely perish unless something was done soon.

The council of the elders decided that they should drain the accumulated words, and in the course of their deliberations they realized that the words falling from the sky slowed down. So they decreed that it was the civic duty of every citizen to use up as many words as possible.

They bought telephones, and started telemarketing campaigns; they complained about their health and spun long tales for their children; they took to poetry.

Within days, the rain stopped; in the next month, the sea ran dry. Today, the inhabitants of this sea are mute, and the basin is empty—unless it rains nightingale songs or tiny blue iridescent fish.

3. *The Sea of Clouds (Mare Nubium)*

The Sea of Clouds is entirely contained by mountains, so high above the blue moon surface that the clouds fill the basin. Mermaids from all over the world make their yearly pilgrimage to this sea— they crawl over land, their tails trailing furrows in the blue dust, their breasts and elbows scuffed on the flat lunar stones. They leave traces of pale mermaid blood, its smell tinged with copper.

They cross the extensive ice fields, and their scales shine with the hoarfrost under the fickle lights of Aurora Borealis. Their breath clouds the air, so much so that the natives rarely travel in the thick fog of mermaid breath, lest they be lost forever.

In the end, the mermaids come to the Sea of Clouds, so just for a day they can swim in the sky and think themselves birds.

---

4. *The Sea of Crises (Mare Crisium)*

This sea looks deceptively calm if viewed from the surface, but on the bottom, where only the greenest of sunrays can penetrate, there is a city. Red algae line the streets, undulating in the current, and green, yellow, and white snails stud the sidewalks.

Every day, war rages in the streets. When the sun rises, opposing armies march along the storefronts and the boarded-up vacation houses. They meet at the corner, and the battle begins. By sunset, very few are left standing, and even they fade as the sun disappears behind the horizon. The next morning, they will start again.

There is no Valhalla on the Moon.

5. *The Sea of Fertility (Mare Fecunditatis)*

It is widely believed that the properties of this sea were discovered by accident, when the fresh waters ran red with blood, and poor women had nowhere to do their laundry. Out of despair, they turned to the sea. The clothes washed there turned stiff from the salt, and the hands of the women turned raw from scrubbing, the salt eating away at their joints and skin. Whoever wore these clothes caked with salt and blood found themselves blessed with many children, and this is how the sea received its name. A less known part of this legend is that those who were blessed by the sea cannot love their children—the salt is too bitter, and the blood burns too deep. They don't tell you this, because what parent would admit that their children are loathed monsters?

6. *The Sea of Tranquility (Mare Tranquillitatis)*

Those who live on the shores of the sea still remember the first moon landing. They remember two men clambering in their elaborate costumes, raising clouds of precious blue dust with every step. The natives stood dumbfounded, and then went to greet the visitors. But the Moon folk are difficult to see, even to their own kind, and the visitors ignored them, leaping with jubilation in the world where gravity was kind.

The natives laughed then, because the Earth men did not realize that if they only shed their heavy equipment, they could leap high enough to achieve nirvana.

7. *The Sea of Moisture (Mare Humorum)*

Everything rots in this climate. Even the precious stones and metals, brought for good luck, disintegrate in the damp air, leaving nothing but handfuls of soggy rust. But the plants love it. A single seed was brought by a basket merchant Eshlev as a gift to his young wife, and she planted it in a flowerpot.

The next morning, a green succulent stalk emerged; by the afternoon it had branched. The seedling gulped moisture from the air, and swelled with every passing minute. Its leaves unfurled like banners, and the stems pushed through every window and door and chimney. In a week's time, the plant had engulfed the house, burying Eshlev and his dogs and baskets deep inside. His wife sat outside, looking at the green hill that used to be her home with dazed eyes, waiting for her plant to bloom.

8. *The Sea of Ingenuity (Mare Ingenii)*

There once was an old man who built robots out of driftwood, seashells, and straw. His robots were clever machines, although even their creator wouldn't be able to tell you exactly how they worked. But worked they did, and when they were done with their chores, they went behind the old man's house, and built inventions of their own. To the untrained eyes, their project appeared as one long wing, and people laughed at the robots, for everyone knows that the atmosphere of the Moon is not dense enough to support flight. Even birds have to walk here.

But the robots were not deterred, and their wing grew larger by the day. They polished its surface and inlaid it with mother-of-pearl. The wing was ready, and when the robots held it up to the rising sun, the wing shuddered and took off.

All the people watched in wonderment as the wing shone in the sun and carried off the robots, propelled by the strength of the sunrays. The robots worked in unison, tilting their sail this way and that way to navigate, but nobody knows where they went. Some say, Mars.

9. The Sea of Serenity (Mare Serenitatis)

Widows come to this sea to cry, and they keep it full, brimming with water that forms a noticeable convex surface in the weak gravity of the Moon. The widows come from all over, icicles in their unbraided hair, empty hands folded over their empty wombs. They sit on the shore and weep, until their eyes turn red, and their lips crack and their breasts wither.

When they cannot cry any longer, they leave, their souls purged and as empty as their hands. Serenity is what is left when all the tears are cried out.

10. The Sea of Vapors (Mare Vaporum)

The steam of geysers and fonts of hot water conceals the outlines of this sea and the adjacent landmarks. No one is exactly sure what lies within the dense fog. But it is accepted as a likely speculation that the geysers are just a clever disguise, and that all the runaway children found a home there.

There are carnivals and circuses, trained elephants and tigers that do not bite, but eagerly lick every hand that offers them marzipans. There are merry-go-rounds, seesaws, fish tanks with the biggest fattest goldfish you have ever imagined, but no clowns. The witch's oven is far too small to fit even a scrawniest child.

There is not a single adult on the Moon who did not contemplate running away to the Sea of Vapors, but the fog is too dense.

11. *The Sea of the Known (Mare Cognitum)*

If one were to sit on the shore of this sea and peer deep into its transparent waters, one would see that the bottom is covered with a multitude of marbles—red, yellow, green, powder-blue, and clear with a blue spiral inside, the best of all. The marbles shift constantly in the current, and arrange themselves in elaborate patterns. If one were to assign them a numerical or alphabetic value, one would soon realize that the patterns only speak of the things that are true.

One would spend day after day, enraptured over all the facts in the universe revealed in no particular order. One would learn that the diameter of Phobos is 22.2 kilometers, that the ducks have a special gland at the base of their tails to keep their feathers waterproof, that cobalt melts at 1495°C, and that in 1495 Russia invaded Sweden.

Then inevitably one would grow impatient and stare at the marbles, frowning. None of the facts the sea tells have anything to do with the Moon itself. One could spend eternity staring into the Sea of the Known, yet learn nothing about it.

12. *The Eastern Sea (Mare Orientale)*

The Yellow Emperor washes all of his animals in this sea. They stare with their liquid eyes of every shade of jade, amber, and topaz, and their crested and maned heads bob obediently as the calm, warm waters lap at their sides. The salt stings a bit, but the Emperor likes his animals clean. They squint their eyes and dream of the days when they will be able to walk into the sea all by themselves, without whips and demanding clicks of human tongues.

13. *The Southern Sea (Mare Australe)*

The Southern Sea is warm and shallow, and the beach is soft sand. Starfish wander through the lapping waves, and suck the mussels dry. Old people like this sea. They chase advancing and retreating waves and toss oversized striped beach balls, and then they sit on the sand and drink Pepsi from warm glass bottles. They listen to the radio and aggregate in small groups, talking and whispering, and casting sideways glances at each other. They laugh, throwing back their heads, their hands covering the grinning lips.

It is always the summer of your thirteenth year by the Southern Sea.

14. *The Sea of Waves (Mare Undarum)*

A weighty galleon would seem a toy atop these waves. The endless moonquakes shake its bottom, and gigantic waves, unconstrained by gravity, pound the shores.

Those who have perished in earthquakes and tsunamis

make settlements here. Nobody forces them to, but many of the ghosts are unable to conceive of anything other than their own death. They stand and stare as the waves roll over the ground, swallowing their houses and oxen whole, poisoning their fields, ripping their life from them again and again.

Some move elsewhere, but there are always the new ones arriving.

15. *The Sea of Nectar (Mare Nectaris)*

The legends of this sea had long existed among the native folks, transmitted in fleeting whispers and shy glances from under lowered eyelashes. A few men, fed up with the stories, longed for sweetness on their lips—and sweetness was the concept only, for nothing on the Moon was ever sweet. Driven by the imaginary taste they could not fathom, they crossed vast empty plains and bristling mountain ranges. Many of them wandered into deep snow, a few more were crushed by falling boulders, one was sucked in by the mud, two released their grasp on their souls, three drowned, and one contracted diphtheria. All of them died, but continued on their way, unable to let go of what they could not even dream about. They reached the sea and cried, because the dead are unable to taste it.

16. *The Sea of the Edge (Mare Marginis)*

Here, the horizon is a razorblade, cutting the sky in two, and it bleeds at sundown and sunset. The cliffs are sharp, and the bottom of the sea is filled with jagged shards of broken mirrors.

Suicides come here, and wait in the piercing wind, looking at the precipitous drop in front of them. They imagine their slow fall and their flesh rent by the teeth of the universe all around them.

And then they jump. It takes a long time to fall on the Moon, and they see themselves reflected in the broken mirrors below.

17. *The Sea of Cold (Mare Frigoris)*

A long time ago, Emissary Togril sat by the shore of the sea and watched out of his slanted eyes as the sky lit up in streaks of blue and white, and the ribbons of color crackled and danced across the night. The light undulated and grew brighter, then faded and dispersed, like a drop of milk in a water bucket.

When only a faint glow remained of the former splendor, a weak phosphorescent shadow stretched downward. The air grew colder, and Togril smelled the spicy, sun-heated wormwood and tamarisk. The tentacles of light grew thicker, until white roads stretched between heaven and the lunar steppe.

Eleven columns of somber riders descended, their horses' hooves clanking, just above the edge of hearing, on the solid milky surface. Their breath did not cloud the air, and their armor—intricately decorated over the breastplate—was made of green translucent ice.

The procession of the warriors showed no sign of stemming, and streamed onto the ground. A cheetah sat behind each warrior, their eyes glowing frozen gold, their pink tongues hanging out, as if they had just vaulted into their masters' saddles after a chase. The leashes chaining the cats to the back bows of the saddles were spun out of thin links of the same green ice as the rest of the tack and armor.

The first rider approached Togril, and he flinched as a hoof caught him square in the chest. With a sharp stab of cold, the horse's leg pierced his chest and exited through his back. His scream froze in his throat as one after another spirit passed through him. The passage of the spirits inflicted no bodily harm, except the cold that settled deeper into his bones, so deep that it never left. The Sea too had retained the cold of the passage of dead Persian warriors forever.

18. *The Sea of Serpents (Mare Anguis)*

It is well known that the serpents with female breasts are the deadliest of all. They raise their narrow poisonous heads above the water, and their breasts bob in the waves.

The travelers know to avoid these monsters when the snakes haul themselves onto the beach and sunbathe under the grey lunar sky. The blue sand of the beach bears the scars in the shape of the snakes.

When the snakes lay their eggs on the beach, they coil around them in a protective spiral, and wait for the sound of faint cracking. Free of their shells, the newborn snakes drink once of their mothers' venomous milk, and swim into the sea. And woe is to the swimmer who comes across a mother snake who has just watched her brood disappear under the waves.

19. *The Sea of Islands (Mare Insularum)*

The islands that stud the calm surface of the sea, smooth as green glass, have long beckoned lovers and mariners. People looked at the round and oblong shapes rising from the sea, and dreamed of fragrant woods and glacial lakes, of buzzing of the bees suckling heavy roses, and metallic dragonflies perched atop nodding stems of lilies.

But the islands are really the humps of ancient monsters with leaden dead eyes and slow, rumbling thoughts. Occasionally, they whisper to each other in softest voices, but they never move or come up for a gulp of air or a taste of fish. They exhale cautiously, and the gentle waves raised by their breath lap at the shores of the islands. They die slowly, too shy to reveal themselves, their embarrassment the foundation of an exquisite illusion.

No matter how horrifying these monsters are, they know the value of appearing beautiful.

20. *The Sea of Foam (Mare Spumans)*

Everyone knows that when mermaids die they turn into foam, because they have no soul. On the Moon, however, every creature shares the fate of the mermaids.

The sea brims with multicolored bubbles, each of them reflecting all others for a short moment before bursting.

They do not visit graves on the Moon. Indeed, there are no graves at all. Those who tire of being dead blink out, and reappear in the Sea of Foam. Everything that has ever existed finds it way here, and the Sea of Foam contains, or will contain in a near future, all of the Moon.

CITIZEN KOMAROVA FINDS LOVE

The very little town of N. was largely bypassed by the revolution—the red cavalries thundered by, stopping only to appropriate the ill-gotten wealth of Countess Komarova, the lone survivor of N.'s only noble family. The wealth was somewhat less than the appropriators had anticipated—a ruined mansion and no funds to repair it. The Countess fled to the N.'s only inn, and the red cavalry moved on, but not before breaking all the windows of Komarov's mansion and allocating it for the local youth club.

Everyone knows what N.'s youth is like, and by fall most of the Countess' furniture was turned into firewood, and by mid-December the mansion stood abandoned and decrepit, and a turd frozen to its parquet floors served as its only furnishing and a testament of gloria mundi transiting hastily.

The countess herself, stripped of her title and now a simple Citizen Komarova, was used to poverty—before the revolution, she made her living as a piano teacher, but that winter, savage and bloody, pianos were turned into firewood, their strings now disembodied garrotes. In search of new means of genteel sustenance, she turned to seamstress shops, but no one was hiring. Nearing despair, she finally settled as a clerk in a consignment shop at the outskirts of N.

The owner of the shop, a man as old a he was ornery, let her rent the room above the shop, where the wind howled under the roof thatched with a ragtag team of tiles and shingles. There was a small and round metal stove, known colloquially as "bourgeoisie," as indiscriminate and insatiable as its namesake: it burned books, pianos, furniture, twigs, and entire palmate fir branches, crackling birch logs. It gave back cherry-red heat that spread in waves through the room over the shop, and broke over the stained walls, much like the distant Mediterranean over its rocky shores.

Citizen Komarova thought of the Mediterranean often— these were the vague memories of early childhood and its naive surprise at the shiny, tough leaves of the olive trees, over the white wide-brimmed hats and mustachioed men on the beach, over the mingling of salt and sun; memories almost obscene in the frozen and landlocked N. It was the only frivolity she allowed herself, and only when the metal stove made the air shimmer with concentrated heat before it dissipated in the cold cold winter nights. Then, Citizen Komarova hugged her bony shoulders, wrapped in the spiderweb of pilling, black crocheted shawl over the spiderweb of wrinkles etched in her dry parchment skin, and rocked back and forth on her bed and cried. The rusted springs beneath her, wrapped in a thin layer of torn and colorless rags, cried in unison.

During the day, when she was done crying over her lost Mediterranean family vacation, she minded the shop downstairs. It was a single room, but much larger than her garret above it, and its contents ebbed and flowed depending on the fortunes of the citizens of N.

By the middle of January, the lone room, echoey just this past December, became stifled with all the things people brought in, hoping that Citizen Komarova would somehow manage to sell them to someone more fortunate, even though whose fortunes were good remained to be seen. There were leather-wrapped yokes the collectivized farmers managed to keep for themselves and now were forced to let go off by bitter cold and steadily declining expectations; there were books with pages forever gone to hand-rolled cigarettes and missing title plates. Chipped china, pockmarked kettles, knives, scissors, ribbons, baskets, and moth-ravaged furs. Whatever nobility survived in the environs had gravitated towards N., bringing with them heavy brocade and monogrammed silverware. Several fox skins, both platinum and regular, stared at Citizen Komarova with their amber-colored glass eyes from dusty corners. She moved between the shelves, adjusting this and that, and casually swatting at pottery with a feather duster.

The first customer of the day surprised her—he stomped his feet and clapped his hands on the threshold, dislodging a small mound of snow off his boots held together by long cloth wrappings and his long military coat, its chest although still covered in white powder sporting recognizable chevrons and ribbons of the red cavalryman, one of Budyonny's fighters. His hat and a red star decorating it gave Komarova momentary chills and her knotted fingers curled around the feather duster defensively. She took a deep breath and stepped forth from behind the shelves, to meet the gaze of the cavalryman's clear eyes. The dead foxes stared too, transfixing the people in the crosshairs of their amber pupils.

"What can I do for you?" said Komarova. The flame of the kerosene lamp on the counter guttered in the draft from the door, and the cavalryman shut it without being told to.

"I have something I'd like to pawn," he said.

"It's a consignment store," she answered. "Which means we can sell it for you, but we cannot offer you any payment straight away."

"I can take it to the market then."

"You could, I suppose."

The two of them considered each other at length.

"What is it then?" citizen Komarova asked eventually; by then, the shadows had grown longer, and the fox eyes glittered in their corners.

The cavalryman dug through the deep pockets of his overcoat. The snow on his clothes had melted, and only tiny droplets clung to the tips of the stray woolen hair on his sleeves, like fur of a cat that came in from the rain and was about to irritably shake off the moisture. From his pocket, the man extracted four horseshoes from his pockets. "For good luck," he said.

"I can give you a copper," said citizen Komarova.

"It's a deal." The man smiled for the first time then, and she was startled by the glint of his teeth in the shadow of the shaggy unkempt beard, which looked unintentional to begin with. When he smiled like that, his eyes sunk and his mouth pulled back, and she felt a chill. She wrapped her shawl tighter still, and offered the payment on the palm of her hand.

He took it with cold fingers and was gone on a swirl of the coat, just as the four heavy horseshoes tumbled ringing to the floor. Citizen Komarova picked them up gingerly, and spent the rest of the afternoon stacking and unstacking them, and sometimes hanging them on the nails over the door for good luck. She was glad when the sun set and no one stepped foot into the shop for the rest of the day, leaving her to her thoughts and the visibly unlucky horseshoes.

The rest of January passed in the sparse slow sifting of snow from the clouds, grey and heavy like quicksilver. The stock of the consignment shop increased: every dress and fur coat and petticoat and necklace, every ring and feathered hat had made its way there, as the former nobility grew hungrier and less optimistic about the possible return of the old order of things. The corners were now filled with rustling of lace and slow undulations of peacock feathers, their unblinking green and azure eyes nodding in the drafts. Countess Komarova, who in her entire lifetime never experienced such luxury, stroked the ermine muffs and guarded them jealously from marauding moths.

She picked up delicate dresses, the lace ruffling on the chest white as foam, or the ones that were light as air, held together by the silken golden stitching. These were the dresses for waists much younger and slimmer than that of the former countess, their skirts long and stiff with golden thread, puffed with petticoats. And still she held them to her bust and looked at herself in the mirror, parallel wrinkles running along her cheeks made more severe by the ruffled collars, by the artificial flowers, feathers, colored buttons. Her eyes shone at her from the mirror and she reminded herself of a hungry cat, not a clear-eyed child of the Mediterranean vacation.

The last day of January brought with it a howling wind, a bitter cold, and another visit from the cavalryman. Citizen Komarova was a bit puzzled by his repeat visit—unlike most, he was already paid for his horseshoes, and the army of which he was a part had moved on a long time ago, so there was no reason for him lingering behind. With him, he brought the cutting wind and the sense of great desolation. As citizen Komarova stared into his eyes, she felt the awful sucking void tugging at her soul, and the whispers ebbed in her skull like the distant Mediterranean in a pink shell pressed against her child memory ear.

"I have something else," the cavalryman said.

"A copper," she answered without even asking what it was, as if some force nudged her from the inside.

His gaze lingered on her face and traveled down, softening. "It becomes you," he said, his hand motioning vaguely at her chest.

She looked down and blushed, suddenly aware of the lace shawl over the dress that neither belonged to nor fit her.

His large, square hand touched her elbow. "I'm Vasily Kropotkin," he said.

"Like the Prince."

"Exactly."

"What do you have for me then?"

Metal clanged to the ground—two sabers in rusted sheaths and a horseshoe, a set of gold-embroidered epaulettes and several medals citizen Komarova did not recognize. "Surely it's worth more than just one copper," Vasily said.

She gave him two. Her fingers, gathered into a pinch as if for a blessing, touched his palm as if it was a holy font, and again her mind was momentarily invaded by whispers and bubbling, hissing screams. She took a step back and he disappeared again— she could never see him actually leave, it was him and then the opened door and a swirl of snow, the ringing of his spurred boots on the frozen ground, his long coat sweeping the path in the snow. And then she was alone, among the glassy staring eyes of foxes and the silently accumulating dust. As soon as the sun went down, she fled up the stair into her small, virginal apartment where the heat from the potbellied stove chased away her fears that crowded so densely and so coldly in the shop downstairs, where the dresses rustled and the imaginary whispers grew louder after the sundown.

Vasily came back in the middle of February, when the wind chased the twisting snow serpents close to the cold ground, and the icicles fringing every doorway and window frame pointed down like transparent daggers, threatening to break off and pierce at any moment. The door clanged open, and the cavalryman—gaunter and sadder but unmistakably himself—smiled at her. His lips, bloodless and thin, pulled away from his teeth, and his cheekbones became suddenly prominent, and the thousand ghost eyes—sharp as the icicles sparkling along the top edge of the doorway—looked through his, grey and cold.

Citizen Komarova felt a chill, and yet her fingers reached out, a greening copper held between them. She touched his callused palm before he had a chance to chase horrors from his eyes and he smiled again, warming, becoming human at her mere touch. The foxes in the corners reared and whispered, baring their teeth, their weak dangling paws clenching, their eyes clear amber and malice. She paid them no mind.

"What do you have for me today?"

He gave her a burlap sack, its bottom dark and crusted. She looked inside, into the pink lace of frozen frothy blood to see a horse's leg, chopped off at the knee, its fetlock covered in long matted hair. She noticed round holes studding the circumference of the hoof and no horseshoe.

She looked away swallowing hard, fighting back a wave of nausea, a riptide of swirling blackness that edged into the field of her vision threatening to swallow it whole. His callused, working-class hand took hers, steadying her on her feet, and she blushed bright-crimson at his touch.

"I cannot give you more than one," she said.

"It's all right." He smiled. "I will bring more."

And before she could protest, before she could stop him, he was gone.

She had disturbing dreams that night—her usual memories of that one perfect summer overlapping over the more desolate and recent events, and one moment it was warm sand and smell of olive blooms, the next she felt callused working-class genitals pressed against the small of her back and she arched, sighed, and woke up, blushing, too hot to go back to sleep. And yet soon the waves pounded and the bed rocked under her, with the rhythm of the sea or something even more forgotten and unknowable, the warmth, the salt.

The shop downstairs caught the mild contagion of her dreams, the faint malaise—it behaved in the mornings, but as soon as darkened afternoons demanded that she lit the kerosene lamp on the counter, the shadows agitated the dresses, and the fox skins, shameless, wandered around the shop on their soft woolen legs. The severed horse's leg thumped on the hardwood tiles haughtily, searching for its missing horseshoe. The lace unraveled and the dresses paired up and twirled in a dance or flailing panic, and fur coats chased away the moths with their long sleeves and then silently stalked the fox skins, who had the advantages of having body shapes rather than being flayed and stitched to others like themselves. They also had eyes, unlike almost everything else in the shop, and they did a better job avoiding Citizen Komarova and not blundering blindly into her.

By the time of Great Lent, on Clean Monday, almost everyone in N. was hungry, and the fast seemed a necessity more than an imposition. When Citizen Komarova left the shop, chased away by the disturbing goings-on, she walked down the snow-paved streets, wondering to herself at how quiet everything was, before realizing that the missing sounds were those that used to belong to livestock—there was no mooing, bleating, nor clucking; no hissing nor barking nor quacking nor meowing, for that matter. Even the human voices were few and subdued. She walked to the bakery and bought a loaf of bread, dry and raspy with mixed-in chaff. She took it to her garret and crumbled it into a bowl of water, with just a splash of precious sunflower oil, and ate it slowly, chewing each bite a hundred times, stretching it, stretching like a winter night when the sleep would not come. The skin on her neck hung looser, a long sad flap. Her waist however had grown slimmer, and now most of the dresses in the shop were too large for her, their full skirts swirling of their own volition about her feet, and sometimes swaying with enough force to make her stumble or almost knock her off her feet. She wore them all the time now, never sure when Vasily Kropotkin would show up but confident that he would. She did not bother to explain to herself why his arrival was important, and why it mattered if he complimented her flowing skirts and delicate crocheted flowers winding about her throat, so beautiful.

He arrived late at night. The kerosene lamp was blown out and Citizen Komarova lay sleepless in her narrow bed in her narrow garret, one side of the roof above her slanting at a sharp angle, memories of past snowfalls whispering in the rafters.

She heard the heavy footsteps in the shop downstairs and lay on her back, listening intently, trying not to breathe so as not to miss the slightest sound—neither the jingling of spurs nor the creaking of the steps, nor the thump of a new burlap sack. It fell to the floor heavily and wetly, with a sucking thwack that made her skin crawl. She knew that she would never dare to look inside, but that the disembodied horse leg would probably investigate and lean against the sack forlornly, its furry fetlock matting with the slow seeping of thick black blood.

Of course he would want his payment—the steps creaked, closer and closer, and the chills and the whispers followed, reluctant to let him go.

The door creaked. Citizen Komarova licked her lips, and said in a small, croaking voice, squashed with terror and sadness, "I have no coppers to give you."

"It's too bad," he said. The bed creaked and shifted as he sat on its edge, invisible in the darkness but solid.

"There are some downstairs, in the shop," she said. "Come back in the morning."

His wide, warm palm touched her face gently but with a hidden threat of superior strength and class position. "Can I stay here?"

She nodded wordlessly, her lips and eyelashes brushing against the leathery contours of his open hand.

The bed creaked again, and she felt his weight pressed against her then on top of her, his fingers indenting the thin parchment skin of her inner thighs, pushing them apart. Their fumblings were short and dry and bruised, but citizen Komarova barely noticed: with every thrust of the knotted, gnarled body on top of her, her vision filled to brimming with unfamiliar sights.

She saw row after row of the red cavalrymen, their horses gone, lined along the darkened riverbank. She could not see their faces, shrouded in shadow as they were; only occasionally she caught a glint from under the visor of a red-starred hat. A glint of copper, she thought, before the man on top of her pulled away and she saw the ceiling of her garret, awash in the grey premonition of the morning, and then her eyes closed and she stared at the frothy waves of the sea, as they covered the white sand and retreated, leaving in their wake perfect lacy patterns of foam, even and complex like crocheted doilies the local nobility left by the dozen in the shop downstairs.

Then there was the ceiling and warm breath on her face, and then it all drowned in the clanging of metal and sparks flying from clashing of the sabers, the whinnying of the horses, and the quick stuttering ta-ta-ta of the machine gun. There was mud and a slippery road, and a lightweight cart with a mounted machine gun but no rider, pulled by a single spooked horse. The two-wheeled cart tilted and tipped over, and the horse slid, its hooves (devoid of horseshoes) splattering mud and mustard-yellow clay over its hide dark with sweat, before it tumbled down, its hind right leg giving under it awkwardly, with a crack that resonated through her bones.

The man on top of her exhaled a muffled curse and pulled away for one last time, leaving her with a brief but searing impression of several cavalrymen surrounding her bed in a semicircle, pressing closer intently as if they wanted to see better. She pulled the covers all the way to her chin and they leered at her, a few of them smirking under the coppers on their eyelids.

"Is this why you need money?" she whispered, and nodded at the silent invisible throng. "For them?"

He seemed neither surprised nor perturbed by citizen Komarova's observation. He rolled on his back, hands under his head and sighed. "Yes. They need coppers to cross over, and I am supposed to get it for them."

"Why you?"

(The dead in her mind's eye stared, some with copper, others—with eyes white as boiled eggs.)

"I was the only one who survived." He sighed. "The White Army, the Black Army—goddamn Makhno!—too many, too many. When there's only one man left alive from the entire regiment, he has to take care of his dead. They sure aren't taking care of themselves."

"I can help you," she whispered, the skin on her throat unusually tight, constricting.

They came downstairs when it was still barely light. The air colored whisper grey, like a dove's underside, pooled in the corners, and soft cold drafts moved the heavy folds of dresses— all but one, a white lacy number that twirled in a dance with a shearling overcoat, oblivious to a gruesome beast that was busily self-assembling from the dismembered horse parts and a fox pelt, all mismatched fur and yellow glow of glassy eyes, teeth and hooves and frozen blood, pink like cherry petals in the spring that was too far away, too hungry and cold to even dream about.

"I know where the owner keeps the shop's take," she said. "He never takes it home—afraid of the thieves. He thinks here no one will find it."

"He'll know it was you."

She sighed and patted his head—lumpy, old scars bulging like veins under his greying and short and badly cut hair. There were probably lice, she thought with only a distant shudder of disgust. There were always lice on these people, no wonder they were so eager to call everyone "bloodsuckers" and appropriate the appropriators, or whatever nonsensical phrase they were using nowadays. Worse yet, they were right. She closed her eyes for a second, to gather her courage. It was the least she could do. "It doesn't matter," she said. "I will show them."

The small chest, wrapped in copper straps mostly for show, was hidden in its usual place—in the bottom of a larger, almost identical chest filled to overflowing with spotted linens, torn doilies, and torn drapes, with broken flowers of white silk and yellowing muffs. She took the little chest out of its soft nest and blew on it, gently displacing stray threads and cobwebs.

They left the paper money—who had use for it anyway, in the town where it would only buy a loaf of stale bread and a jar of sunflower oil?—and took all the coins, all colors, all sizes. Copper and silver, the old Tsar coins and the new ones. Ghostly fingers reached for them and the red stars of the ghosts' hats flashed in the morning light multiplied by many faces of the coins, and soon all their white eyes were hidden under the soft shine or green patina of metal.

"It is time," citizen Komarova said softly.

He gave her a puzzled look.

"I told you I would show them. Only you will have to help me."

They went back up the rickety stairs, with the composite horse-fox pawing at her hems with its toes and hooves and barking piteously. Soon, the strange beast was left behind, and citizen Komarova lay on her maiden-narrow bed. The ruffles brushed her chin and hid her neck, and the lace over her breast lay smooth, virginal-white.

She closed her eyes and told Vasily Kropotkin what he must do. He hesitated a while, but he was a soldier and she was a parasite, no matter how appropriated. He found the class strength within him, and his heavy hands stroked her throat. There were a few minutes of blind kicking panic, and the sound of either a crushed trachea or of broken bones of the fox-horse as it lost its footing and tumbled down the stairs.

But soon enough her eyes closed under two coppers, and she stood on the Mediterranean shore, a pink shell clasped in her hands, and an entire regiment of the Red Army crowding behind her, eager like children to see the white sand and the gentle waves and sea, blue as nothing they had ever seen before.

TIN CANS

I am an old man—too old to really care. My wife died on the day the Moscow Olympics opened, and my dick had not done anything interesting since the too optimistic Chechen independence. I shock people when I tell them how young I was when the battleship Aurora gave its fateful blast announcing the Revolution. And yet, life feels so short, and this is why I'm telling you this story.

My grand-nephew Danila—smug and slippery, like all young people nowadays, convinced they know the score even though they don't know shit, and I always get an urge to take off my belt and wail some humility on their asses—called and asked if I needed a job. Tunisian Embassy, he said, easy enough. Night watchman duty only, since for business hours they had their own guards, tall and square-chested, shining and black like well-polished boots, their teeth like piano keys. You get to guard at night, old man, old husk, when no one would see you.

Now, I needed a job; of course I did, who didn't? After the horrible and hungry 1990, even years later, I was just one blind drunken stagger of the inflation away from picking empty bottles in the streets or playing my accordion by the subway station. So of course I said yes, even though Danila's combination of ignorance and smarm irritated me deeply, just like many things did—and it wasn't my age, it was these stupid times.

The Embassy was located in Malaya Nikitskaya, in a large mansion surrounded by a park with nice shady trees and flowerbeds, all tucked away behind a thirty-foot brick fence. I saw it often enough. The fence, I mean. I had never been inside before the day of my interview. All I knew about Tunisia was that they used to be Carthage at some point, very long ago, and that they used to have Hannibal and his elephants—I thought of elephants in the zoo when I paused by the flowerbeds to straighten my jacket and adjust the bar ribbons on my lapel. There used to be a time when war was good and sensible, or at the very least there were elephants involved.

There were no lines snaking around the building, like you would see at the American embassy—not surprising really, because no one wanted to immigrate to Tunisia and everyone was gagging for Brooklyn. I've been, I traveled—and I don't know why anyone would voluntarily live in Brighton Beach, that sad and gray throwback to the provincial towns of the USSR in the seventies, fringed by the dirty hem of a particularly desperate ocean. The irony is of course that every time you're running from something, it follows you around, like a tin can tied to dog's shaggy tail. Those Brooklyn inhabitants, they brought everything they hated with them.

That was the only reason I stayed here, in this cursed country, in this cursed house, and now stood at the threshold, staring at the blue uniforms and shining buttons of two strapping Tunisians—guards or attachés, I wasn't sure—and I wasn't running anywhere, not to Brooklyn, nor to distant and bright Tunisia with its ochre sands and suffocating nights. Instead, I said, "I heard you're hiring night watchmen."

They showed me in and let me fill out the application. There were no pens, and I filled it out with the stubby pencil I usually carried with me, wetting its blunt soapy tip on my tongue every few letters—this way, my words came out bright and convincing. As much as it chafed me, I put Danila's name as a reference.

They called me the next day to offer me the job, and told me to come by after hours two days later.

It was May then. May with its late sunsets and long inky shadows, pooling darkness underneath the blooming lilac bushes, and clanging of trams reaching into the courtyard of the house in Malaya Nikitskaya from the cruel and dirty world beyond its walls. I entered in a shuffling slow walk—not the walk of old age, but of experience.

And yet, soon enough there I was. As soon as the wrought iron gates slammed shut behind my back, I felt cut off from everything, as if I had really escaped into glorious Carthage squeezed into a five-storied mansion and the small garden surrounding it. A tall diplomat and his wife, her head wrapped in a colorful scarf, strolled arm in arm, as out of place in Moscow as I would be in Tunisia. They did not notice me, of course—after you reach a certain age, people's eyes slide right off of you, afraid that the sight of you will corrupt and age their vision, and who wants that?

So I started at the embassy—guarding empty corridors, strolling with my flashlight along the short but convoluted paths in the garden, ascending and descending stairs in no particular order. Sometimes I saw one diplomat or another walking down the hall to the bathroom, their eyes half-closed and filled with sleep. They moved right past me, and I knew better than to say anything—because who wants to be acknowledged while hurrying to the john in the middle of the night. So I pretended that I was invisible, until the day I saw the naked girl.

Of course I knew whose house it was—whose house it used to be. I remembered Lavrentiy Beria's arrest, back in the fifties, his fat sausage fingers on the buttonless fly, holding up his pants. Khrushchev was so afraid of him, he instructed Marshal Zhukov and his men who made the arrest to cut off the buttons so that his terrible hands would be occupied. It should've been comical, but it was terrible instead, those small ridiculous motions of the man whose name no one said aloud, for fear of summoning him. Worse than Stalin, they said, and after Stalin was dead they dared to arrest Beria, his right hand, citing some ridiculous excuses like British espionage and imaginary plots. The man who murdered Russians, Georgians, Polacks with equal and indiscriminating efficiency when he was the head of NKVD, before it softened up into the KGB. And there he was then, being led out of the Presidium session, unclean and repulsive like a carrion fly.

He was shot soon after, they said, but it was still murder; at least, I thought so, seeking to if not justify, then comprehend, thinking around and around and hastening my step involuntarily.

Sometimes the attachés, while rushing for the bathrooms, left their doors ajar, illuminated by the brass sconces on the walls, their semicircles of light snatching the buttery gloss of mahogany furniture and the slightly indecent spillage of stiff linen, the burden of excess. But mostly I walked the hallways, thinking of everything that happened in this house, so I wasn't all that surprised or shocked when I first saw the naked girl.

She must've been barely thirteen—her breasts uncomfortable little hillocks, her hips narrow and long. She ran down the hall, and I guessed that she did not belong—she did not seem

Tunisian, or alive, for that matter. She just ran, her mouth a black distorted silent hole in her face, her eyes bruised. Her hair, shoulder-length, wheat-colored, streamed behind her, and I remember the hollow on the side of her smooth lean hip, the way it reflected light from my flashlight, the working of ropy muscles under her smooth skin. Oh, she really ran, her heels digging into the hardwood floors as if they were soft dirt, her fists pumping.

I followed her with the beam of my flashlight. I stopped dead in my tracks, did not dare to think about it yet, just watched and felt my breathing grow lighter. She reached the end of the hallway and I expected her to disappear or take off up or down the stairs, or turn around; instead, she stopped just before the stairwell, and started striking the air in front of her with both fists, as if there was a door.

She turned once, her face half-melting in the deluge of ghost tears, her fists still pummeling against the invisible door, but without conviction, her heart ready to give out. Then an invisible but rough hand jerked her away from the door—I could not see who was doing it, but I saw her feet leave the ground, and then she was dragged along the hardwood floors through the nearest closed door.

I stood in the hallway for a while, letting it all sink in. Of course I knew who she was—not her name or anything, but what happened to her. I stared at the locked door; I knew that behind it the consul and his wife slept in a four-postered bed. And yet, in the very same bed, there was that ghost girl, hairs on her thin arms standing on end and her mouth still torn by a scream, invisible hands pressing her face into a pillow, her legs jerking and kicking at the invisible assailant . . . I was almost relieved that I could not see him, even though the moment I turned and started down the hallway again, his bespectacled face slowly materialized, like a photo being developed, on the inside of my eyelids, and I could not shake the sense of his presence until the sun rose.

I soon found a routine with my new job: all night I walked through the stairwells and the corridors, sometimes dodging the ghosts of girls—there were so many, so many, all of them between twelve and eighteen, all of them terrible in their nudity—and living diplomats who stayed at the Embassy stumbling past the soft shine of their gold-plated fixtures on their way to the bathrooms. In the mornings, I went to a small coffee house to have a cup of very hot and sweet and black coffee with a thick layer of sludge in the bottom. I drank it in deliberate sips and thought of the heavy doors with iron bolts and the basement with too many chambers and lopsided cement walls no one dared to disturb because of what they were afraid to find buried under and inside of them. And then I hurried home, in case my son decided to call from his time zone eight hours behind, before he went to bed.

You know that you're old when your children are old, when they have heart trouble and sciatica, when their hearing is going too so that both of you yell into the shell of the phone receiver. But most often, he doesn't call—and I do not blame him, I wouldn't call me either. He hadn't forgiven and he never fully will, except maybe on his deathbed—and it saddens me to think that he might be arriving there before me, like it saddens me that my grandchildren cannot read Cyrillic.

I come home and wait for the phone to speak to me in its low sentimental treble, and then I go to bed. I close my eyes and I watch the images from the previous night. I watch seven girls, none of whom can be older than fourteen, all on their hands and knees in a circle, their heads pressed together, their naked bottoms raised high, I watch them flinch away from the invisible presence that circles and circles them, endlessly. I think that I can feel the gust of Beria's stroll on my face, but that too passes.

I only turn away when one of them jerks as her leg rises high in the air—and from the depressions on the ghostly flesh I know that there's a hand seizing her by the ankle. He drags her away from the circle as she tries to kick with her free foot, grabbing at the long nap of the rug, as her elbows and breasts leave troughs in it, as her fingers tangle in the Persian luxury and then let go with the breaking of already short nails. I turn away because I know what happens next, and even though I cannot see him, I cannot watch.

Morning comes eventually, and always at the time when I lose hope that the sun will ever rise again. I swear to myself that I will not come back here. *Never again*, I whisper—the same oath I gave to myself back before the war, and just like back then I know that I will break it over and over, every night.

On my way out of the light blue embassy house, I occasionally run into the cook, a Pakistani who has been working there for a few years. We sometimes stop for a smoke and he tells me about a bag of bones he found in the wall behind the stove some years back. He offers to show it to me but I refuse politely, scared of the stupid urban legend about a man who buys a hotdog and inside finds his wife's finger bone with her wedding ring still on. The ghosts are bad enough.

During this time, my son only called once. He complained at length, speaking hastily, as if trying to prevent me from talking back. I waited. I did not really expect him to talk about things we did not talk about—why he left or why he never told his wife where I was working. In turn, I made sympathetic noises and never mentioned how angry I was that his emigration back in the '70s fucked me over. What was the point? I did not blame him for his mother's death, and he didn't blame me for anything. He just complained that his grandkids don't understand Russian. I don't even remember what they, or their parents, my own grandchildren, look like.

When he was done talking, I went to bed and even slept until the voices of children outside woke me in the early afternoon. They always carried so far in this weather, those first warm days of not-quite summer, and I lay awake on my back listening to the high-pitched squealing outside, too warm in my long underwear. And if your life is like mine—if it's as long as mine, that is—then you find yourself thinking about a lot of shit. You start remembering the terrible sludge of life at the bottom of your memory, and if you stir it by too much thinking, too much listening to the shouts and bicycle bells outside, then woe is you, and the ghosts of teenage girls will keep you up all night and all day.

The cars NKVD drove were called black ravens, named for both color and the ominous nature of their arrival in one's neighborhood. *Narodniy Komissariat Vnutrennih Del*—it's a habit, to sound out the entire name in my head. Abbreviations just don't terrify me. The modern yellow canaries of the police seemed harmless in comparison, quaint even. But those black ravens . . . I remembered the sinister yellow beams of the headlights like I remembered the squeaking of leather against leather, uniform against the seats, like I remembered the roundness of the hard wheel under my gloved hands.

Being a chauffeur was never a prestigious job, but driving him—driving Beria—filled one with quiet dread. I remember the blue dusk and the snowdrifts of late February, the bright pinpricks of the streetlamps as they lit up ahead of my car, one by one, as if running from us—from him, I think. I have never done anything wrong, but my neck prickles with freshly cut hairs, and my head sweats under my leather cap. I can feel his gaze on me, like a touch of greasy fingers. Funny, that: one can live ninety years, such a long life, and still shiver in the warm May afternoon just thinking about that one February night.

It started to snow soon after the streetlights all flickered on, lining along the facades of the houses—all old mansions, being in the center of the city and all, painted pale blues and yellows and greens. The flight of the lights reminded me of a poem I read some years ago; only I could not remember it but tried nonetheless—anything to avoid the sensation of the sticky unclean stare on the back of my head, at the base of my skull, and I felt cold, as if a gun barrel rested there.

"Slow down," he tells me in a soft voice. There's no one but him in the car, and I am grateful for small mercies, I am grateful that except for directions he does not talk to me.

I slow down. The wind is kicking up the snow and it writhes, serpentine, close to the ground, barely reaching up high enough to get snagged in the lights of the car beams.

"Turn off the lights."

I do, and then I see her—bundled up in an old, moth-eaten fur coat, her head swaddled in a thick kerchief. I recognize her—Ninochka, a neighbor who is rumored to be a bit addled in the head, but she always says hello to me and she is always friendly. The coat and kerchief disfigure and bloat her as she trundles through the snow, her walk waddling in her thick felt boots that look like they used to belong to her grandfather. I hope that this misshapen, ugly disguise would be enough to save her.

I pick up the speed slightly, to save her, to drive past her and perhaps find another girl walking home from work late, find another one—someone I do not know, and it is unfair that I am so willing to trade one for another but here we are—just God please, let us pass her. In my head, I make deals with God, promises I would never be able to keep. I do not know why it's so important, but it feels that if I could just save her, just this one, then things would be all right again, the world would be revealed as a little bit just and at least somewhat sensible. Just this one, please god.

"Slow down," he says again, and I feel the leather on the back of my seat shift as he grips the top of it. "Stop right there." He points just ahead, at the pool of darkness between two cones of light, where the snow changes color from white to blue. The wind is swirling around his shoes as he steps out, and the girl, Ninochka, looks up for the first time. She does not recognize him—not at first, not later when she is sobbing quietly in the back seat of the car, her arms twisted behind her so that she cannot even wipe her face and her tears drip off the reddened tip off her nose, like a melting icicle. I still cannot remember the poem—something about the running streetlights, and I concentrate on the elusive rhythm and stare straight ahead, until I stop by the wrought iron gates of his house and let him and Ninochka out. I am not allowed beyond that point, being just a chauffeur and not an NKVD man. I am grateful.

So I thought that my presence in the sky-blue house was not coincidental, and the fact that I kept seeing the dead naked girls everywhere I looked meant something. I tried to not look into their faces, not when they were clumped, heads together, in a circle. I did not need to see their faces to know that Ninochka was somewhere among them, a transparent long-limbed apparition being hauled off into some secret dungeon to undergo things best not thought about—and I squeezed my eyes shut and shook my head, just not to think about that, not to think.

My son was a dissident, and to him there was no poison more bitter than the knowledge that his father used to work for NKVD, used to turn people in, used to sit on people's tribunals that condemned enemies of the state. His shame for my sins forced his pointless flight into the place that offered none of the freedoms it had previously promised, the illusory comforts of the familiar language and the same conversations, of the slowly corrupting English words and the joys of capitalism as small and trivial as the cockroaches in a Brighton Beach kitchen. He still does not see the irony in that.

But he does manage to feel superior to me; he feels like he is better because he's not the one with naked dead girls chasing him through dreams and working hours, crowding in his head during the precious few minutes of leisure. The bar ribbons of all my medals and orders are of no consequence, as if there had been no war after the slow stealthy drives through the streets. Seasons changed but not the girls, forever trapped in the precarious land between adolescence and maturity, and if there were no victories and marching through mud all the way to Germany and back, as if there was nothing else after these girls. Time stopped in 1938, I suspect, and now it just keeps replaying in the house in Malaya Nikitskaya. And I cannot look away and I cannot quit the job in the embassy—not until I either figure out why this is happening or decide that I do not care enough to find out.

I remember the last week I worked in the Tunisian Embassy. The dead girls infected everything, and even the diplomats and the security saw them out of the corners of their eyes—I saw them tossing up their heads on the way to the bathroom, their eyes wide and awake like those of spooked horses. The girls—long-limbed, bruised-pale—ran down every hallway, their faces looming up from every stairwell, every corner, every glass of sweet dark tea the Pakistani cook brewed for me in the mornings.

The diplomats whispered in their strange tongue, the tongue, I imagined, that remained unchanged since Hannibal and his elephants. I guessed that the girls were getting to them too, and for a brief while I was relating to these foreign dignitaries. Then they decided to deal with the problem, something I had not really considered, content in my unrelenting terror. They decided to take apart the fake partitions in the basement.

I was told to not come to work for a few days, and that damn near killed me. I could not sleep at night, thinking of the pale wraiths streaming in the dark paneled hallways of the sky-blue house. But the heart, the heart of it were all these dead girls, and I worried about them—I feared that they would exorcise them, would chase them away, leaving me no reason to ever go back, no reason to wake up every day, shave, leave the house. I could not know whether the semblance of life granted to them was torturous, and yet I hoped that they would survive.

They did not. When I came back, I found the basement devoid of its fake cement partitions, and the bricks in the basement walls were held together with fresh mortar. The corridors and the rooms were empty too—I often turned, having imagined a flick of movement on the periphery of my vision. I looked into the empty rooms, hoping to catch a glimpse of long legs shredding the air into long, sickle-shaped slivers.

I found them after morning came and the cook offered me the usual glass of tea, dark and sweet and fragrant.

"They found all these bones," he told me, his voice regretful. "Even more than my bag, the one I told you about before."

"Where did they take them?"

He shrugged and shook his head, opening his arms palms-out in a pantomime of sincere puzzlement. I already knew that they were not in the house, because of course I already looked everywhere I could look without disturbing any of the diplomats' sleep.

Before I left for the day, I looked in the yard. It was so quiet there, so separate from the world outside. So peaceful. I found the skulls lined under the trees behind the building, where the graveled path traveled between the house and the wall.

I looked at the row of skulls, all of them with one hole through the base, and I regretted that I had never seen Ninochka's face among the silent wraiths. I did not know which one of these skulls was hers; all of them looked at me with black holes of their sockets, and I thought I heard the faint rattling of the bullets inside them, the cluttering that grew louder like that of the tin cans dragging behind a running dog.

I turned away and walked toward the gates, trying to keep my steps slow and calm, trying to ignore the rattling of the skulls that had been dragging behind me for the last sixty years.

ONE, TWO, THREE

When Anton and Claudia moved into their new house in an Ohio suburb, they thought it was a sign of how things would be from now on—new and clean and brilliant. Now they could start a family, although Claudia disliked that expression.

"It's not like we're not a family," she told Anton after another phone conversation with her mother. Claudia's relatives, a loud clan of sun-baked, stocky Bulgars, intimidated Anton to such an extent that he loathed disagreeing with them, even in their absence.

"You know what she means," he told his wife, and put his arm around her slender hips. "It's just not the same without children."

Claudia nodded and gently wrestled from under his heavy arm. "I better get the dinner started," she said. She slipped into the kitchen and chopped onions and carrots, then tenderized chicken cutlets with a wooden mallet. She would never be enough for him, she thought. She wanted a baby, sure enough, but she wished it were not required to be complete.

When Anton started his new job, she stayed home, working in the garden, building a chicken coop, embroidering curtains and knitting baby jumpers, striped green, yellow, and red—her only rebellion against tradition, but she just couldn't stomach any pink and blue. She fed the chickens, and made pancakes and crepes for Fat Tuesday. When March came, she made martenitsas—little red and white yarn dolls—and hung them over windows and doors to greet the arrival of spring. But she just couldn't get pregnant.

At first, Claudia resisted seeing the doctor, afraid to give Anton more ammunition he would use to blame her for her inadequacy. Soon she ran out of excuses, and sat in the doctor's office as the doctor explained the common causes of infertility. Anton's gray gaze hung over Claudia like a rain cloud, and she knew he was not paying attention to the doctor, but quietly smoldering, furious that his wife was defective.

A few weeks later, when the doctor informed them that there was nothing wrong with her, Claudia felt a short-lived burst of satisfaction. It was Anton who had the problem.

The doctor suggested artificial insemination, anonymous donors. Claudia looked at Anton with hope. She did want a baby, after all, but Anton would not hear of it. Claudia proposed adoption, but he only sighed and shook his dark-haired head. It was expensive, he said; Claudia did not argue, knowing that Anton would not raise a child that was not his.

By the time March came again, Claudia busied herself with tying together bundles of red and white yarn, and hanging her martenitsas above every window and doorway. Most of the residents in Somerville, Ohio did not know what these dolls were, but other Bulgarians instantly recognized the traditional greeting of the springtime. And so did other Slavs, even those that weren't quite human.

The first sign that something was amiss came when Claudia went into the basement to fetch some pickles and raspberry preserves she'd made last fall. She skipped down the steps, invigorated by the fresh bite in the air, and a large onion flew past her head.

Claudia gave a small cry of alarm, and squinted into the dusk of the basement. Another onion hit her in the shoulder, with little force but startling nonetheless.

"Who's there?" Claudia said, in English and then Bulgarian.

Another onion (that missed badly) was her only answer.

Claudia ran over to the barrel with onions, and dodged another projectile. Her assailant, moving with such speed that its outline blurred, rushed past her and up the stairs. She chased after, encouraged by the fact that her assailant was rather small.

Outside, there was no sign of the attacker, and when Anton came home, he only laughed at her story. However when a horrid racket woke them up in the middle of the night, Anton was not laughing. He grabbed the baseball bat he kept by the bed for such an occasion, and tiptoed into the kitchen, hitching up his pajama bottoms nervously. Claudia followed, less alarmed, feeling vindicated.

Their best china—wedding gifts from countless relatives— lay in shards on the kitchen tiles, glistening in the moonlight seeping through the window. The screen door flapped in the wind. The mysterious little troublemaker was nowhere in sight, but high-pitched shrieks and ululations started outside.

"What the hell?" Anton hefted his bat and headed outside.

The screams came from the chicken coop in the back yard, but quieted as soon as Anton and Claudia reached the door.

"Shh," Claudia whispered. "Listen."

"One, two, three," came a little stuttering voice from inside the coop. "One, two, three . . ."

Anton threw the door open, and in the swath of moonlight they saw a little girl, dressed in a poorly patched potato sack. She was counting chickens, but turned toward the sound of the opening door, her eyes flashing huge and dark, and shrieked.

Before Claudia or Anton could react, she rushed outside, running so close to Claudia that she felt a brush of cloth and a gust of icy wind, but no flesh.

The mysterious girl carried on like that, throwing onions and potatoes, breaking dishes and preserve jars, and shrieking in the coop. She could only count to three, but that did not stop her obsessive attempts to count clucking, ruffled chickens.

"One, two, three," she screamed, sending them into a wild flapping panic. "One, two, three!" All attempts to chase her away brought only temporary relief.

Claudia became convinced that the wild girl was not of any earthly agency. She asked her mother to send any and all books of fairytales and folk superstitions she could find. Claudia found the answer in one of the books describing the pagan Slavic traditions. Eastern peoples spoke of the malevolent house spirit called Kikimora. Claudia could not wait to tell Anton about her discovery.

For once, he listened. Dark circles under his eyes spoke of his lack of rest, and Claudia was certain that his willingness to listen was due to his exhaustion.

"See?" Claudia showed him the picture of a lopsided girl. "It says here, the kikimoras throw onions, break dishes and count livestock, but can't go past three."

"Yep," Anton said. "Sounds like one of those things. What else does it say?"

"It says that they can't sew, but try anyway. The stitches all come out crooked and weak. It says that before misfortune they make lace, and clicking and rattling of their bobbins keeps the inhabitants of the possessed house up all night."

Anton yawned and rubbed his face. "Does it say how to get rid of them?"

Claudia paused for a moment, thinking of the best way to translate the words on the page in front of her. "If you catch her and cut the shape of a cross into her hair, she will become human."

"What else?"

Claudia flipped through the book. "Doesn't say anything else."

"I suppose it could work," Anton said. "If she becomes a person, we can hand her over to the police."

Claudia nodded. *Or we can keep her*, she thought. Some things were best left unsaid, and thought about only in Bulgarian.

"How do we catch it?"

"It says the kikimoras can't resist bobbins, warm milk, and unfinished sewing."

"Let's try all of those," Anton said, his eyes glinting with unexpected enthusiasm.

Before they went to bed, they laid out their enticements on the kitchen table: Claudia's mother's birchwood bobbins, a cup of microwaved milk, and one of Anton's shirts Claudia began to hem, but never got around to finishing. Next to the shirt they left thread and needles, turned off the lights, and stomped to the bedroom with an overwrought display of fatigue. They stretched, yawned, and told each other how tired they were; they giggled like children at their deceit, and whispered conspiratorially, their lips brushing past the other's ears. Claudia could not remember the last time she felt so close to him; they lay in bed, listening, whispering, holding hands.

At midnight, the kikimora started her habitual wailing and screeching and shattering of now sparse glass, but soon she fell quiet. There was a brief clatter of the bobbins, and Claudia tensed and sat up, grabbing a pair of scissors from the bedside table. Anton and Claudia tiptoed back to the kitchen, and watched silently as the kikimora drained the milk in one long thirsty swallow, and started on sewing. She was no better at it than at counting, but persisted, quickly covering the bottom of Anton's shirt in mismatched tracks of stitches and crooked seams that weaved through the fabric like the footprints of a drunk in the snow. She was so preoccupied with her task, her small soiled hands flying, that she did not notice when Claudia snuck up behind her.

Claudia grabbed the small body, disconcertingly cold and slippery, and hugged it tight to her chest. The kikimora shrieked and flailed with the strength surprising in someone so small. She almost kicked free, but Anton grabbed her reed-thin shoulders and pinned them to the floor. Her legs kicked up, blurring with speed, and she screamed and screamed, like a wounded animal. Claudia's hands shook as she took the scissors to the creature's wispy hair, and with two swift strokes exposed a cross-shaped patch of her white skull.

The girl went quiet and limp, her eyes rolling back in her head. For one dreary moment, Claudia feared that they killed her, and she shook the girl—so tiny, she couldn't be more than three years old—until her eyes swiveled back and met Claudia's. "Ba-ba," the girl said.

"Where did you find her?" said the social worker, looking up with tired eyes from his paper-littered desk.

"She was hiding in our cellar," Anton answered. "We found her yesterday."

"We'll check her against all missing persons reports," the social worker said. "Thanks for bringing her in."

The little girl, sensing that something was amiss, grabbed onto Claudia's hand, looking at her with pleading dark eyes. She had quite a bit of a lazy eye, but Claudia did not care. To her, the little changeling was the most precious thing, no matter how lopsided or cross-eyed.

Claudia squeezed the girl's hand. "What if no one claims her?" she said. "What will happen to her?"

"Foster care," said the social worker. "What, you're interested?"

"Yes," Claudia said, avoiding looking at Anton. "Please keep us posted—I don't want someone else taking her in."

"Okay," he said, and gave the little kikimora a thorough looking over. "Don't worry, I'm sure the competition won't be stiff."

As they left the social services building, Claudia listened absently to the girl's crying inside.

"Well?" Anton said. "What's that foster nonsense?"

"She's ours," Claudia whispered fiercely. "She chose us, and we are not turning her away."

"But—"

She spun around, cutting him off. "Anton, I never asked you for anything. I put up with a lot of shit. But you can't deny me this." She stared at Anton, silently challenging him. The cars passed by in the broad streets without sidewalks, and above them the cloudless May sky bloomed azure. The birds twittered in a few perfunctory maples lining the parking lot.

"I guess she did come to us," Anton said, and patted his pockets for the car keys. "Maybe it is a sign."

Satisfied, Claudia nodded and walked to the car. At home,

she resumed her busy routine, but never strayed away from the phone for more than a few minutes at a time.

Despite her irrational fears, there were no living relatives uncovered, and no desperate couples rushed to adopt the girl. She had scoliosis, and her eyes were badly crossed. She did not speak, but seemed relieved to be brought back to the home where she first became human, comforted by familiar sounds of the chickens clucking in the back yard, and smells of the first preserves of the season.

Anton never took more than a perfunctory interest in the child, but Claudia did not mind. Tina, as she named the girl, seemed content to follow Claudia around the house and the backyard, and watched her every movement with quiet intensity. For a few weeks Claudia felt happy—as happy as she was when she and Anton first moved into the house, full of hope. And just as then, the happiness soon gave way to discontent.

She could've coped with an ill child—she could've spent nights sitting up soothing fevers, administering injections, giving sponge baths. But she did not know what to do when Tina went rigid and screamed and screamed without any visible provocation, without an end, growing hoarse but still screaming and moaning, the back of her throat shredded with exertion. She couldn't cope when the girl banged her head against the table, the pulsing blue vein in her forehead vehemently searching for the sharp edge, when the girl clawed her own face, gouging deep parallel ravines into her translucent skin.

"What will we do?" Claudia asked Anton, as Tina napped in her lap, temporarily consoled, curled up like a shrimp.

"I don't know," Anton said. He had good grace not to add, *You wanted this.* "Maybe she needs to see a doctor."

Claudia's fingers ran through the girl's hair absently. "Maybe."

Tina did not like the idea of leaving the house—she kicked when they loaded her into the car and strapped her down in a plastic safety seat. She bit Anton's arm as he buckled the seatbelt over her. Two crescent wounds swelled with blood. He frowned and got into the driver's seat.

Claudia looked out of the window at the fluffy clouds littering the sky and kept quiet. She did not want to admit that Anton was right, and stubbornly hoped that things would work out. They just had to.

They had to wait in the reception area, and Claudia blushed and lowered her head under the disapproving eyes of the receptionist and a few parents. Tina twisted and hissed, slid off her chair as if she had no bones, and tried to bang her head on the coffee table, littered with colorful fans of magazines.

"Shh," Claudia whispered, and held Tina's head. "It's all right, it's all right."

Anton stared at the wall opposite him, his hands thrust deep into his pockets. He wanted nothing to do with either of them, and didn't even try to hide it.

When they were finally called in, Claudia had to resist an urge to jerk Tina by her arm, just drag her along like a floppy doll. Instead, she carried her. The girl tried to slide through her arms like soap.

The doctor, a nice young woman just a little older than Claudia, listened to her sympathetically, every now and again giving Tina a penetrating look. Tina still hissed, but remained still in the cocoon formed by Claudia's arms and lap, squirming only occasionally.

The doctor told them that Tina had an autism spectrum disorder—they were not sure exactly which one. "But they are pretty similar," the doctor said.

Anton spoke for the first time since they got there. "Can you fix it?"

"Unfortunately, no," the young doctor said. "There are therapies that can help her adjust. We can teach her to relate to other people."

"But she's not going to get better," Anton said, standing up. He turned to Claudia. "Let's go."

The doctor gave him a card. "This is our behavioral therapy center," she said. "You may want to check it out."

As they were leaving, the doctor caught Claudia's sleeve. "She's in your foster care, correct?"

Claudia nodded. "What does it have to do with anything?"

"There are institutions for autistic children," the doctor said. "The state will take care of it if you need it."

"Thanks," Anton said, and left.

"The book said she would become human." Anton paced across the kitchen floor, and when he turned his shoes squeaked on the polished tiles.

"She did," Claudia said, in a whisper, afraid to wake up Tina, who napped on the floor by the kitchen table. "It's not her fault that she's ill." She sat down next to the child, running her fingers through the wisps of her light hair, all signs of the cross shorn into it obliterated by the new willful growth. *It's my fault,* Claudia thought. *I wanted to make her human, and I broke her.*

Tina shifted in her sleep, and uttered a wordless whimper. "Don't worry," Claudia said to her, even though the girl could neither hear nor understand her. "We're not giving you away. You're ours now."

Anton sat on the floor next to them, watching Tina as if she were an exotic animal, impossible to comprehend. Claudia supposed she was, just like everyone else. She was grateful that her husband put in an effort, at least. Most didn't bother at all.

"Her hair is growing back," Claudia said. "Do you think it'll make a difference?"

Anton shrugged and yawned. "Let's go to bed."

She tucked the blanket around Tina and followed him to the bedroom. Both of them lay sleepless, listening to the small tired noises houses make at night. They heard Tina waking up and whimpering, then her shuffling footsteps across the kitchen floor, the clicking of the screen door latch.

The screen door banged in the wind. Anton shifted but didn't get up. Claudia balled the sheet in her fist as she heard the angry clucking of chickens and a small, halting voice. "One, two, three," Tina counted and laughed. "One, two, three." Then the clicking of the bobbins started, portending a disaster.

YOU DREAM

This is a recurring dream, the kind that lingers, and lately it has become more frequent. And it takes a while to realize that you are not, in fact, standing in front of the brick apartment building, its doorway cavernous and warm, your hands in your pockets, cigarette smoke leaking slowly between your lips and into the frozen air. It takes you a while to even remember that you've quit smoking years ago. And yet, here it is, clinging to the collar of your winter coat in a persistent, suffocating cloud, and you can taste it still.

It takes you even longer to remember why you dreamt about this building on the outskirts of Moscow—that you used to live there, but this is not why; you're there because of the boy who used to live in the same building but the other entrance. You cannot remember his name or whether you were really friends or just nodded at each other, passing by like boats in the lonely concrete sea of the yard, a fringe of consumptive poplars looking nothing like the palms of the tropical isles neither of you were ever likely to see. You know, though, that there was never any unpleasant physicality between the two of you, even after you learned to throw your body between yourself and whomever was trying to get too close.

You sit up in your bed and want a smoke, and whisper to yourself, *It was never sex. Never.* It was a defensive reflex, the same as a lizard that aborts its tail and escapes while some predator dumbly noses around the mysteriously wriggling appendage. You'd learned to do it with your entire body, and only the spirit escaped, not watching from the distance, running instead for the hills and the razor slash of the distant horizon. It was always about escaping.

Anyway, the boy: as far as you can recall, he had an average and pale face, he was short and slouched, his hands always in the pockets of his ratty hand-me-down winter coat, too short for him. His straight dark hair was always falling ungracefully across his forehead, and the only thing even remotely remarkable about him was the fact that even in the deadest winter cold his eyes remained warm and soft and brown, and he looked at everything with the same subdued delight. Finding oneself in the diffuse cone of his nearsighted gaze was both disconcerting and comforting, since he seemed to be the only person in the entire universe who honestly didn't want anything from you.

You try to remember what happened to him—you think vaguely that he died as a teen after being drafted, died somewhere in Chechnya; or maybe it was his older brother, and the boy just disappeared one day. Maybe he is still there, at his old apartment, and the memory of his death is a confabulated excuse for not having kept in touch. That seems likely.

It's time to get up anyway, and you stare out the window; you've moved from the grey suburbs to the sort-of center, near the Moscow River's bend, where it is somewhat less grey and the lights of opulence are visible across the river. You try to be satisfied with your lot in life, but discontent lingers, so you eye your pantyhose, tangled and twisted into a noose, and your short skirt, the one you're getting too old for, and you keep getting a sneaking suspicion that your immediate boss feels the same way and soon enough he'll trade you for a newer model, like he does with his BMWs.

So you call in sick. No one minds since there's yet another economic crisis in progress, and chances are no one will be paid until right before the New Year. And they can type their own damn reports, those twelve managers and only two of you to do the actual work. It doesn't matter. You dig through your wardrobe and find half-forgotten woolly tights, scratchy and severe and thick, and a long gabardine skirt with a broken zipper, which you fix with a safety pin. You wrap your head in the flowery kerchief every Russian woman owns—even if she never bought one, it was given as a gift, or, barring all normal means of acquisition, spontaneously generated in her apartment. You suspect that yours is one of those, an immaculately gotten kerchief with fat cabbage roses on a velvet-black background with tangled fringe.

It is warmer outside than you expected, what with the dreams of winter and whatnot, but the wind is still cutting and it throws handfuls of bright yellow poplar leaves in your face as you walk away from the embankment. Your shoulders stoop under a grey woolen cardigan, and your walk is awkward, unnatural in flat shoes, and you feel as if you keep falling heavily on your heels, the familiar support elevating them above ground missing. Your face feels naked without the makeup.

St. Nicholas' church is open and empty, the smell of frankincense and whatever church incense they use there tickling your nostrils and yet infusing you with reflexive peace, conditioned like a dog that salivates at the sound of the bell. You buy a thin brown candle and plop it in front an icon, wherever there's space, and mumble something prayer-like under your breath.

The mass is long over and only black-clad old women are there, rearranging and correcting falling candles, sweeping the heavy stone tiles of the floor. They look at you with their cataracts, blue like skimmed milk, and mumble under their breath. You catch the word "whore" and try not to take it personally—after all, this is what they call every woman who is not them, whether she is mortifying her flesh with woolen tights or not. You try to will your legs to not itch and end up backing behind a column and scratching discreetly.

You are not sure what brought on this religious impulse, except for the boy you miss without having known him. Then you think of the rest of his family, his numerous siblings, always hungry and underdressed, and it resolves in your memory, finally: he was a son of a defrocked priest who was forced into disgrace and living in a common apartment building instead of a parish house, no longer surviving off tithes, but the very modest salary of a night watchman. His wife worked at the meat factory across the street and always brought home bulging sacks dripping with blood, filled with tripe and bones and stomachs, and it was never enough for their brood, which, by your estimate, was somewhere between seven and nine. Poorer and more fecund than real priests, even.

"May I help you?" A soft, stuttering voice startles you from your reverie and you spook upright, your head springing back and almost breaking the nose of the speaker.

The young priest steps back, calm, his hands behind his back. "You look spiritually wrought," he says, smile bristling his soft beard, light as flax. "You need guidance."

"I don't," you say with unnecessary force, the wraiths of your twelve bosses rearing their heads, the images of people always telling you what you need. "I need information. Why would a priest be defrocked?"

"Depends," he answers with the same softness, the change of topic barely breaking his cadence. "Are we talking about now, or in the past? Because the synod just defrocked a priest the other day, for marrying two men."

"No," you say. "Before—in the seventies or early eighties. A priest in Moscow was defrocked. He had children."

"Most of us do," young Father says, musing. "Back then, that would've been insubordination, most likely. Failure to respect the hierarchy. Talking badly about the hierarchy. Or possibly a failure to inform—or maybe informing on the wrong people, the wrong things." He sighs heavily, his grey eyes misting over. "You know, I grew up in the church. I'm not afraid of ever losing my faith—when I was young, I saw one priest beating another up with an icon."

Normally you would laugh at the image, but his thoughtful sincerity stops you. "I see," you say.

"Do you know that priest's name?"

"Father Dmitri," you say.

"No last name?"

You shake your head and feel stupid.

"Do you know what church he was assigned to before his defrocking?"

"No. I was just thinking about his son . . . they used to live in the same apartment building as I did."

"Go visit them, then," he says flatly. "They were probably too poor to buy another apartment."

"I don't . . . " You want to tell him that you really don't want to see anyone from your past, anyone who would recognize you and put together the images of you—then and now, past and present—and find the comparison lacking.

But he is already losing interest, backing away. "You need to get baptized," he says before turning away, toward the old women who wait for his glance as if it were a blessing.

"How do you know I'm not?" you call after, raising your voice unacceptably.

"You're tormented," he calls back, just as loud.

The priest is wrong—your mother had baptized you at birth, even though such things were frowned upon back in the 1970s. She even took you to the Easter and Christmas masses, where you stood on your aching feet for hours, holding a candle that dripped hot wax on your hands. The memory brings only boredom and unease and doesn't lessen whatever spiritual torment the priest saw in you. He doesn't know that the church with its battling priests isn't as calming to you as it is to him— you worry that you will now have comical nightmares of priests in their long black robes and tall hats pummeling each other with icons and candlesticks. You are really not looking for salvation from them, but from that quiet boy in your childhood. No one else had such kind eyes. You sigh, regretful that your young self was so unaware of how rare a treasure this kindness was—and you're not even sure if such optimism should be commended.

By the time you were twelve, you certainly knew enough of those who were not kind, of the tiny cave under the very first flight of stairs by the apartment building's entrance, the cave you always had to run past because of those who hid there—boys who would reach out and hold you against the wall and put their hands under your skirt and down your sweater. You never told your mom why you would wait for her to come home from work, when the shadows grew long, and she couldn't understand that you were not afraid to be home alone—you were afraid of the dash up the flight of stairs, and your two-room apartment could've as well been located on the moon.

You do not remember the faces of those boys, just that one who never laid a finger on you; instead, he walked with you sometimes, and watched you get into the elevator, safe. Sometimes the boys under the stairs would beat him, and once they held his face down in the large puddle that manifested in your paved yard every spring and fall—held him until bubbles coming from his silted lips turned into stifled screams and only a chance passerby spooked the hooligans.

When you get home, you unwrap the kerchief and hate it for a while because your hair is now flattened and tangled and you'll have to wash it again. Then you pick up the phone, since there's nothing else to do but to hurl yourself toward the past, since the present refuses to surrender any answers or even passable lies.

Your mother sounds older than she did the last time you spoke, and you try not to feel guilty about her unseen decline in some sanatorium that costs you most of your uncertain salary, and of course it would be cheaper to have her live with you, here, over the black river that smells of gasoline and foams white in the wake of leisure boats. You sigh into the phone and try to ignore all of her unvoiced complaints.

"Mom," you finally say, "do you remember that family that used to live next door, when I was little? The one with seven kids?"

"Vorobyev," she says, her memory as flawless as always. "The youngest boy, Vasya, was such a sweet kid. Always running around in those girls' coats from his older sisters."

That's right, you now remember, those were plaid, too-short girl coats. No wonder everyone teased him; no wonder his unperturbed demeanor incited them to violence—there was no point in such savage humiliation as a girl's coat unless its victim would acknowledge it as such.

"Vasya Vorobyev," she repeats. "Too sad about him."

"What have you heard?" Your heart seizes up and it's ridiculous, you haven't thought about that kid in decades. In forever. "What happened?"

"Anya, his mother, used to call me sometimes," she says. "He's dead, in Osetia last year. Now she's dead too—her heart gave out after that."

"Too bad." You are numb now, numb to the tips of your fingers, and they almost drop the receiver. A deep chill settles in at the loss you aren't sure you've suffered. "Do you remember why was his father was defrocked?"

"No. Why would you care about something like that?"

"I don't," you whisper, and say goodbye. You spend the rest of the day watching TV and pacing and drinking buttermilk straight out of the bottle that fits so comfortably into one hand, and you keep thinking back to the days when you needed two to hold it.

The boy who defended you sometimes. You're glad to have a name, but in your mind he's still that boy—the boy. You're glad to be dreaming about him the next night—at least there he is alive and little, even as other people's hands press his face into the dirty pavement, his teeth making an awful scraping sound that makes you cringe in your sleep. They leave, but not before making lewd gestures in your direction, and you wait for the boy to stagger up, his feet shuffly and his knees buckling under him. He totters but remains standing. You feel lucid even though it is a dream and in it you are still small. "Why was your father defrocked?"

"Why does it matter?" He lisps a bit, his tongue thoughtfully exploring the ragged edge of the chipped front tooth. He doesn't seem to know that he is in your dream.

"Because I need to know what did he do that was so awful, to bring you here. What was it that you were paying for?"

"Looking for the prime mover, huh?" He drops the pretense of childhood and for a second becomes terrifying—still a kid, but somehow older and deader. "I don't know why. Who knows why shit happens, huh? Who knows why you don't tell anyone about them dragging you under the stairs. Why you never told them—"

Your face burns with exposed shame and you snap away from him, the hem of your gabardine dress twirling around your legs, long and smooth and brown in your first pair of nylon pantyhose. "Fuck off," you mutter darkly. And yet you understand his point, the essential impossibility of revealing one's secrets—especially if those secrets are not one's fault. We can get over the wrongs we do, but we cannot forgive ourselves for the wrongs done to us, for our own helplessness.

"Don't be like that." He catches up to you and walks with you across the paved yard, the large puddle in its center only nascent. It must remind him, you think, and then you are suddenly not sure whether the puddle incident happened before or after the chipped tooth.

You sit in your bed upright, your heart strumming against your ribs. You have to go to sleep, you tell yourself, you have to get up early tomorrow, but then you remember it'll be Saturday. So you give up and pull on a pair of jeans and tuck your nightgown into them, throw on a jacket and run down the stairs and across the street—like a wayward moth that woke up in the fall by mistake—toward the fluorescent glimmer of an all-night kiosk.

You buy a gin and tonic in a can—make that two—and a pack of Dunhill's, the red one. You buy a translated detective novel for good measure, and the guy behind the bulletproof glass smiles crookedly. "Got a wild night planned?"

You ignore the familiar sarcasm, so integrated into the national discourse that you notice its absence more than its presence. You spend the rest of the night sitting on the windowsill, the right angle of your legs reflected in the dark windowpane, drinking bitter gin and tonics and smoking with abandon, stuffing the butts into an empty can.

You wait until six in the morning, when the subway is open, and you walk to the station and take the subway and the bus to the street where you grew up. You hope that there's no one there who will recognize you, and you get off at the familiar stop—forgotten just enough to feel uncanny, as if its coincidence with your memory is a miracle, like Jesus seen in a sandwich. Your hopes are dashed the moment your foot touches the asphalt—a high female voice calls your name.

"Look at you," babbles a middle-aged woman, red coat, face painted with too much enthusiasm and not enough artifice. "You haven't changed a bit." She clearly expects you to say the same, and the lie would be easier if you could remember who she was.

"Natasha," she reminds you. "Romanova. We used to be in the same class through the sixth grade. I live one building from yours." She walks along with you, oblivious to your cringing away from her. "What are you doing here? Visiting someone?"

"Vorobyev family," you say before you can come up with a decent lie.

"Oh," she says. "I think they moved—well, the kids had all moved out."

"I heard Vasya's dead," you say.

She looks at you strangely. "Well, stop the presses."

"I just heard."

She looks at you, concerned. "What do you mean? I thought it was you who had found him."

You shake your head at her nonsense, and yet the quiet nightmare dread grabs you by the heart and squeezes harder, as you mumble excuses and break away from the talkative friend you don't remember having and you race ahead to the poplar row that seems fatter and taller and more decayed than before. The asphalted path leads between the trees to the yard surrounded by six identical brick buildings, each nine stories tall with two separate entrances. Your house is the last one on the right, and you race past your entrance. You find their apartment not by the number but by muscle memory—your legs remember how to run to the fourth floor, taking two steps at a time, how to swing abruptly left and skid to a stop in front of a brown door upholstered with quilted peeling pleather diamonds, how to press the doorbell that is lower than you expected—you can reach it without getting on your tiptoes.

It rings deep within the cavern of the apartment, and you know by the apartment's position (you've never been inside) that it has three rooms—barely enough for nine people—not counting a kitchen, and that the balcony looks out into the yard, above the puddle.

A boy with soft brown eyes opens the door, still the same, still in his coat, water dripping down his sallow face, his hair slicked into a toothed fringe over his forehead. You are mostly surprised by the differential in your heights now—something that was just beginning to manifest around the time you left home, when you were sixteen, and would rather have moved in with your first boyfriend (so much older than you) than stayed here, near those stairs that trained you in your lizard defense. Now you're towering over him with your adult, aging self, crow's feet and sagging jeans and all, and he is still twelve (thirteen?), and he looks up at you nearsightedly, his pale face looming up at you as if from under water. You accept it with the fatalism of someone who has bad dreams too often to even attempt to wake up.

"It's you," he says without much surprise. "Come on in."

You do, as you would in a dream. The apartment has suffered some damage—there are water stains on the ceiling and water seeps through the whitewash, dripping down the browned tracks over bubbling, peeling wallpaper. The windows also weep, and the hardwood floors buckle and swell, then squish underfoot like mushrooms.

The boy stands next to you by the window, looking through the water-streaked glass at the sunshine and fluffy clouds outside, at the butter-yellow poplar leaves tossed across the yard by the rising wind. "What is it that you want?"

You are well familiar with the logic of dreams and fairy tales, of the importance of choosing your words wisely, of the fragility of the moment—waste your breath on a wrong question and you will never know anything. "How did you die?" you finally ask. "I cannot remember." Other questions will just have to go unanswered.

He points to the puddle outside, wordlessly, and you remember the hands pressing his face into the water, and you standing there, watching, helpless, until there are no more bubbles. Afterward, you tell the grownups that you found him like that, and you don't know who did it.

"Why didn't you tell them?"

You're an adult now, and the words come out awkwardly. "I was afraid of what they would do to me if I told. I'm sorry."

He's too much of a gentleman to rub it in your face that he had been defending you then, that he could've walked past and stayed alive.

"It wouldn't have mattered," he says instead. Dead in Chechnya. Dead in Osetia. Disappeared one night without a trace. Dead in a kayaking accident. You remember all his deaths and they crowd around the two of you, suffocating and clammy.

And then it's just you again, standing on the sidewalk outside, watching the eddies of yellow leaves spiraling around the ankles of your brown boots with worn, lopsided heels. And then it is just you, walking to the bus stop, promising to yourself to never return here, to never look back at the fourth story window and all the dead faces of the boy pressed against the weeping glass.

ZOMBIE LENIN

1.

It all started when I was eight years old, on a school trip to the Mausoleum. My mom was there to chaperon my class, and it was nice, because she held me when I got nauseous on the bus. I remember the cotton tights all the girls wore, and how they bunched on our knees and slid down, so that we had to hike them up, as discreetly as eight-year-olds could. It was October, and my coat was too short; mom said it was fine even though its belt came disconcertingly close to my underarms, and the coat didn't even cover my butt. I didn't believe her; I frowned at the photographer as he aligned his camera, pinning my mom and me against the backdrop of the St. Basil's Cathedral. "Smile," mom whispered. We watched the change of guard in front of the Mausoleum.

Then we went inside. At that time, I was still vague on what it was that we were supposed to see. I followed in small mincing steps down the grim marble staircase along with the line of people as they descended and filed into a large hall and looked to their right. I looked too, to see a small yellowing man in a dark suit under a glass bell. His eyes were closed, and he was undeniably dead. The air of an inanimate object hung dense, like the smell of artificial flowers. When I shuffled past him, looking, looking, unable to turn away, his eyes snapped open and he sat up in a jerking motion of a marionette, shattering the glass bubble around him. I screamed.

2.

"A dead woman is the ultimate sex symbol," someone behind me says.

His interlocutor laughs. "Right. To a necrophile maybe."

"No, no," the first man says, heatedly. "Think of every old novel you've ever read. The heroine who's too sexually liberated for her time usually dies. Ergo, a dead woman is dead because she was too sexually transgressive."

"This is just dumb, Fedya," says the second man. "What, Anna Karenina is a sex symbol?"

"Of course. That one's trivial. But also every other woman who ever died."

I stare at the surface of the plastic cafeteria table. It's cheap and pockmarked with burns, their edges rough under my fingers. I drink my coffee and listen intently for the two men behind me to speak again.

"Undine," the first one says. "Rusalki. All of them dead, all of them irresistible to men."

I finish my coffee and stand up. I glance at the guy who spoke—he's young, my age, with light clear eyes of a madman.

"Euridice," I whisper as I pass.

3.

The lecturer is old, his beard dirty-yellow with age, his trembling fingers stained with nicotine. I sit all the way in the back, my eyes closed, listening, and occasionally drifting off to dream-sleep.

"Chthonic deities," he says. "The motif of resurrection. Who can tell me what is the relationship between the two?"

We remain wisely silent.

"The obstacle," he says. "The obstacle to resurrection. Ereshkigal, Hades, Hel. All of them hold the hero hostage and demand a ransom of some sort."

His voice drones on, talking about the price one pays, and about Persephone being an exception as she's not quite dead. But Euridice, oh she gets it big time. I wonder if Persephone or Euridice is a better sex symbol and if one should compare the two.

"Zombies," the voice says, "are in violation. Their resurrection bears no price and has no meaning. The soul and the body separated are a terrible thing. It is punitive, not curative." His yellow beard trembles, bald patch on his skull shines in a slick of parchment skin, one of his eyes fake and popping. He sits up and reaches for me.

I scream and jerk awake.

"Bad dream?" the lecturer says, without any particular mockery or displeasure. "It happens. When you dream your soul travels to the Underworld."

"Chthonic deities," I mumble. "I'm sorry."

"That's right," he says. "Chthonic."

4.

When I was eight, I had nightmares about that visit. I dreamt of the dead yellowing man chasing me up and down the stairs of our apartment building. I still have those dreams. I'm running past the squeezing couples and smokers exiled to the stairwell, and mincing steps are chasing after me. I skip over the steps, jumping over two at once, three at once, throwing myself into each stairwell as if it were a pool. Soon my feet are barely touching the steps as I rush downward in an endless spiral of chipped stairs.

I'm flying in fear as the dead man is following. He's much slower than me but he does not stop, so I cannot stop either.

"Zombies," he calls after me into the echoey stairwell, "are the breach of covenant. If the chthonic deities do not get their blood-price, there can be no true resurrection."

I wake up with a start. My stomach hurts.

5.

I take the subway to the university. I usually read so I don't have to meet people's eyes. "Station Lenin Hills," the announcer on the intercom says. "The doors are closing. Next station is the University."

I look up and see the guy who spoke of dead women sitting across from me. His eyes, bleached with insanity, stare at me with the black pinpricks of the pupils. He pointedly ignores the old woman in a black kerchief standing too close to him, trying to guilt him into surrendering his seat. He doesn't get up until I do, when the train pulls into the station. "The University," the announcer says.

We exit together.

"I'm Fedya," he says.

"I'm afraid of zombies," I answer.

He doesn't look away.

6.

The lecturer's eyes water with age. He speaks directly to me when he asks, "Any other resurrection myths you know of?"

"Jesus?" someone from the first row says.

He nods. "And what was the price paid for his resurrection?"

"There wasn't one," I say, startling myself. "He was a zombie."

This time everyone stares.

"Talk to me after class," the lecturer says.

7.

The chase across all the stairwells in the world becomes a game. He catches up to me now. I'm too tired to be afraid enough to wake up. My stomach hurts.

"You cannot break the covenant with chthonic gods," he tells me. "Some resurrection is the punishment."

"Leave me alone," I plead. "What have I ever done to you?"

His fake eye, icy-blue, steely-grey, slides down his ruined cheek. "You can't save them," he says. "They always look back. They always stay dead."

"Like with Euridice."

"Like with every dead woman."

8.

Fedya sits on my bed, heavily although he's not a large man but slender, birdlike.

"I could never drive a car," I tell him.

He looks at the yellowing medical chart, dog-eared pages fanned on the bed covers. "Sluggish schizophrenia?" he says. "This is a bullshit diagnosis. You know it as well as I do. Delusions of reformism? You know that they invented it as a punitive thing."

"It's not bullshit," I murmur. It's not. Injections of sulfazine and the rubber room had to have a reason behind them.

"They kept you in the Serbsky hospital," he observes. "Serbsky? I didn't know you were a dissident."

"Lenin is a zombie," I tell him. "He talks to me." All these years. All this medication.

He stares. "I can't believe they let you into the university."

I shrug. "They don't pay attention to that anymore."

"Maybe things are changing," he says.

9.

"Are you feeling all right?" the lecturer says, his yellow hands shaking, filling me with quiet dread. Same beard, same bald patch.

I nod.

"Where did that zombie thing come from?" he asks, concerned.

"You said it yourself. Chthonic deities always ask for a price. If you don't pay, you stay dead or become a zombie. Women stay dead."

He lifts his eyebrows encouragingly. "Oh?"

"Dead are objects," I tell him. "Don't you know that? Some would rather become zombies than objects. Only zombies are still objects, even though they don't think they are."

I can see that he wants to laugh but decides not to. "And why do you think women decide to stay dead?"

I feel nauseous and think of Inanna who kind of ruins my thesis. I ignore her. "It has something to do with sex," I say miserably.

He really tries not to laugh.

10.

In the hospital, when I lay in a sulfazine-and-neuroleptics coma, he would sit on the edge of my bed. "You know what they say about me."

"Yes," I whispered, my cheeks so swollen that they squeezed my eyes shut. "Lenin is more alive than any of the living."

"And what is life?"

"According to Engels, it's a mode of existence of protein bodies."

"I am a protein body," he said. "What do you have to say to that?"

"I want to go home," I whispered with swollen lips. "Why can't you leave me alone?"

He didn't answer, but his waxen fingers stroked my cheek, leaving a warm melting trail behind them.

11.

"I thought for sure you were a cutter," Fedya says.

I shiver in my underwear and hug my shoulders. My skin puckers in the cold breeze from the window. "I'm not." I feel compelled to add, "Sorry."

"You can get dressed now," he says.

I do.

He watches.

12.

The professor is done with chthonic deities, and I lose interest. I drift through the dark hallways, where the walls are so thick that they still retain the cold of some winter from many years ago. I poke my head into one auditorium, and listen a bit to a small sparrow of a woman chatter about Kant. I stop by the stairwell on the second floor, to bum a cigarette off a fellow student with black horn-rimmed glasses.

"Skipping class?" she says.

"Just looking for something to do."

"You can come to my class," she says. "It's pretty interesting."

"What is it about?"

"Economics."

I finish my smoke and tag along.

This lecturer looks like mine, and I take for a sign. I sit in an empty seat in the back, and listen. "The idea of capitalism rests on the concept of free market," he says. "Who can tell me what it is?"

No one can, or wants to.

The lecturer notices me. "What do you think? Yes, you, the young lady who thinks it's a good idea to waltz in in the middle of the class. What is free market?"

"It's when you pay the right price," I say. "To the chthonic deities. If you don't pay you become a zombie or just stay dead."

He stares at me. "I don't think you're in the right class."

13.

I sit in the stairwell of the second floor. Lenin emerges from the brass stationary ashtray and sits next to me. There's one floor up and one down, and nowhere really to run.

"What have you learned today?" he asks in an almost paternal voice.

"Free market," I tell him.

He shakes his head. "It will end the existence of the protein bodies in a certain mode." A part of his cheek is peeling off.

"Remember when I was in the hospital?"

"Of course. Those needles hurt. You cried a lot."

I nod. "My boyfriend doesn't like me."

"I'm sorry," he says. "If it makes it any better, I will leave soon."

I realize that I would miss him. He followed me since I was little. "Is it because of the free market?" I ask. "I'm sorry. I'll go back to the chthonic deities."

"It's not easy," he says and stands up, his joints whirring, his skin shedding like sheets of wax paper. He walks away on soft rubbery legs.

14.

"Things die eventually," I tell Fedya. "Even those that are not quite dead to begin with."

"Yeah, and?" he answers and drinks his coffee.

I stroke the melted circles in the plastic, like craters on the lunar surface. "One doesn't have to be special to die. One has to be special to stay dead. This is why you like Euridice, don't you?"

He frowns. "Is that the one Orpheus followed to Hades?"

"Yes. Only he followed her the wrong way."

15.

There is a commotion on the second floor, and the stairwell is isolated from the corridor by a black sheet. The ambulances are howling outside, and distraught smokers crowd the hallway, cut off from their usual smoking place.

I ask a student from my class what's going on. He tells me that the chthonic lecturer has collapsed during the lecture about the hero's journey. "Heart attack, probably."

I push my way through the crowd, just in time to see the paramedics carry him off. I see the stooped back of a balding dead man following the paramedics and their burden, not looking back. Some students cry.

"He just died during the lecture," a girl's voice behind me says. "He just hit the floor and died."

I watch the familiar figure on uncertain soft legs walk downstairs in a slow mincing shuffle, looking to his right at the waxen profile with an upturned beard staring into the sky from the gurney. The lecturer and zombie Lenin disappear from my sight, and I turn away. "Stay dead," I whisper. "Don't look back."

The rest is up to them and chthonic deities.

EBB AND FLOW

I sit in my underwater palace, looking through the window at the schools of bright, silent fish drifting in the crystal water, I listen to the sweet music played by jellyfish and seahorses, and I remember. After the love is gone and all the tears are cried out, what else is left to do?

This story does not have a happy ending; they almost never do. The only happy stories you will ever hear are told by men—they spin their lies, trying to convince themselves that they cause no devastation, and that the hearts they break were never worth much to begin with. But I am the one who lives under the sea, keeping it full and salty. I, the daughter of the Sea *kami* Watatsumi. I, who once had a sister and a husband.

I wouldn't have met my husband Hoori no *mikoto* if it weren't for his foolishness. Back on land, he was a ruler of Central Land of Reed Plains, but still he loved to hunt. His brother, Hoderi no *mikoto*, was the best fisherman their young country had ever known. But Hoori was not content with what he had. He talked his brother into trading their jobs for a day.

Hoderi could not use his brother's bow and arrows and found no game. Hoori was even less successful: not only did he fail to catch any fish, he also lost the fishhook his brother prized above every other possession. Hoderi was upset at the loss, and Hoori swore that he would find it.

He spent days searching the beaches, digging through the mounds of withered kelp, looking under the weightless pieces of driftwood pale like the moon, turning over every stone, round and polished by the sea into the brightest azure shine. But he didn't find the hook.

He went home and looked at his favorite sword for a long time. It was a katana of the highest craftsmanship, worth more than half of all Japan. Hoori always talked about his weapon with tears in his eyes, as if it were a child or a dear friend. And yet, his love for his brother was stronger than his love for his weapon. He shattered the katana into a thousand pieces and molded each into a sharp fishing hook that shone in the sun and were strong enough to hook a whale.

But Hoderi was not consoled. No matter what Hoori did and how much he pleaded, Hoderi remained firm: he wanted his hook, and no other.

Hoori grew despondent and spent his days wandering along the shore. The soft susurrus of the waves calmed his troubled heart as they lay themselves by his feet, lapping at his shoes like tame foxes.

He noticed an old man sitting on the beach, throwing pebble after pebble into the pale green waters. Hoori recognized the old man as Shiotsuchi no *kami*, the God of Tides.

"Why are you so sad?" the old *kami* asked.

"I lost my brother's fishhook," Hoori said. "And he would neither talk to me nor look me in the eye."

Shiotsuchi nodded and snapped his fingers at the waves. Obedient to his will, they brought him many stems of pliable green bamboo. Fascinated, Hoori watched as the waves reared and spun, shaping the bamboo stems into a giant basket with their watery fingers.

When the bamboo basket was ready, Shiotsuchi helped Hoori

into it. "I'll command the tides to carry you to the palace of the Sea God, Watatsumi no *kami*. There is a well by the palace, and a katsura tree growing there. Climb into the tree, and you will be taken to Watatsumi no *kami*. He will be able to help you find the hook, for he is the ruler of all sea creatures."

Hoori thanked the *kami* and settled into the basket. It carried him along with the tides, and the small round waves tossed his bamboo vessel about, playfully but gently.

They carried him all the way to the palace made of fish scales. My home, my life, where my sister and I sang and played under the watchful eye of our father, where all the creatures were our playmates, and even rays would never hurt us but let us ride on their shining backs. Seahorses tangled in our hair, and jellyfish subserviently let us pummel their bells as if they were drums. We dressed in finest silks and sealskin, and never knew a worry in the world.

We didn't know that he was coming.

On that fateful day, you did as you were told. My maid came to the well to fetch me a cup of water—even under the sea we need sweet water to drink. She saw your reflection in the well, and she ran, fearful of strangers, but not before you tore a piece of your jade necklace and dropped it into the cup she carried.

She brought the cup to me and told me about the stranger in the well. I barely listened as I tilted my cup this way and that, watching the sun play across its golden sides, reflecting from the sparkling jade through the transparent water. It was green and beautiful, and I smiled as the reflected sun dappled my face, warming it. Surely, no evil can come from someone who had a stone like that, I thought.

I called my sister, Tamayoribime, and showed her the stone.

She beamed. "Where did it come from, Toyotamabime?" she asked me.

I told her of what my maid told me, and we went to investigate, our arms twined about each other's waists. We found you in the branches of the katsura tree, the spicy fragrance of its leaves giving you the aura of danger and excitement. You smiled at us and spoke as if you were our equal.

"Come down from that tree," Tamayoribime said.

You did as she told you, although the smile wilted on your face, and your forehead wrinkled in consternation. I guessed that you were not used to being ordered about.

"Please, honored guest," I said. "Come with us so we may introduce you to our father, Watatsumi no *kami*."

You nodded and looked at me with affection. I lowered my gaze before yours, and you smiled.

We led you through our palace, and you grinned in wonderment, tilting your head up to see the cupping roof of the palace, inlaid with mother-of-pearl and decorated with fine drawings done in the octopus ink. You gaped at the tall posts of sandstone and whale ivory holding up the roof, at the twining kelp around them, at the bright lionfish that guarded access to my father's throne room. The guardian let us through, and you stood in astonishment in my father's awesome presence.

He was a great *kami*, and he lay coiled atop a sealskin and silk *tatami*, his skin shining bronze and green, his great bearded head, larger than your entire body, resting on a mound of silk pillows and red and blue jellyfish. A jade incense burner exhaled great clouds of pungent smoke, masking the strong salty smell of my father.

"Come in, Land Prince," my father boomed, his voice shaking the intricate panels of fishbone decorating the walls. "Come in and sit down on my fine *tatami*, and tell me what brings you here."

But you kept silent, your mouth half-open in fascinated attention. My father winked at me, and I called in our entertainers—singing fish, dancing crocodiles, and squid who did magic tricks. Flying fish, tuna, and octopus put on a play for you, and two eels played *koto* and *shamisen* by twining their flexible bodies around the instruments' necks and plucking the strings with their tails. You clapped your hands in time with music and laughed like a child. Then your eyes met mine, and you blushed.

My father, who never missed anything that occurred in his palace, sent Tamayoribime and me out with a flick of his tail. He wanted to talk to you *kami* to *mikoto*, I guessed and obeyed. We left the palace and ran through the forest of kelp, shouting for all the fish to come out and chase us on a pretend hunt. It was dark when we came back, and my father announced that I was to become your wife.

I looked into the marble floor studded with starfish and did not answer. I never argued with my father; I did not know how.

And so we were married, and I came to love Hoori. I showed him all the secret places my sister and I loved: a grotto of pink stone with a white sand floor, adorned by pearly yellow and blue snails that dotted the walls, gleaming like precious stones; I showed him a large smooth rock where octopi wrote their secret letters in black ink, their tentacles as skillful as the finest brushes; and a dark cave that went down into the bottom of the ocean for miles, gilded with shining algae and populated by phosphorescent moray eels. For our amusement, seahorses staged battles and races, and squid swam in formation, shooting giant ink clouds shaped as flowers to celebrate our love.

Tamayoribime, my sister, rarely joined us on these excursions. Although still young, she understood that the bond the land prince and I shared was not for her to enjoy. She smiled every time she saw me, but I could see the sorrow of her hunched shoulders as she fled to the kelp forest, alone, with only fish for company. My heart ached for her loss, and I wished that gaining a husband did not mean losing my sister. Hoori and I were inseparable, and she grew more distant from me every day, her face close but unreachable, as if it were hidden behind a pane of glass. Hoori had severed the only bond I've ever known and thus increased my attachment to him; all the love I used to lavish upon my sister was his now.

Days passed, and before we knew it, three years had passed since Hoori first entered our palace. I realized that I was pregnant, and told Hoori that he was soon to become a father. He was jubilant at first, but as my belly grew so did the unease in his eyes. He sighed often, and one day I asked what was wrong.

He told me that he missed the land and was thinking about returning home. "Only," he added, "I still haven't found my brother's fishhook. I cannot go back without it."

"Is this why you came to my father's palace?" I asked.

He bowed his head. "Yes. Only the time here was so delightful that I have forgotten my purpose. Please, Toyotamabime, talk to your father on my behalf."

I obeyed his wishes, as I always did; he was the pearl of my heart, my beloved, so how could I refuse him, even though he wanted nothing more than to return home and leave me behind? I cried as I told my father of Hoori's plea.

His great fins fanned slowly as he listened to my words. "Well," he said. "I will find that hook for him."

My father's great roar summoned forth all the sea creatures, and Hoori watched with delight as they swam and slithered into the palace, filling it almost to bursting. Fins, tentacles, scales and claws in every imaginable color shimmered and moved everywhere. My father surveyed this living tapestry and asked everyone in turn whether they've seen the hook.

The fish swore that they haven't, and the crabs and shrimps and scallops promised to sieve through the ocean sand, grain by grain, to find the hook. Only the sea bream remained silent, although his mouth opened and closed as he strained to speak.

"What's wrong with him?" my father asked the tuna and the ocean perch.

"He hasn't spoken in a while," they said. "Something's been caught in his throat for a long time, and he can neither eat nor speak."

My father extended one of his great but slender claws into the bream's obediently opened wide mouth, and soon it emerged with a shining hook caught in it. The bream breathed a sigh of relief and apologized for his mistake. But Hoori was so delighted to have recovered his brother's treasure that he paid no mind to the bream's mumbling.

"Thank you, O great Watatsumi no *kami*," Hoori said to my father. "Now I can return home."

I turned away, biting my lip, cradling my bulging belly in my arms. I would not argue, I thought, I would not beg. If the kelp forests and hidden underwater caves were not enough to keep him, what could I do? If the music and singing of the perches and moray eels did not bind him to our palace, what would my feeble voice achieve?

He took my hands and looked into me eyes. "Toyotamabime, my beloved," he told me. "Will you follow me to the land?"

I'd never been on land before, and the thought filled me with fearful apprehension. Moreover, that would mean breaking away from my father and my sister, from my entire life. But what was I to do? "Let me wait here until it is time for our child to be born," I begged. "Then, build me a parturition hut thatched with cormorant feathers on the beach. I will come there to give birth."

"I'll do as you ask," he said.

"Just promise one thing," I said. "Promise that you will not look into the hut when I am giving birth. Promise me."

His face reflected surprise, but he agreed. "I will send a maid to attend to you," he said.

I shook my head. "My sister will attend to me."

"As you wish," he said, already turning away from me to face my father. "Will you help me get back home?"

"But of course," my father boomed. "One of my fastest *wani* will carry you home. But before you go, please accept this gift from me." With these words, my father produced two jewels, the size of a bream's head, one green, and one pink.

Hoori accepted the gifts with tremulous hands.

My father explained. "The green one is a tide-raising jewel Shiomitsu-Tama, and the other is the tide-lowering jewel Shiohuru-Tama. Use them if you need them."

I smiled at both of them through my tears. In my naiveté, I thought that the jewels were to make our meetings easier, so that Hoori could bring the sea to his doorstep and me with it.

But I was wrong.

When Hoori returned home, born on the back of our swiftest shark, he discovered that Hoderi had a hidden purpose in sending him away to find his hook. While Hoori was away, Hoderi had taken over the land, installing himself as an Emperor, usurping Hoori's place. I do not know what it is that men usually do to hurt each other; but I do know that Hoori used Shiomitsu-Tama, the jewel of flow, to call the ocean forth and flood his brother's fields, poisoning the land with salt, to steal the breath of Hoderi's men. The ocean flowed onto the land, drowned the fields and people who worked in them, until it rose all the way to the doorstep of Hoderi no *mikoto*'s house.

And we, the inhabitants of the ocean, we suffered too. The ocean fell so low that many of the shallow places were exposed, killing the coral and the slow starfish and sea urchins. Jellyfish flopped on the exposed rocks and collapsed into sad puddles of death. The secret grotto grew too shallow for the snails, and they fled, their mantles rustling on the dry sand. That was the price of your triumph.

And when you succeeded in subduing your willful sibling, you lowered the tides, filling back the ocean. Oh, how happy we were that day, and how we mourned those we had lost! But there was little time for mourning; it was time for our child to be born.

Tamayoribime and I dressed in our finest silks and mounted our loyal whale who took us to the shores of your country. Tamayoribime sang and tried to make conversation, laughing a little desperately, trying to recapture the carefree days of our childhood and failing. Soon, she gave up, leaving me to my thoughts. I worried if you remembered to build the hut and fretted that you wouldn't be able to resist the temptation to look. And I felt guilty about my deception, about hiding my true nature from you, but when one was born a princess, a daughter of the Sea *kami*, one was bound to have some secrets even one's husband was not meant know.

The night had descended, setting the ocean aflame with many tiny candles lit for us by the tiniest of our subjects, and they reflected in the fine sky canopy of black velvet stretching far above us. The roaring of the waves signaled that the shore was close, and anxiously I searched the outline of the dark beach against the darker sky for the sign of my beloved. I saw a flickering of a lantern mounted on the cormorant-feathered roof of a hut. The hut was small but warm and dry and richly decorated on the inside. You waited for me there, and the moment our hands met I felt the first pangs of birth pain.

Tamayoribime ushered you outside, into the darkness, where the waves crashed on the shore with a hungry roar and the air tasted of salt spumes. When she returned, she wiped the sweat off my forehead and comforted me as the contractions grew stronger, and I was no longer able to maintain my human form.

My hair unwound like the seaweed in the current and fell off, and my nose elongated as my mouth jutted forward, pushed wide open by the gleaming triangular teeth. My smooth skin turned into sand and leather, my arms turned into fins, and my legs fused into a muscular tail armored with a crescent fin. As a shark, I writhed in agony of childbirth, my entire body convulsing and my tail whipping the *tatami* covering the earthen floor.

Just as the head of our son, open-eyed and screaming, pushed out of my body and my insides ripped and bled, I heard another scream. With my shark eyes I saw your face, pale against the sky, looking at me through the hole in the roof. Oh, the horror on your face would've been easier to bear than the disgust. Tears rolled from my lidless fish eyes, and with a downward maw, teeth gnashing, I begged and pleaded for your forgiveness, for you to love me again.

The color drained from your face, and I saw that with it all the memories of our life under the ocean drained out of you, as if they never existed. You forgot everything and could only see the loathsome monster writhing on the ground between your son and pretty Tamayoribime. What was left for me to do? I fled, lumbering, flopping, awkward, my gills full of sand. I struggled across the beach and into the waiting welcoming arms of the surf. It embraced me, washing away dirt and blood, forgiving, comforting.

I did not look back.

I returned to my father's palace, leaving Tamayoribime to care for my son Ugayafukiaezu. The bond between us had been broken, and even she chose you and the child over me. I could not bear to look at my child or at you, and so I blocked the passage between land and sea, so that the journey between our realms would never again be easy. Only Tamayoribime passed freely, bringing me news of my son's growth and an occasional poem from you.

I could not bear to hear the singing of fish anymore and could not forgive them for telling you about the whereabouts of the cursed fishhook, so I took away their voices. Now, they are forever silent, and only the mournful songs of their *koto* and *shamisen* and the silver bells of the jellyfish break the silence of our realm. I listen to their music, so sad, and yet not sadder than my heart. When all the tears are cried out and only memories are left, I wander like a ghost in the grand palace made of fish scales, dreaming of the voices of my sister and my husband.

And every time the ocean water churns, I am reminded of the ebb and flow of the tides, of the jewels you still have in your possession. You never use them anymore, not even to bring me closer to you. But every time the water turns toward land, I grow hopeful, and my love for you ebbs and flows with the ocean.

THERE IS A MONSTER
UNDER HELEN'S BED

Moth flutters against the billowing curtains—white on white—
and Helen knows it's there only because of the sound its wings
make, quick little beats, dry and rustling. Helen imagines the
moth scream in a silent high pitch.

Helen wants to get up and untangle the little wings carefully,
avoiding the powdery scales, but she cannot let her feet touch the
floor. She imagines the cool wide boards, polished to a smooth shine,
so good to slide across in her white socks she has to change every day
now—but that's for daytime, when monsters are asleep and sated,
and retreat under the floorboards and behind the wallpaper covered
in deceitfully bright flowers. Monsters sleep behind the flowers, in
the narrow interstices between the wallpaper and the drywall, under
the nodding shadows of printed daisies and poppies.

But at night they wait for Helen, and she does not dare to
set foot on the smooth floor. The moth flutters, and Helen digs
herself deeper under the covers.

Helen has to go to the bathroom. The monster senses her
restless shifting and breathes heavily, moving closer to the edge,
its claws scrabbling on the wood of the floorboards. Helen can
hear the wet gurgling of its saliva and phlegm, and shivers. She
will wet her bed again tonight.

Helen's new mom, Janis, listens to the sounds upstairs. The circle of yellow light from the lamp clings to the shaggy rug Janis wants removed but never gets around to.

Her husband Tom follows her gaze with his own and smiles sheepishly.

"How long do you think until she learns English?"

Tom shrugs. "Children pick up languages pretty fast."

"But she's . . . older," Janis says. There is carefully hidden disappointment in her voice. She tries to love Helen; most of all, she tries not to regret her decision to adopt her. She did not want to wait for a younger child to become available, not in that horrid hotel with frozen pipes and non-flushing toilet, not in Siberia, where snow covered the ground in October. She grabbed Helen and ran back to the semblance of civilization in Moscow and then back to New Jersey—much like one would grab a sweater one did not particularly like, just to not spend another hour in a mall. She now regretted her panic, she regretted—even though she would never admit it to herself—bringing back Helen and not someone else. She is older, and like so many orphanage kids, she has developed an attachment disorder, or so her psychiatrist said.

She is a pretty child though, Janis consoles herself. Thin and blond, with dark blue eyes that have a habit of staring at any adult with thoughtful intensity, as if sizing them up for parental role. But everyone said how pretty she was. Janis sighs and returns to her reading. It's a parenting book, something she never thought she would be reading.

There's rustling upstairs, and both Janis and Tom look up, as if expecting to be able to see through the vaulted ceiling.

"Should we check on her?" Janis says.

Tom shakes his head. "She's old enough to sleep by herself."

Janis remembers the orphanage—ten beds to a room. Helen is not used to being by herself.

"She better not wet her bed again," Tom says.

Janis nods. The book is not helping.

Helen thinks back to the day when the monsters first appeared. She had to go to the bathroom, and she felt (or imagined) a quick touch of hot breath when her feet touched the cold linoleum tiles of the orphanage floor. She listened to the even breathing of eight other girls—one had been recently adopted, the youngest, who went home with her new mom and dad. There were no monsters and no hidden breathing, just a general unfairness of the situation: the longer one waited for the parents to show up, the smaller one's chances grew.

Helen went to the door, into the long hallway lit by dead fluorescent lights, and all the way to the bathroom where the toilet gurgled habitually.

On her way back, Helen heard voices—husky voices of the older boys, too old to be adopted, too young for the vocational training school where they would be sent once they turned fourteen. The boys everyone knew would grow up to be bad, and already well on their way to fulfilling the expectations. Helen pressed against the wall and listened to their whispers and laughter.

She passed the door of her dormitory and peeked around the corner. They were by the lockers, five or six of them, and there were no adults in sight.

Helen can see it now: there is a girl with them—Tanya, who is older than Helen. She is ten, and she hangs out with the boys; she smokes and drinks with them after the lights-out. But they do not act as her friends. Tanya is crying.

The boys push her against the solid wall of the lockers, and Helen imagines how the cold metal feels against a cheek wet with tears, the faint smell of green paint lingering since last summer.

The boys tell Tanya to shut up, and press harder, her face and chest flat against metal; they lift her dress and pull down her underwear, they force her legs open.

One of the boys, red-headed, cold-eyed, puts his hand between Tanya's legs; his shoulder is moving as if his hand is searching for something, and his breath is loud in the silence broken only by the occasional sob. He then pulls down his pants and presses against Tanya who cries more as he thrusts with his hips. He steps back and another boy takes his place. Helen thinks she smells the sea, of which she retains a faint memory—she was only two when her real parents took her on vacation.

She stepped away from the corner and ran to her room on light feet, barely touching the linoleum. She ran to her bed and then the monster lunged. She felt its fetid breath on her knees, its clawed hands grabbing her ankles.

She cried and wrestled free, and dove under the covers; until morning she dreamt about cold eyes and sharp claws sliding up her legs and forcing them apart.

Janis tries to be a good mother; even as she finds Helen awake and curled up among the bunched and wet sheets, she does not scold. She only sighs and tosses the soiled sheets into the hamper. She then tells Helen to go eat breakfast.

At the table, Helen is still subdued but wrinkles her nose at slices of toast—she does not like Wonderbread, she misses the chewy thick slices with a golden crust. Janis makes a mental note to pick up some loaves of Italian bread, and butters the toast for her impossible girl.

"Eat," she says, even as Helen stares at her with uncomprehending eyes. "We're going to see the doctor."

Helen smiles at that word. "Papa," she says.

Janis shakes her head. "No. Nyet. Tom is your papa," she says. "Not the doctor, not any anyone else. You can't choose your family, you know."

Helen does not understand, but Janis does, and she mentally admonishes herself to practice what she preaches, to remember this little adage. Like it or not, she is stuck with Helen; she's not going to return her like an unloved puppy to the pound. If only she were easier to love.

Janis shakes her head and cleans the table. She nudges Helen up the stairs, and she goes, obedient, to brush her teeth and put on her clothes. Helen does everything quickly, the motions precise and fluid, trained by half a decade of synchronized grooming, dressing, and eating. She makes her bed neatly with hospital corners—even though she still seems baffled by the second sheet instead of the white cloth envelope enclosing the blanket that so vexed Janis during her hotel stay in Siberia.

Janis drives to the doctor. In this part of Edison, there are many Russians and other Slavic nationals—she can hear their rough, guttural speech reaching for her through the open car window, trying to drag Janis back to the snow-covered town in Siberia, run-down buildings parasitically attached to some industrial monstrosity of secretive purpose.

Helen, on the other hand, perks up and sticks her head out of the window, smiling and waving. Janis purses her lips and pulls her inside, and rolls up the windows. Helen has to learn English, not to cling to a misplaced remnant of the life she had left.

The doctor is Russian too—he laughs with an avuncular roll, and reassures Janis in his heavily accented English. He takes Helen to his office on the third floor of the office building, where the windows offer up a view of the adjacent strip mall. Janis follows even though she cannot understand them. They seem to conspire against her—the doctor at his ostentatious mahogany desk (he sits next to it, not behind it) and Helen, sunken into a plush red chair, a box of tissues thoughtfully placed on the small stand by her elbow. Janis sits awkwardly on an uncomfortable ottoman by the door, feeling like a poor relation, an unwelcome intruder.

The doctor and the girl look at her simultaneously, laugh, and resume their conversation. What an ugly language, Janis thinks. There are no tissues by her ottoman.

Helen likes the doctor, the same way she likes all bearded men with calloused hands and a faint smell of cologne and leather clinging to them. She wishes for a new father like that—not her current flabby, pasty one. Helen knows that despite what the doctor says, the family is not permanent—she remembers children who went home with their new parents, only to be returned and given to different ones. The trouble is, Helen does not want to go back to the orphanage where the monsters are relentless and walk freely at all hours. She prefers the ones that stay under the bed and sleep during the day. Helen devises plans to become a monster herself.

"Why are you unhappy?" the doctor asks. His eyes behind the lenses of his spectacles are kind. He often asks this question.

Helen shrugs.

"Aren't your parents nice to you?"

"They are," she says. "They are nice."

"What's the problem then? Do you miss your friends?"

"No." She shakes her head. She does not miss anyone. "I want new parents."

"Some would say you are lucky to have the parents you do. They give you everything you want."

She nods. She knows she is being ungrateful—always has been, even back in the orphanage where she was lucky to have a roof over her head and a bed to sleep in, where she did not have to freeze to death in the streets. "I know."

"Then what?" The kindness in the doctor's voice cracks, about to let something else through. "What's the problem?"

"There is a monster under my bed," she says. "It wouldn't let me go to the bathroom."

"Is this why you wet your bed?" the doctor asks.

Helen feels her cheeks grow hot—she cannot believe Janis has told on her. Her eyes flash indignation, but the doctor does not notice.

"What kind of monster is it?" he asks.

Helen hikes up her trouser leg and shows him deep bruises the color of plums, the wide gashes barely healed over, running from her kneecap to the top of her white sock. She hears Janis gasp on her ottoman.

Then the doctor starts asking Janis questions Helen does not understand. She only hears fear in Janis's voice, and feels guilty. Now she knows about the monster too, and probably worries.

Janis looks at the newspaper clipping the doctor has photocopied for her. Some are printouts of the internet articles, and Janis wonders if he collects this stuff and why. But she knows the answer—there are enough of these adopted children and their anxious parents to pay for his office and the mahogany desk and the red plush chairs. Of course he collects the clippings about child murders.

Janis reads the small, too dark print of a poor photocopy, she looks at the photograph that doesn't look like a child's face—just a Rorschach of black and white planes; it's such a bad copy of the picture. Could be a little boy with black pools where his eyes should have been.

She reads the articles—they all say the same thing. An adopted child beaten to death by his parents in Switzerland. Countries and names change from one article to the next, but the story is the same—beaten, dismembered, thrown out of windows, moving vehicles, off bridges. She flips through the clippings, face after face after face in severe black and white. Janis cries then, not for them but for Helen.

The monster growls so softly it sounds like a purr. Its claws tap on the floorboards like castanets. Helen sits on her bed hugging the bruised knees to her chest.

The doctor did not seem to believe the story of the monster, and instead seemed to think that her mom and dad were the ones who hurt Helen. He even said that if they beat her, she should tell him that now and the police would find her new parents. While the proposal seemed tempting, Helen decided that lying was still wrong. The monster growls louder, reminding her of her mistake.

Helen cannot sleep and she thinks back, to what she can remember of the orphanage—so much of it is fading from her memory already. But the monsters she remembers, their long shadows stretching across the chipping walls. The nannies tell her that these are not shadows, just stains from the age-old plumbing leaks. Just blemishes of an unknown origin. They rumble in the pipes, they spread in the puddles of gray light that move across the floor of the classroom as the day wears on. They hide under desks and chairs in the common room, they follow the children outside to the swings and the monkey bars.

The monsters look out of the eyes of the parents who come to take away children; they all speak unfamiliar languages. They look out of the eyes of the nannies and especially the older boys, all teeth and clawed fingers. Helen avoided them and kept her head down, dreading the day she would be tall enough to push against the lockers.

She dangles her foot off the bed and pulls it back up right away, teasing the monster. She hears it lunge and miss and dig its claws into the floorboards. Its breathing is heavy now, upset. If she weren't so afraid, she would've descended to the floor and let the monster devour her—every bone, every morsel—and lick the floor clean of blood with its red tongue, rough enough to strip the paint and varnish off wood. Her parents would find no trace of her, as if she simply vanished from the world.

It would be a good death, she thinks, not at all like the girl they've found hanging off the curtain rod, her red tights wrapped around her neck. Helen remembers her purple tongue teasing between white sharp teeth; she remembers the missing incisor and the swollen tissue squeezing through the gap. Or like the boy who snuck off to go swimming in the lake a few kilometers away. They brought him back, blue and naked and wet like a creature from a horror movie. Like a monster.

She dangles the edge of the blanket and hears the tearing of fabric. She pulls back the long twisting shreds. She hears the footfalls on the staircase, and hides the torn blanket from sight. She pretends to sleep as the door squeals open and Janis stands in the doorway. Helen feels her worried look with the back of her neck.

"This is ridiculous," Tom says, and turns off the TV to illustrate his seriousness on the matter. "They think that we are hurting her?"

Janis nods and shows him the clippings. They do not say it out loud, but they both are thinking the same thing: these children are impossible, they are messed up and they cannot be fixed. They do not speak English, and yet they demand, they want things, they require tutors and psychiatrists, and their medical bills are piling up. The orphanages have the secret policy of adopting the most damaged children abroad, and Janis cannot decide if it is out of kindness, trying to get them help they cannot get at home, or cynicism, getting rid of the defectives and the unwanted.

She thinks of the people in the adoption agency and the orphanage staff, and she does not know if those people even know their own motives. She only knows that the doctors at the orphanage give all the children a clean bill of health, afraid to spook the potential parents. In any case, they find out soon enough.

Helen came with a heart murmur and bed wetting; the latter does not seem too bad compared to the congenital heart defect that is too late to fix. But even that fades in comparison to her acting out and scratching, to her fears, to her reluctance let them touch her. Even that fades in comparison to the unexplained bruises and cuts.

"I think she did it to herself," Tom says. "The doctors checked her out before—there wasn't a problem then. Maybe she fell or banged against something in the playground?"

Janis shakes her head. "I don't know. But those bruises . . . they look like fingerprints. Adult fingerprints, and nail scratches." She draws a deep breath, dreading the question she has to ask. "Tom . . . You wouldn't . . . "

He looks at her open-mouthed, not indignant, just surprised. "No. Of course not." Of course not, Janis scolds herself. How could she even think that?

He stares at her, clears his throat. "Janis, we really need to talk."

She knows what it's about—the child is a problem, like the children in the clippings. The problem. They never fought before, never suspected one another of anything unsavory. They used to have leisure and spare cash, they never used to argue like that. Janis just cannot bear to think about admitting defeat, to tolerate the smug *I-told-you-so*s from family and friends. "It's different when it's your own," they will say. "What did you expect? She's too old, too mixed up. It's not the same as having your own baby. It's sad, but you can't save them, Janis, you can't save them all."

She thought she could save just one, but even that is apparently too much for them.

"Yes," she says out loud. "We need to talk. Let me just check on her."

Helen squeezes her eyes shut and waits for the woman to close the door, cutting off the thick slab of light reaching in from the hallway. The light makes the monster retreat into its den somewhere between the bed and the floorboards, where its eyes glow with quiet red ferocity in the darkness. She wants to ask the woman—Janis, mom—to leave the door open, to put the lights on, but she cannot, and she cries silently, her salty tears sliding down her cheek and into her hair, soaking into the pillow.

The woman does not leave. Instead she comes in and sits on the bed, the white texture of her cable-knit sweater exaggerated by the light from the hallway and darkness inside the room. It is cold tonight—the cold has finally caught up with Helen. It chased her across the unfathomable chasm of the ocean and nine hours of flying through the air over the stationary clouds. The autumn is here now, and there are no more moths fluttering in the curtains.

Helen peeks between the tear-soaked eyelashes, and the beam of light twinkles and breaks into a myriad of tiny stars. The woman looks back at Helen but does not smile like she usually does when their eyes meet. Instead she sighs and strokes Helen's hair. She feels the moisture under her fingertips, and she looks like she's about to cry herself.

Helen considers opening her eyes completely but decides against it and squeezes them shut, feigning sleep. If she looks at her new mom directly, she will start talking, and then Helen would cry in earnest at her inability to understand, to explain about the monsters and shadows and fear.

Helen wants to talk about summers in Siberia—so short and so intense, so full of high-pitched whining of mosquitoes and the smell of pine trees oozing fresh sap, of spongy bogs studded with butter-yellow cloudberries. About the lake where the runaway boy drowned but which becomes transformed by a cloudless blue sky overhead into a swath of precious smooth silk surrounded by soft, succulent-green branches of firs.

But Helen cannot explain these things and she forces her eyelids tighter together, until her eyes burn.

Janis gives up and rises to her feet, the springs of the mattress squeaking in relief. The door closes behind her, cutting off the light.

In the darkness, there is shifting and stirring. Helen watches the sheet of wallpaper peel away, admitting a thin beam of bluish light into the room.

Helen sits up and peers into the widening gap—carefully at first, wary of the monsters. She sees a small man, no bigger than a cat, crouching on the other side of the wallpaper barrier. His withered narrow face looks at Helen over his shoulder, and then he turns away and draws on the inside of the wall—a chain of tiny cranes, dwarfed by the shadows of daisies and poppies. They seem paler on the other side but alive, nodding in the invisible breeze.

Helen pulls the sheets of the wallpaper apart, and she sees a bright blue lake surrounded by yellow-needled larches. The monster crawls from under the bed and stands beside her, panting like a dog, the black fur between its wing-like shoulder blades bristling. Helen is surprised to not be afraid of it anymore.

The monster leaps into the gap and Helen follows, timid at first. She turns to look back and watches the wallpaper fold back with a quiet rustling and grow together, fusing. She sees the ghostly flowers, and behind them—her room, a shadow image from a magic lantern.

The monster growls and bounds ahead, then stops and waits for her by the tiny man and his cranes, which are flying in place, their wings sweeping up and down in a graceful motion. She watches them for a while, never moving and yet flying south among the daisies and poppies which are still blooming despite the autumn and its cold fingers reaching even behind the wallpaper, where the monsters sleep during the day.

The monster barks and laughs and leaps to the right, then to the left; then it gallops toward the lake, looking over its shoulder, inviting Helen to follow. Helen sighs and walks through the fallen leaves, rubbery under her white socks, she walks to the lake where a blue boy with sharp teeth is waiting for her, the monster by his side like a hound.

YAKOV AND THE CROWS

Yakov is glad to see that the crow has come back. He watches it out of his office window, five stories up above a frozen Moscow street; just another window on the flat, uniform façade of the square building. They call places like this one "the box"—not just because of its shape, but also because no one really knows what goes on in there. Government buildings. Yakov knows, he works here. He proofreads blueprints. Now they pile on his desk, and Yakov watches the crow.

He has noticed it a few days back, when he cracked the window and took his lunch bag from the ledge just outside. Many did this—it saved a trip down to the refrigerator in the common room. Yakov noticed that the ham sandwich lacked ham, and the entire neat package has been eviscerated with surgical precision. He looked outside, as if hoping to glimpse a thief. He saw a crow.

The crow does its usual rounds—it flies level with the sixth story, from one end of the building to the other, inspecting every window for a paper bag. The crow disdains hardboiled eggs and laughs at bread, but savors meat and cheese. Yakov waits for it.

It alights on the ledge and looks at Yakov, its head tilted, one roguish eye studying him. The black of the crow's head looks like a beret, and its body is of dull but somehow shiny grey. Black feathers on the tips of its wings are folded primly, like laced fingers. What a gypsy eye, Yakov thinks. How familiar. Maria used to have black gypsy eyes like that, until they closed, forever weighted by dull copper coins.

The crow watches him, the glimmer in its eye almost humorous. It seems indifferent to Yakov's lunch bag. It moves closer, with short hops along the ledge, until its black rogue eye is aligned with Yakov's blue. The crow shakes with suppressed laughter.

"Maria?" he says before he even realizes his lips are moving.

The crow flaps its wings and continues its solitary patrol. Yakov returns to his desk. There are three other desks in the room, covered with dust, empty since the budget cut last year, in 1989. They still keep Yakov.

Five o'clock rolls by, and he takes the subway home. It's crowded, and he leans against the doors, thinking about the crow, as the train carries him away from the hateful wind-scourged outskirts, towards the center, the old city, where his home is.

It is dark as he walks down the frozen boulevard, past the sleeping bums and squeezing couples undeterred by the cold and the frigid iron of the benches. Streetlamps light his way with their wan mercury glow.

He ascends to the third story, and listens outside of the door. Young voices and music reach into the stony stairwell full of echoes. His son Mitya has some friends over. Yakov likes the music—one of the new bands, Aquarium it's called. He listens to the lyrics from outside; they have nice imagery. Gold on blue, flame-maned lions, wolves and ravens. He turns the key.

Mitya and two of his friends, Andrey and Slava, greet him with fake moans of disappointment. Yakov smiles—he likes the kids, and they seem to like him back, despite their many differences.

"Yakov Mihailovich," Slava says. "We did some nice business today. I just thought I'd tell you that." He knows how much

Yakov disapproves of all the recent wheelings and dealings, and never misses a chance to tease him.

Yakov bites. "There's more to life than money, boys."

All three giggle.

"Dad," Mitya says, grinning from ear to ear, his eyes as dark and mischievous as those of the crow. "Don't you want to know how?"

Yakov nods.

"This morning, we bought a case of beer at seven rubles a can. And this afternoon the prices went up, all the way to fifteen."

"And you sold it," Yakov guesses.

The three laugh.

"No," Mitya says. "We're drinking it. Want some?"

Yakov laughs too. They all think that the inflation is funny. "You call that business?"

"Life's too short to drink cheap beer," Andrey says.

Mitya notices that Yakov is preoccupied. "You want anything to eat?" he says.

Yakov shakes his head. "You go ahead. I'll just read."

"Want us to turn the music down?"

"No, I like it. Reminds me of the Akmeists."

"Who?" Slava says.

Yakov sighs. These kids have their heads so full of money, they forgot everything else. "The school of poets in the early 20th century," he says. "They wrote poetry centered around imagery. You heard of Gumilev, I presume."

"Yeah," Andrey says. "Wasn't he executed by the firing squad in 1921?"

Yakov rolls his eyes. "Yes. And before that, he was a poet. A good one, too. There's more to people than the way they died."

He goes to his room, changes into his threadbare sweats and reads a Rex Stout novel. A few pages into it, he realizes that he has no idea of what he has just read—the crow is still on his mind. He doesn't believe in reincarnation, but still, those eyes . . .

Mitya's friends leave, and he pokes his head in, concern on his sharp dark face, so unlike Yakov's pale and placid one. "Dad, are you all right?"

"Yeah," Yakov says.

"Everything all right at work?"

Yakov nods, looking into the book with emphasis.

Mitya comes in and sits on Yakov's bed. "Did I do something?"

Yakov gives up and closes the book. "No, Mitya." He starts to tell him about the crow, but feels silly and cuts himself off. "How was school?"

"Fine," Mitya says. "I just wish I majored in computers, like Andrey."

Yakov nods. Andrey will have an easier time finding work. "Still," he says. "The world needs art history majors."

"Only it's not going to pay them," Mitya says. "You know it and I know it. As soon as I graduate, I'll be selling cigarettes in the kiosk across the street."

Yakov wishes he had comfort to offer. This is really his biggest problem with the new times—money. So much time is spent thinking about it, people hardly pay attention to anything else anymore. "There's more to life than money," he says feebly.

"I know." Mitya sighs. "I'm surprised that you're so reactionary. I thought you hated the communists."

Yakov nods. "Still do. But I like free education and healthcare, and guaranteed employment."

Mitya has heard all this before. "I know. But the free healthcare didn't save Mom."

Yakov sits up. "Don't say that. It was cancer, no one could have done anything for her." He sighs. "At least, the doctors who cared for her were not there for the money, but because they wanted to help people."

They sit in silence for a while. Yakov feels like a failure. All the things he dreamt of, all the hopes are dashed and ridiculed. He wanted freedom, he wanted the yoke off his neck. He didn't want this soulless vacuum, he didn't want fear.

"It's all right, Mitya," he answers his thoughts. "When I'm gone, you can sell this apartment. It costs a lot."

"Dad, don't say that."

"Sorry." It's not fair, Yakov thinks. He just wants his son to be able to do what he loves. He wonders what the crow would think about that.

The next morning, Yakov sits on the windowsill, waiting for the crow. His heart skips a beat when it appears. But not alone—there's a whole murder. He counts them. Twelve. They patrol the windows in formation. Every now and again, one breaks off to rummage through a paper bag and emerge with a hotdog or a slice of ham in its beak. Yakov watches his crow. He can tell it apart from all the others.

The crows arrive to his window. He's waiting for them, holding out a plastic container full of beef chunks. The crows demur at first, but soon grow bold and eat. He talks to them. He tells them of all the things that bother him—that the politics have changed but the politicians are still the same exact people as back in the sixties, only balder and fatter; he tells them that nobody cares about anything important anymore. He tells them that freedom has nothing to do with money, or the McDonald's restaurants. The crows stop eating and listen.

They leave, but come back the next day, a dozen of them. The blueprints are still piling up on his desk, but Yakov doesn't care. He finally found someone who would listen to him.

One of the crows seems agitated, and flaps its wings. The others caw, and Yakov stops talking, perplexed. The crows gather around their discomfited fellow. They grow silent and watch, until the crow falls on its side, its wings beating, and its feet scraping the ledge. It twitches and becomes still, its upturned gypsy eye milking over with death.

Eleven crows look at Yakov for a moment, and take wing.

"Wait," he calls after them. "Come back!"

The door opens, and Luganov, his boss, looks in. "Yakov," he says. "Do you have a crow problem?"

"No," Yakov says. "Why?"

"People were complaining they steal lunches," Luganov says. "I put rat poison in mine, and told everyone else to do the same. You need some?"

"No," Yakov says, shaking. "Why would you do something like that?"

Luganov barks a laugh. "I figured, rat poison would work even on winged rats, no?"

The door closes, and Yakov sits on his chair, his face in his hands. Poisoned. No doubt, the crows blame him. He prays that they would come back tomorrow, so he can explain.

The crows come the next day, just eleven of them. They start their patrol.

"No," Yakov screams from his window. "No! It's poisoned!"

They either do not hear, or choose to ignore him.

Yakov throws the window open and waves his arms. He makes so much noise that heads appear in the windows above and below him. He calls to the crows, imploring, warning, and apologizing. They don't seem to care.

Yakov climbs onto the high windowsill and stands there for a moment, his knees trembling under him. "It's poison," he calls again in a breathless voice. "Leave it alone! They're trying to kill you!"

He steps out on the ledge. The heads in the windows gape and gasp, and disappear. He hears footsteps in the hallway—his coworkers running to intercept him, to drag him inside, to silence him. Yakov will not submit to that; he has been silenced before, but he won't let it happen again. He takes a step along the ledge, his arms still waving, his voice growing hoarse.

Yakov's knees shake and he feels sick to his stomach. "Come back," he screams. "Please come back!"

His foot slides from under him, and his arms flap like wings. Then, it's only the exhilaration of the flight and the pinch of frozen air.

People gather around the dead body, clucking their tongues and telling each other to call the police. They are too busy to see a dozen crows that circle high above the square building, cawing.

HECTOR MEETS THE KING

"I never was good at saying goodbye, and you were never good at letting go. So it starts, between me and you, and so it will end. I and you, inhale and exhale, a sigh and a kiss into a flat, adenoid face of the world.

"I know, I do not look much like a hero nowadays—gravity, the eternal bitch, has me in its hold, my fingertips are stained with ink, and my shoulders wrap around my chest as a pair of wide, anemic wings. But believe me, I am a hero.

"There are ties in the world, son. Nothing binds more securely than another's pain. I watch your mother sleeping, her translucent skin flushed with dreams, her stately knees drawn at the pit of her stomach. I would have loved her even if she were short of leg and black of tooth; even then hurting her would not be a possibility. Mediocrity is the only painless state in the world, or so I thought.

"There is a finite, immutable amount of pain in the world, and what you spare others you must swallow yourself. I swallowed my pride and my honor. I did not walk through the gates that day, unable to hurt her. I would rather be a coward than a torturer. The legends lie—they tell the story as it should have been, they tell of Hector felled in the spray of warm sticky blood and splintered bone, they tell of his body dragged behind a chariot, of his orphaned son. The truth is sadder. Hector lived to see his son grow up. He watched him through the shroud of swallowed shame, and his eyes teared, as if from acrid smoke of burning Troy. And so it ends."

I sing of what has not been sung before. I sing of Hector and his sacrifice, I sing his unlamented mediocrity. I sing his cowering, and I sing his end.

I sing the dry wooden rain of arrows that drummed on the roofs of the palace and the hovels, monotonous, growing too familiar to be noticed. I sing the braying of donkeys in their stables, the crowing of rooster at dawn, and lowing of oxen. Smells of manure and hay. Incessant gnawing of saws and hacking of axes outside the city walls. The siege. I sing guilt like manacles.

Hector took off his helm with horsehair crest that had scared the infant. With this gesture he dispensed with the heroism forever. He took his son into the crook of his arm, and his wife—by her hand. He was familiar with the labyrinth of narrow streets, and with vast open space by the city walls.

As Cassandra's mad cries hung over the city like a cloud, he led them to the well-hidden entrance into an underground tunnel that took them outside, into the thicket of scrub and hazelnuts. Swift, straight branches—future arrows—lashed their faces as they walked away from the doomed city.

I sing Hector, as he cranes his neck surveying a tall, gleaming building, and I sing his new job, I sing eight hours at the office, every day, excepting the holidays and two-week vacation. I sing the plastic smile of the receptionist that greets him every morning, as the elevator spews him forth, in the crowd of other overheated bodies. I sing Hector's sacrifice.

I put on my helm, the horsehair crest of it moth-eaten and ready to fall apart into dust. I fold the note addressed to my son and leave it on the kitchen table. I do not dare to kiss Andromache, for fear of waking her and letting the yoke of her white arms hold me back again.

I find my spear in the back of a coat closet, and my arthritic fingers close over its smooth, cool shaft. I do not even attempt to put on my old armor—my girth is too great now, and my back is too bent and weakened by years at the desk to bear its terrible weight. But I brush my fingertips against polished bronze of the breastplate. I pick up my shield and strap on my sword.

I pause in the driveway, thinking whether I should take my car. I decide against it—it seems undignified somehow. I let my feet carry me past and out of the sleeping development.

I pass green lawns and neatly trimmed hedges; somebody's dog follows me, its docked tail wagging in tentative friendship. I do not know where I am going, but I am certain that I will find it, and all mistakes of the past will be rectified. I think of what will become of Andromache, of her delayed widowhood. I find comfort in thoughts about pension, Social Security, life insurance. With all that, she won't have to do any more telemarketing, and she will drop her pretense of happiness. As I think, I do not notice as I arrive here, at the miniature golf course.

Hector stopped, the trimmed grass soft and submissive under the soles of his scuffed brown shoes. He surveyed the battlefield from under drawn greying eyebrows. His eyes squinted against the lashings of the wind and hardened to narrow slits.

A windmill chopped the air into thick, humid slices, and the wind whistled between its four wings. A giant ape, its low forehead wrinkled with malice, grinned with bright wooden teeth and shuffled its massive foot back and forth, exposing and covering a narrow pipe, just wide enough for a golf ball. A dinosaur reared up as its mouth opened in and closed in silent screams of presumed pain.

These were the only worthy adversaries, and Hector hefted his spear, choosing his target. The ape seemed the most malignant of all, and he shouted his challenge to it. The ape grinned and shuffled in one place, too dumb or too conceited to take cover.

Hector's arm felt weak as he raised his spear and hurled it toward the ape. The spear hit its shoulder and sunk into the wooden flesh, trembling from impact. The shaft swayed, and the spear fell to the ground.

The ape roared and cowered for a moment, and then stood to its full height, its fists the size of millstones pounding on its chest. It swung at Hector, but he ducked the blow. The giant fist passed inches over his head, and his grey hair ruffled in the wind.

Hector ripped his sword from the sheath, and lunged for the ape's unprotected side. The gash his blade left dripped with ichor the color of papier-mâché, and the ape howled in pain.

Hector retreated, waiting for his chance to strike, as the enraged ape chased after him, its cries piercing like Andromache's tears. Hector was running out of breath, weighed as he was by age and manacles of guilt. He remembered the ape's name: King Kong. It was too young and too strong for him, and he retreated until the back wall of the windmill blocked his passage—he could feel it with his shoulder blades. The ape's fists swung in an easy rhythm: king-kong, sigh-kill, maim-kiss.

Hector's sword slashed across the ape's knuckles, making it cry out again, but inflicted as little damage as a toothpick. He still waved his weapon about as the ape picked him into one of its fists, as his ribs cracked, as his world narrowed to a swirling, rolling singularity of darkness.

In his last moments his thoughts sped up so that his short time of lingering lucidity between blindness and death stretched forever. Hector dreamed of Achilles, guilt, and ape, of the forces that grinded him into a bloodied, limp husk, of the destiny of loss and defeat. He dreamed of Andromache's peppy voice traveling over the telephone wires, "Have you considered switching your long-distance provider?" He had spared her degradation in the Grecian hands, he had saved her from a lifetime of slavery. She would be grateful.

And he thought of his son, of his legacy, of a sigh and a kiss. He would graduate from college and enter a law school, and become a king—like King Menelaus, King Priam, the King o'Cats, King Kong. And Hector smiled.

CHAPAEV AND THE COCONUT GIRL

I discovered that my mom left for Indonesia (Bali, to be exact) on her birthday. I called to wish her a happy one, but my dad answered the phone instead and informed me that she was traveling. To Bali. "She told me to tell you that she is in paradise," he said.

"Give her my best," I said.

Now, don't get me wrong. I'm thrilled for my mom to be able to travel like this, because really, for people of her generation and ethnic disposition (she was born in 1942, in German-occupied Lithuania) life never promised anything remotely tropical or whimsical. Yet, I was a little troubled as I had been since 1989, when the world shifted askew cracking the foundation of our existence, and the cracks spread all over the formerly impenetrable and imaginary air bubble that surrounded the then-USSR. I found myself among those who somehow slipped through those cracks, like a goldfish in a temporary prison of a plastic bag, right into the cold and big world—or a fish tank; not that it made that much difference. And this was really the crux of the issue: people like me left so that the change around them would be explainable by travel and culture shock rather than by the impossible overturning if the world which suddenly folded, did a little flip, and pulled itself from under their securely planted feet. Travel lets you pretend that the world didn't really change, that you just chose your terms. My terms include working in an AI lab at MIT; could be worse.

My parents stayed behind then, as they still do every time I visit, and when I leave them at the airport, I always look back, at how small they are, and my heart fractures anew. So I'm thrilled now that mom is getting to travel a little, and she doesn't feel quite as abandoned to me when she does. She gets to do some abandoning of her own, and I console dad over the phone. Of course he can cook his own dinner, but he appreciates the sympathy. I think he does—at least, as effective as sympathy across the Atlantic can be, conveyed by sighs whispering through the impossible length of telephone wires.

And after we hung up, I was still pensive, thinking of my mom in such a distant place, even more distant than before. The positive thing about travel though is that if you go away sufficiently far, at some point you start getting closer. And of course distance was conducive of deceit: for all I knew, mom could've still been at home, giggling on the couch, and not at all in Indonesia. Distances are tricky like that.

There is a secret I have, a really embarrassing thing: I worship Chapaev. Despite the jokes that are his later legacy and the revolutionary terror of his earlier days, these people, their horses, the Red Army, and all that elementary school-level propaganda is lodged deep in my heart, like a metal splinter. Horses and steppes and wars fought with sabers rather than guns. They probably did have guns though; wouldn't they? Of course they had guns. It's just this is not how I imagined it in my childhood or now, for that matter. Temporal distances are tricky as well.

Dealing with the dead is frustrating because you can never ask them anything—you could, but they wouldn't answer. So I compose long conversations in my head, asking about the Red

Army and how did it all really happen, what the dirt under the horses' hooves smelled like, if they were crawling with lice, this sort of thing. If he really drowned in the end, trying to swim across River Ural, or did he fake it, tired of war and fame, tired of being a hero. If he decided to quit the revolution gig and instead grow pumpkins somewhere. I wonder if he's still alive, even though he would be over a hundred years old, hundred and twenty, to be exact, but that doesn't seem too old for a hero. Come and think about it, all heroes of the revolutions are relatively young in historical terms. And I'm left to my own yarns, recursive narratives I spin as I drink my tea and stare out of the window at the houses across the street and imagine Charles River far behind them. I squint and the buildings disappear and I can see in my mind's eye Charles, thick and green, speckled with oil slicks like a multicolored serpent, and if I squint further, it becomes Ural on the shores of which my stories either end or begin—it all depends on a day.

Today, I wait for the rooftops to turn molten yellow and orange, like a pumpkin, and I imagine him emerging from the freezing water, dripping wet, his teeth clattering, and the right sleeve of his uniform dark with blood. Then he walks, like giants walk, each leap taking him over a hill or a small river, the blood drips spawning lakes and craters in his wake, leaving the earth steaming and scorched, scars that it will take centuries to heal in the unforgiving Siberian climate. The pine and fir forest that gradually rises around him does nothing to impede his progress as he pushes the trees aside like mere branches, and pulls his feet out of the sucking morasses of swamps with ease.

This is the thing that makes daydreaming so pleasant: one can keep the details vague and imagine tall firs and green meadows, serpentine rivers and lakes like mirrors, fields yellow with heavy nodding wheat—everything, everything. And his walk can take him anywhere, and today I imagine him walking like that, strides of a giant, a red star on his hat illuminating his way with a crimson strobe, across Siberia and past China, all the way to the Sea of Japan. I imagine him jumping off the edge of Kamchatka as if it it was a springboard, and then—Sakhalin, Japan. I watch him treading on islands and land formations as if they were mere stepping stones, all the way to the East China Sea where the islands grow a bit scarce and he has to swim a little. Then in the Philippines, he's picking up his inhuman stride again, and there, finally, he reaches Indonesia. My mom said it was a paradise.

Coconut Girl is a myth common in Indonesia, my mom says. Suddenly, she is a folklorist who's eager to educate me on foreign mythologies. She also emails me pictures of alien birds and large lizards—who is this woman?—and talks about where she would like to go next year. Right now, it's a toss-up between Thailand and New Zealand. But for now she talks about the Coconut Girl and laughs, and I assume blushes a little, because it is really a dirty story. Girl shitting out stuff like that—of course, my mom doesn't say "shitting out." She says "excreting," and that makes me giggle over the phone.

So, the Coconut Girl: there was a farmer named Ameta who found a coconut when it washed ashore. No one ever saw such things before on his island (called Seram). The next night he dreamt about planting it—a shadowy voice instructed him how to do such a thing. He planted the coconut and soon the coconut grew into a beautiful palm tree, and many flowers clustered between its feathered leaves. Ameta climbed the tree but cut his hand, and one of the flowers became stained with his blood. As such tales go, the flower stained with blood became a coconut that then became a girl, named Hainuwele.

Hainuwele, as it turned out, wasn't just any coconut girl: every time she went to the bathroom, instead of regular human turds she dropped all sorts of interesting objects: earrings, serving dishes, coral statuettes, dinner plates, jewelry, stones, shells. Copper gongs and other treasures. And she gave all of those wonderful things to the villagers.

We all know how these stories go. Coconut Girl was the original Giving Tree, Rainbow Fish, and whatever other propaganda they're feeding the kids nowadays. In her case, however, the story is truthful—after all her giving, she was killed, since we do not like those who make us feel grateful, and there's no greater contempt than that for someone whom we owe a debt of gratitude. The Indonesian version tells it right.

I of course don't tell this to my mom, because she would only get upset at my negativity. She thinks I'm cynical, but I am not. I'm normal. It is her who is abnormally naïve, and after all the crap she had to go through it is a small miracle that she manages to be happy, bouncy, and wanting to see New Zealand. "Will you walk the path to Mordor?" I ask her.

"A path to what, dear?" she asks, sweetly.

"Never mind," I say. "Listen, I have to go."

"Save your money," she says. "International phone calls are expensive."

I want to tell her that money has nothing to do with it, it's just that I have to go to work, but change my mind. It doesn't matter and she will never remember anyway. And as dad says, there's just no point in arguing—I can stand being wrong as long as it makes her happy. I hope it does.

I take the subway to work, and while riding I consider the rest of the tale. Its sad sad end, especially.

So what did the villagers do to the girl who gave everything to them, the precious things she made come out of her own body? They dug a pit and pushed her into it, and then they danced and trampled the dirt over her. I can imagine a death like that—suffocation and lungs filled with mud, a broken sternum and ribs bristling with white shattered edges. Loss of consciousness and its black relief. Being buried alive not accidentally but intentionally. Hands grasping and failing, nails breaking.

Ameta found her body and cut it into pieces and buried it all over the place. Mom didn't tell me why would he do such a thing—I can understand exhumation, but not dismemberment, but I'm sure he had his reasons and I'm just blinded by my own prejudices. Whatever the case, he dismembered her and buried her parts all over, and then they grew into various tuberous plants, yams etcetera. Mom is hazy on what exact plants they are, and she also said something about goddess and how people started having sex only after Hainuwele died. If I were in the mood, I would think how cool it is that the story manages to conflate the Eve's apple with Jesus and throw in some creation to boot, but today I'm uninterested in Westernizing folklore and reducing everything to Christianity. Instead I sit and stare at my own reflection in the window across, as the subway train sways and hurtles itself closer and closer to MIT, my station, while thinking about how Chapaev fits into it and what would he do. He is an indispensable part of the Revolution—and as such, a creation mythology. The world he belonged to was forged in a celestial fire, a new world to which a very bloody creation myth was entirely appropriate, and heroes of the revolution were its sacrifices.

The mythology of the Red Cavalry is a pervasive one—no matter how many post-Communist years we accumulate, his image is always there, saved in the collective un- and semiconscioius, in jokes, old movies, books some of us had to read. They are the heroes, the martyrs, the creators. They are our Coconut Girl—without the fertility.

Why do I want to save Chapaev so badly? Two reasons: first, ambiguity of his death. If someone's body is never found, you cannot really be sure that they are dead. Second, I want him to be alive so that he doesn't end up like the stupid giving tree. We hate those who help us, and the only way to deal with that guilt is to kill them—like they did with the Coconut Girl, Hainuwele. Better yet if the benefactors kill themselves (we call it self-sacrifice, and this is our favorite) sparing us the mess. In my mind, heroes that live are a vindication, a heartfelt slap in the face of our collective greed. So I make him live, and I make him settle in Indonesia.

"So you made him an immigrant." I don't have many friends, except Veronica and Cecilia, two Brazilian grad students who are way too much fun for me, and I'm not even sure how to deal with them. But I just follow them around, awkwardly, and buy them drinks in any of Boston's pubs if the opportunity presents itself. It presents itself after work today, and we all drink in the Bow and Arrow. Cecilia is downing fuzzy navels and Veronica is sticking with sweet wine; I drink Sam Adams, out of some guilty obligation of someone who knows they don't really belong in

Boston but appreciates the opportunity anyway. After a few, I tell them about Chapaev and Indonesia. They seem amused.

"So you made him an immigrant," Cecilia says and laughs.

Veronica, who has a cold, laughs too in a sexy deep throaty way that makes me insanely jealous. "Everyone's an immigrant somewhere. Except the people who stay home."

"And who would want that?" Cecilia laughs and laughs. I'm jealous of how lanky and long she is, how her neck elongates and strains as she tosses back her head and finishes her drink. This is something about these two that I want so desperately and yet have no prospects of achieving: being in the center of attention, attracting people no matter where they go, having seemingly hundreds of friends. I always feel so honored when they choose to hang out with my own insignificant self.

"What are you working on now, Elena?" Veronica asks. "Besides rewriting history, of course."

"Still cockroaches," I say and sigh. The AI lab I work in, the Minsky lab, is world famous for our research. I get to be a nameless collaborator, the one who equips our robotic cockroaches with sensors and simple programming, little chips that allow them to teach themselves to avoid light and scatter at the sound of footsteps. So they scatter and are a huge pain in my ass to catch and fix. "I'm doing vibration sensitivity programming now."

Cecilia nods, politely. Or maybe she is genuinely interested. "They act like real ones?"

"Yeah," I say and drink my beer. "It's not much, and I've been in the lab for five years now, and I still do cockroaches. It's something, I guess."

They agree.

"What's next for you?" Veronica asks. "Rats?"

I'm not sure if she's mocking or not. "Probably more cockroaches. I want to make something that can learn more things, you know? More patterns. Like, not just light and sound and vibration, but the time of day, something that can make decisions. And not just react but to anticipate, to affect . . . " I stumble over my words and fall silent, afraid to bore, to take up too much of their valuable attention. Besides, they are training to become neuroscientists, and I expect them to have some contempt for those of us who try to replicate a great complexity of a brain via computer chips and switches linked together, the artificial neural networks that are not at all neural.

"It sounds pretty cool," Veronica says, her white teeth gleaming, her skin the color of an ominous sunset. "This is the problem I have with much of the neurosience—it always interprets living beings as reactive, and you can't really make a breakthrough within those constraints."

I nod and hold my breath—it is not often that Veronica (or Cecilia, for that matter) want to geek out with me. Normally, they just try to give me advice, because apparently to them I look especially helpless and awkward. And I am grateful, I really am, and I hope to learn their effortless laugh and ability to not become tongue-tied when faced with people, and managing to not dress as a dork. Not mangling every English idiom I learn with such effort would also be nice, but I'm not setting the bar high here. At least, in terms of personal social achievement.

"I think most of us are reactive though," I tell Veronica. "It takes a hero to be able to shape the circumstance rather than follow them. You know how only main characters in books manage to shape their own destiny and the rest just follow? I think it's the same in human history."

"I was thinking more about my animals," Veronica says, and mercifully doesn't laugh. With a blistering wave of shame, I remember that she works with bats. "But I take your point. Bats are always scanning their environment for clues, so they are searching for their own shape of being . . . of their spaces. It's one thing to merely perceive the surroundings, and yet quite another to send out the signal to find out what those surroundings are; by choosing direction, they create the reality they want to interact with."

I nod. "This makes sense. Maybe I should equip my cockroaches with a sonar or some echolocation device. This way I can teach them to make decisions about what to explore."

"Let me know how it goes," Veronica says.

Cecilia smoothly interjects, "And meanwhile, we're having a party this Saturday. Our friend Todd will be bringing his band."

"You have something to wear, right?" Veronica says, and their concern with my lack of a cohesive wardrobe forces away all other thoughts, and I bask in their attention and consider highlights. We finish our drinks and Cecilia skips, to prepare the place for the party. Veronica stays with me, and before I can get over the prospect of a one-on-one conversation, she informs me that we have to go to Filene's Basement. "You absolutely cannot wear those palazzo pants again," she tells me firmly. "They're too synthetic, there're sparks flying off the cuffs when you walk."

I want to debate whether it is even possible for something to be too synthetic, isn't it an either-or situation? But Veronica grabs my hand and it makes me melt a little, and we're off to scour the expanse of Mass Ave for proper party outfits.

But before we reach Filene's Basement, something in a store window catches my eye and I freeze despite Veronica's impatient tugging and pulling, and I stare. It looks like some local gallery, one of those shops with hardwood floors polished so even the most modest heel clacks too loudly and the fronts of which are nothing but thick glass. In this window display I see: coral beads, copper gongs, dishes, wonderful objects. This place has Hainuwele all over it, and I go inside, suddenly conquering my fear of these posh and severe places.

Veronica follows, her perfect eyebrows drawn like Scythian bows, and her nose, reddened by the cold, sniffling with irritation. "What gives?"

"I have to see this," I say. Our shoes clack on the parquet, blond and polished, and there's no one but us in there. I look around for clues, for some sign that I'm in the right place. Finally, I see a dinner plate, carved out of soapstone, heavy and perfect, with a bunch of smaller knickknacks piled on it. "Take one," the handwritten sign over the plate invites. I sort through— mostly single earrings (my ears aren't pierced), coral beads, tiny statuettes, until finally I find a tin five-splayed star, painted red. The star Chapaev wore over his helm, I have to assume. I clasp it in my fist and tell Veronica, "Okay, we can go."

At the party, I feel unusually at ease—perhaps because there's a red star hastily sewn onto the bill of the hat I picked up while shopping. It is gray and has copper buttons on the sides, and gives a vaguely military impression. I'm wearing it with my new dress despite Veronica's suggestions. I am at ease.

Cecilia and Veronica went for a tropical theme, and there are piña coladas and pineapples and papayas everywhere. The place is a loft, and they moved most of the furniture into the kitchen, and there's a vast expanse of hardwood floor, like the gallery, but the sounds of heels are muffled by so many bodies packed into the space, their soft heat dissipating any too-clear sounds. The sideboard with drinks and fruit and strong cheeses is stretched along the far wall, by the window, which shows an incredible molten sunset, streaked bronze and pink and red, and soon it is violated and abandoned, cheeses crumbled and left undone on the bamboo cutting boards, the dull flat knives crusted over with white film like murder. I make my way over to the sideboard and pick on crumbs of camambert and smoked gouda, and sneak a grape or two. I would've liked some pineapple, but I know it would only make the corners of my mouth turn red and hurt for days, so I wisely stay away and sip a piña colada. The band is tuning up in the corner and the party surges toward them, leaving me and the cheeseboard in a contented solitude.

Our silent communion is interrupted when someone above me says, "Cecilia tells me you're in Minsky lab."

"Yeah," I say through a mouthful of cheese and give the intruder a hostile look. "What of it?"

He stares down at me through his thick glasses, his face expressing sincere concern. "So do you think AI is really possible?"

I swallow my cheese, and don't enjoy it anymore. "It depends on how you define AI. It probably isn't going to be cute or sexy if that's what you're asking."

He frowns and takes a step back. My mom always tells me that I'm too abrupt; she gave up on the honey and vinegar analogy some years ago, ever since I asked why would I want to catch flies in the first place. I knew, of course, what she meant.

"I'm just being curious," he says, frowning. "You don't have to be . . . like that." He of course means to say "such a bitch," but to his credit doesn't.

I shrug and scope the board for more stray cheese bits. "You don't have to ask inane questions. You asked Cecilia what I did so you could talk to me, but you don't really care. So don't expect a thoughtful well-reasoned answer while making small talk."

"Nothing wrong with small talk."

"Of course not. Just try not to trivialize shit other people care about."

At this point, I expect him to make an exit, but he just shakes his head. "Would asking you about your hat also qualify as trivializing?"

"Depends on why you ask."

He heaves an exaggerated sigh, and it is almost drowned by the first twangs of the garage band guitar. He wrinkles his nose. "I ask because it's an interesting hat, and I want to talk to you, and I want to talk to you because all you do is glower and eat cheese, and stare daggers and wear weird hats with a really pretty dress."

Funny, and I thought I was being friendly. "Fair enough."

"Do you hate this music as much as I do?"

"More."

"Want to get coffee?"

I shake my head. "I really don't want to hang out. It's nothing personal, it's just I'm not looking for more friends." It's better that way; at least so early on he has a chance of believing me. After a few conversations people usually assume that this is just a posture, that I really do want friends and am merely shy. But this is not the case: besides the Brazilian neuroscientists, I don't want anyone.

He sighs again. "Tell me about your hat then."

Iconography is a tricky business. So there's a hat and a star, but how do you explain the depth of its meaning, the sheer cultural weight to a stranger, a foreigner who had never heard of Chapaev, has a very vague notion of the Red Cavalry, and overall perceived the epithet "red" as somewhat derogatory. He just sees a tin star and cannot smell the steppes and the galloping horses, the aroma of their sweat mixing with the sun and dust and wormwood in the air. The light carts the horses are dragging behind them, the backward-facing machine guns, the ringing of hooves. Tarragon and salt and summer, victory and heroism and the heart-aching infatuation with this imagined history, so much more beautiful and clear and taut than the real one, the icons instead of dirt and fleas and lice, the famine, the death. How do you explain something like that? This is why I've given up trying to be friends with the Americans. So instead I befriend Brazilians and other foreigners, and find some measure of cold comfort in the fact that we share the impossibility of proper communication, united in our isolation. At least, Cecilia and Veronica have each other.

And now I have the guy who attached himself to me at the party, and the party is over and I'm still struggling to explain. We're standing outside, in front of the brownstone where Cecilia and Veronica live, and there're no lights in their windows. And it is hopeless, hopeless, and I hear my voice give out and feel my eyelids grow hot, and I feel like crying from the futility. "I have to go," I say.

"Wait—"

But already I flee, my heels striking the convex cobbles, and curse myself for even trying. Communication is only possible with a quick ta-ta-ta of the mounted machine gun, of the ta-ta-ta of feet striking in unison over the tamped down soil, the beating of the heart, the slow bleeding out of Hainuwele buried alive and danced over to death. With the rapid drumming of my running heels, short and stout, made for such running-drumming across the old part of the city, where streets are lined with cobbles and wind up and down invisible hills. And this is all I want to say to this guy as he recedes invisibly behind me, my only message. Let him think what he will.

And yet, the seed is planted. It wasn't anything that he said or I said or the two of us stumbled over, some secretly discovered meaning. Rather, the thought crystallized from the entire muddled day, and as I fall asleep that night, I think of things I could do. Should do. Fuck the cockroaches and their stupid sensors, fuck the Turing and his tests. The lab complex certainly has enough shit lying around, and certainly it'll be all right for me to do a little side project. Building a hero of the revolution will be a better use of my time, not to mention, tons more interesting than the cockroaches.

In the morning, I stop by the store-gallery where I found my star. It is still closed, but I lift the doormat, as if hoping to find a spare key a thoughtful relative may or may not have left for me, and instead I find a small silver fish dangling on a long small gauge chain. I take it with me. Fish means water, and surely there was fish in the Ural River and the ocean surrounding Indonesia.

At work, I am greeted by the familiar skittering of electronic cockroaches who all live in my office. Instead of making me want to slice my wrists as usual, they make me giddy instead. I sit at my desk without moving and watch their flat round bodies cautiously crawl from under the radiators and filing cabinets, and resume their usual blind wanderings around my desk; they will do it until I move. I sit still and plot in my head how to make a hero of the revolution.

In many ways, electronic Chapaev would have to be the opposite of my cockroaches: I even make a list of qualities, but the primary among them is that he would not skitter but remain steadfast, he would be afraid of neither light nor movement. He would not remain in my office but rather would explore widely and wildly, possibly all the way to Indonesia. He would not locomote using tiny wheels, he would have actual limbs and eyes and possibly a mustache. He would enjoy shooting a machine gun and would like horses; perhaps express some interest in riding them. He would be good at war but not bloodthirsty, sociable and easygoing but not obnoxious, and he would be charismatic like a good piece of iconography ought to be.

Achieving this would probably be more difficult than imagining—this is why we've been doing cockroaches for as long as I remember instead of anything interesting. But I have my hat with a star and a silver fish on a chain, and an entire network of computers that think they are neurons or something like it. How difficult can it be? I sit at my console and play with parameters—not quite devising a Turing test but trying to calibrate hypothetical responses. The console buckles at first but soon enough cooperates, and lines of code line up across the screen like obedient soldiers.

I spend weeks writing code, by the skin of my intuition's teeth and by the mysterious mercies of silver fishes and other gifts from the Indonesian gallery. Every time I go, there is something new and mysterious waiting for me—some marbles, some carvings, a few pins. I collect them even if there was no obvious use for them just yet.

Cecilia and Veronica stop by the lab on Friday—and they laugh and nudge each other with their tanned, angular elbows. "There's someone there who wants to see you," Cecilia says.

Veronica rounds her eyes and hisses in a theatrical whisper, "He's really into you."

For a split insane second I hope that it is Chapaev, but that would be stupid. I sigh and look up from the console. "I'm kinda busy."

But already he's entering—the guy from the party—and the cockroaches skitter at his footsteps, and I think of how they learn, of how we taught them to learn—avoid light, then learn to associate light with footfalls (because people come in and turn on the light, see?), and once that simple algorithm is in place they extrapolate and avoid footfalls, clicking of switches, sounds of door, ground vibrations.

"Hi," the guy says. "I'm sorry if I said something to upset you. I—"

I watch Cecilia and Veronica back out of the lab, conspiratorial grins on their faces, and make a mental note to stop by the sixth floor where they're mutilating hamster and rat wetware, to tell them that I really don't need awkwardness in the workplace.

"I forgot your name," I tell him.

"Ryan. You want to get coffee?"

I do and we go to the Au Bon Pain across the street, and I frown and try to tune out his voice. Instead, I think of how to make Chapaev extrapolate from a simple set of premises. In my mind, I compile his set of his likes and dislikes—he should be afraid of water to stay away from rivers and streams and oceans, and he should love horses, war, the revolution. He should like Marx well enough but harbor a secret dislike of the bourgie Engels, and he would like Trotsky . . . of that I'm not really sure, but I hope that he would.

I drink my coffee and catalog the list of traits, and ways of coding them and then teaching him to extrapolate. For example, if he liked Trotsky he should dislike Stalin . . . or so I think. And if he liked the revolution, he would certainly like the Brazilians.

Ryan insists on paying. He really seems oblivious to the fact that I don't need (or even like) him, and that I am only tolerating him for Cecilia's and Veronica's sake. And because I dislike being rude, appearances to the contrary notwithstanding.

"No," I finally say. "I'll pay for my coffee because I don't want to be beholden."

"It's not like that," he says. I of course know better. "You can pay the next time."

"There won't be the next time," I say. "Unless you know something useful about programming, let me be."

"I do," he says. "I know Perl."

I laugh. "I'll call you when I need to conduct a Turing test."

"That has nothing to do with Perl."

"Exactly." As if I would ever let him close to my console and my programs. "I might need volunteers. Look for fliers on campus."

I look away, hoping that I impressed upon him my disinterest. Otherwise, it would have to go to a direct confrontation, and I truly hate those.

"I'll see you around, I guess," he says. He only pays for his coffee.

A week passes, and a feeble AI Chapaev starts flickering in my computer. Trying to talk to it is vastly reminiscent of a nineteenth-century séance with a medium: the AI answers only yes and no, and occasionally gives a low sepulchral moan that makes the speakers vibrate and whisper like falling sheets of paper.

I try to help him, tell him stories. I tell him about my mom coming to visit me and how her plane was so late and then she couldn't find her way through the grave-cold, cavernous interior of the JFK Airport, and when she finally emerged, tired and on the verge of tears, I too cried because I missed her and because I couldn't see her so upset. And then there was a long long drive to Boston, and I wished she could rest. She curled up in the passenger seat, so small, and it was ridiculous to think how large she loomed when I was just a baby, and I tell Chapaev now about something she said back then—on I-95, a long and empty stretch, so dark, so late—how she stared out of the window and whispered, sleepily, "I so like driving at night. It is so sad and alone, as if you are lost in the world, forever, and no one knows where you are and how to find you."

I don't know whether the AI Chapaev understands me, whether he would ever be able to comprehend what it's like, to miss your mom so much even when you yourself an adult. Just as I think that, he whispers, his voice a ghost in the speakers, "Then why did you leave her?"

I avoid the answers and stoke the feeble consciousness, I bring him things I now buy from the Indonesian shop—I bring him seashells pink on the inside and parrot feathers, I bring him bead necklaces and statuettes of the elephants, I bring plates and gongs, marvelous gongs Hainuwele would be proud of.

He is feeble however, and his voice gutters and dies, and I think of ways of stabilizing him. This is all awfully unscientific, but it occurs to me that things in pairs persist better than single units, even though I don't buy the whole rib story. Or the Ark story, for that matter. What I do buy, however, is that Hainuwele is both a creation myth and the genesis and the birth of original sin—before her death, no one had sex. It was only after she died and was buried and sprouted into agriculture did people discover animal husbandry and, by extension, their own. Or so the story goes.

Hainuwele is God, Jesus, and the serpent in this story, and she is everything to my Chapaev's nothing—he's just a whisper from a distant book, in a distant place, in a distant time. He did not beget sin but only a mediocre book, a few movies, and a shitload of jokes. His creation myth guttered out after a few decades, and there's only the dead and wistfulness for something that could've—should've—been that is left in its wake. He's not a god, he's the hero of the failed Revolution, and those creation myths are not the same.

Mom calls the next day, and her voice is weak and distant. She assures me that everything is all right, fine really, and both of my parents are of the age when no news is good news, and I dread it when they call, because they don't call unless there's news. And despite her reassurances, there's a lump in my throat and a knot in my belly.

She talks about travel instead, and about the trip to Estonia her and dad were planning—and I think about how it changed, how Estonia used to be the same country but was now "abroad," grown more distant, while America had moved closer. My head spins as I imagine the stretchings and contractions of the world, the distortions—the way neat squares of criss-crossing parallels and meridians buckle, like wet hardwood floors, and how the surface of the globe itself becomes ridged instead of smooth. And then I see Chapaev stepping from one ridge to the next, as the Earth folds and moves Indonesia just a few steps away from the Ural River.

"You seem distracted," mom says, reproachful.

"Sorry," I say. "I'm just thinking about geopolitics."

"We miss you," mom says, and I suddenly know that it is time for me to go visit. I buy my ticket the next day, for two weeks ahead. I need two weeks to make some headway with Chapaev and the Coconut Girl.

It is time to bite the bullet, and I head for the Indonesian shop and its endless bowl of "take one" freebies. I know I've been relying on its serendipitous nature entirely too much, and I even wonder if my superstition led me astray, away from the proper design of my AIs. I also feel guilty for neglecting my cockroaches, and I buy them some old cookies from the bakery next door. They like food, sugar, darkness, uncleanness. At some point, one has to question the wisdom of turning one's office over to the artificial cockroaches.

To my surprise, I find Ryan of the party and the awkward Au Bon Pain meeting browsing through the store, looking at the sculptures and the copper gongs. Marvelous gongs, I think, my mom called them. Just like in the hotel brochure.

"Hi," he says, not at all surprised to see me.

"Anything good?" I ask, sidestepping his unasked questions—

where have I been, how was work, if I've been talking to Cecilia and Veronica lately.

He jerks his shoulder in a shrug. "Same old. I come here sometimes, just to relax. I love this exotic stuff."

He probably doesn't mean to and it is terribly unfair of me to assume that he does, but I feel my cheeks burning as if from a slap. How I hate that word, exotic. How I loathe it, how stupid I feel not to having realized until now that he spoke to me because I was exotic too, a bored quest for novel experiences with a minimum of investment and always at someone else's expense. This is why I think Chapaev would be good for the Coconut Girl—they would be strange to each other and alien, but never exotic, never animal-like, never to be studied and prodded and ask why they were so sensitive, so worked up about minor stuff. Never to be amusing when one felt like being amused—only to be understood, or at least mutually incomprehensible, the mutuality possible only between equals.

"Oh," I say and step away. "Do they ever have sales help here?"

"There's a bell on the counter," he says.

I ring the bell, regretting it isn't a gong, and I wait, until footfalls shuffle and approach, and an old woman, her parallel wrinkles carved into her cheeks like if they were wood, slips into the store slash gallery through a small door behind the counter. She smiles at me. "You like freebies," she says.

"Who doesn't?" I mumble and blush and hope that Ryan didn't hear.

"Some more than others," she says, and laughs so mirthfully I have to smile too. "What can I get you?"

"Hainuwele," I say.

She frowns. "What about her?"

"If you were to capture her in one object, what would it be—here, I mean, and how much?"

Of course it turns out to be a copper gong wrapped in a cloth decorated with embroidered vegetables (the crops she turned into, I assume), and of course it costs about as much as my monthly rent. But at this point, I don't really care—I need to finish before I go home, and Hainuwele is tricky.

I nod goodbye to Ryan and thank the old woman, and head back for the lab. As I walk, I compile the list of attributes for Hainuwele—afraid of crowds, dancing floors, dirt. Probably not crazy about the club scenes—very much like myself, for I'm afraid of being trampled. Hainuwele likes gongs, coconuts, flowers, root vegetables. Writing an AI is a lot like writing a dating ad, except longer and with actual commands.

My office has become a depository of little tokens from the Indonesian store as well as some old mementos—a VHS of Chapaev the movie, some notes from history classes I dragged with me across the ocean for no other reason but reluctance to throw away any bits of knowledge, no matter how petty and political. Then there are cookies for the AI cockroaches, and I crumble them onto the floor. At night, they gather around the crumbs but don't eat them because they cannot eat, and I passingly worry that the cookie crumbs would attract real cockroaches and consider tidying up a little—maybe just getting rid of cookies and Cheeto dust and empty snack bags that rustle when my cockroaches skitter over them.

The lights are dimmed and the programs are running. Chapaev speaks in a faint whisper, and Hainuwele, small as she is, uncertain, is silent altogether. I take the gong out of its wrapping and put the cloth on top of the monitor, so that the traditional root vegetables flutter in the breeze and festoon around the pale monitor light, like ghosts of harvests past. I do not dare to ring the gong out of fear—I don't want to attract attention of my lab members (are they still working? It seems like I haven't spoken to anyone in so long, it could be a very long night or a four day weekend, who even knows anymore?) So instead of ringing I just brush my fingertips against its convex surface, and the dry skin whispers against polished metal, iron in my blood evoking copper of hers. The ringing of the gong is so faint, it lingers on the very edge of hearing, almost imagined but neverending.

There's a week before I have to go home, and between buying presents and arranging for cat sitters and tweaking the two AIs that now possess my work computer, I manage to call Cecilia and Veronica and ask them to come and to bring Ryan. They bubble with excitement, deceived that their matchmaking skills finally bore shriveled and bitter fruit. I wait for them in the darkened lab, my office windows shuttered with horizontal plastic slats that barely let in little zebra stripes of the sunlight. I drum my fingers on the black surface of the desk and hum to myself, keeping tune with the AIs whispering in the wires. I think idly of making them some sort of physical vehicles, like the little cockroach bodies, and wonder if that would help them develop their personalities. I wonder in Cecilia and Veronica might be able to lend me some rat brains, to play with chips and whatnot. I'd rather my Chapaev be a real rat than a fake cockroach; at least in a rat body he would have whiskers. Ideally of course I would like him to have limbs for locomotion and a mustache for historical accuracy, and a sparkle in his eyes to humor my childhood fantasies.

The three of them arrive, and they all look at me, frowning with concern.

"You okay?" Veronica finally says.

"Yes," I say. "Just a ton of work, and I'm going home for a few weeks so there's a lot of things to finish. Can you help me to test this program?"

"How?" Ryan says.

I have no idea; how do you verify the authenticity of artificial personality, how do you make sure it matches a long-ago dead hero of the revolution or a mythological coconut girl? "Play twenty questions with it," I tell them. "Try to figure it out."

They crowd around the keyboard, taking turns typing and giggling. From their mounting excitement, I'm guessing that the AIs are doing fairly well, but fatigue overwhelms. I rest my head over my folded arms, for just a moment, and the next thing I know I dream about being inside the computer, about flickering along the wires and bursting into sparkling fireballs at the connections, chips and silvery spiders of etched aluminum filigree. It always calms me down to imagine it, and to dream it is an unexpected joy. I sigh with happiness in my sleep and fly faster and faster, turning into pure energy, the resistance of metals my only constraints. And soon enough I feel that I'm not alone—although how can a flow of electrons possibly be alone?—as two discrete entities join me and flow alongside.

I recognize them, of course—one by his mustache and the other by her gong. "We will administer a Turing test," Chapaev says and flashes me a smile bright as stars in the electronic darkness. "Don't worry, you'll be fine." I do what I can not to laugh, and then Hainuwele whispers softly next to me, her voice lilting like the gentle stammering of a forest stream, and I cannot understand her words.

"What are you saying?" I ask, laughing and crying and flying through metal, the distant echo of a jet flight—an echo preceding the event, I think, and imagine humming of wings and the metal guts, the whispering of electronic blood that would take me home.

They speak in unison, and I do not understand. Their words fuse into a lulling melody, into whistling of winds and churning of water, and then it grows lower and and stronger, so that my entire body starts vibrating and humming, like a flower when a bumblebee touches it with its furry legs.

Cecilia shook my shoulder, and I peeled my eyes open, annoyed. I was so close to making out their words, and they were so close to me—so alive, their tingling electric flesh flowing over mine.

"You ok?" Cecilia asks.

I nod and yawn. "Yeah. How's the test?"

"It's a joke, right?" Veronica says, and even Ryan frowns at me. "What?"

"Your program doesn't work," Ryan says and heaves an exasperated sigh. "It looks like an elementary school project . . . what were you trying to do?"

I rub my eyes again, redundantly. "What happened?"

"See for yourself," Cecilia says. "Have you even tried this before? It started out all right, but then it just got stupid and then the computer froze."

They all seem genuinely annoyed with me for wasting their time and I feel sorry about that; yet I wish they would just tell me what exactly went wrong. But already they're leaving, filing out of the lab, and I stare at the screen. The transcript should be autosaved, and I find it quickly enough.

They are right—it is embarrassing. It reads like one of those programs you can have a conversation with, and you can throw it off with any simple question. The transcript soon enough disintegrates into "And what do you want to do?" and "Tell me more about it" and "I don't know." It is embarrassing.

"Why do you do this to me?" I ask the computer, and their voices—their long-ago dead voices—fill my ears like water filling up an empty scallop shell, and their words crowd and lap at my tympanic membranes.

We didn't do anything, they say. *We just didn't know how to talk—their fingers were so awkward on the keyboard, and their ears are too coarse to hear us. We're sorry if we've embarrassed you.*

"It's all right," I whisper back. "Not your fault."

And here we go again, choosing terms for our defeat and creating our own realities as heroes would. I agree with them and blame Cecilia and Veronica and the guy from the party that seems so long ago for their inability to hear, to pay attention properly, rather than myself. I resolve to build them bodies, and this is way beyond my purview, and I saunter to the robotics lab next door.

I make small talk with grad students there, none of whose names I can remember, but nothing seems to be doing since one of them is working on a creepy-looking hand operated by a bundle of strings that replicate motion of human muscles—at least in theory; in reality, it looks like an overly elaborate marionette, and the rest putz about with various simple things that all look like roombas and dryers and other household appliances, I ask to borrow one of the roombas at least, and tell them that I need to try a new program for my cockroaches. As if. They grumble but let me, and for a moment I feel vertiginous, as if standing on a great precipice—and finally, finally, I would be able to give shape to the world, to become active rather than reactive. To choose my own direction.

The roomba I drag to the lab with me is smallish—maybe five pounds of wheels and gears and receptors, light and pressure, with a small knot of electronics for its brain. It takes me the rest of the day to equip it with the twin consciousness of my heroes. The night before it's time for me to go I equip it with a mustache and a gong and pack it into a cardboard box and stuff the box into my carry-on—no way I'm checking them in.

The plane is half-empty, and it is off-season. Most of the passengers are my compatriots, and I avoid talking to them, studiously. The night falls so fast—we are traveling east after all, forever east, like Chapaev searching for a passage to Indonesia— and only when everyone is asleep and the lights are dimmed I let the robot out of its prison.

It hums and feels its way along the aisles, and the plane is cutting through the thick damp air outside like a fat silver knife, carving up space to make a tunnel, to bring me closer to my mom. And at my feet, two AIs shift and whisper nervously in their single shared body, silver and flat like a cockroach, and I can only imagine what will happen when we touch the ground. I feel fevered and elated, and I picture the small silver thing touching the ground and springing up as a handsome mustachioed man (this is how it happens in fairy tales—a bird hits the ground and becomes a hero), and then he would step forth and bring

Hainuwele out by her hand. Her gong would ring, and the sound of it, as impossible as that of the Tsar-Bell, will carry over this new fractured, corrugated world where close things have grown far away, and the far things are smushed together.

The sound of her gong and the roar of his laughter will smooth out the wrinkles and bind what was fractured, and the world will become whole again: my mom will meet me on the tarmac instead of the twisty bowels of the airport, and the horses will gallop through the streets, blood of revolutionary terror washed off by River Ural's waters, sparkling like dew on the hairs of their bay hides, like rain. And the gong and the bell will ring even louder, amplified by a million horseshoes striking the stones, and all those who were trampled over underground will spring up, break through the pavements and stand in sunlight, and the doors of the Mausoleum will swing open and all the heroes of the revolution will toddle outside on their stubborn soft and new legs, squinting at the sunlight, and the root vegetables that will flourish right in the middle of Red Square—and it won't be necessary to bury dismembered bodies to sustain their growth. My Brazilian neuroscientists will fix the decaying brains of the dead and we will install AIs that will whisper shyly in the wires of their new souls, and we will make as many heroes as we need.

THE BANK OF BURKINA FASO

One knows that one was a good ruler when even in exile (accursed, dishonored) one still has a loyal servant who remains, despite the tattered cuffs and disgrace, despite the wax splotches covering the surface of the desk like lichen on tombstones, remains by one's side and lights the candles when darkness coagulates, cold and bitter, outside of one's window.

The deposed Prince of Burundi nodded his gratitude at Emilio, the servant with a dark and hard profile, carved like stone against the white curtains and the shadow of sifting snow behind them, like a restless ghost. The Prince then carefully perched his glasses, held together by blue electrical tape, at the vertiginous hump of his aristocratic nose, and turned on his computer.

The Wi Fi in most Moscow apartment buildings was standard but spotty during snowstorms, and the prince hurried to get out as many emails as he could before the weather made it impossible to send anything out. He saved reading of his email for the very end, until after his messages were hurtled into the electronic ether and he could have the leisure to read through the hundred and twelve messages in his inbox.

None of them were replies—he was not surprised; daily, he steeled himself, preparing for just such outcome. After all, wasn't his own inbox filled with desperate pleas, cries for help he had neither wherewithal nor opportunities to answer? The best he could do was read them all, and let his heart break over and over.

However, after so many years of reading, of writing those letters himself—because what else was there to do for those exiled and dishonored but to reach for the unknown strangers' kindness?—he found himself growing weary, and the words flowed together in a soft, gray susurrus of complaint. So it was surprising for him to click on a name that did not look familiar and to be jolted to awareness by the words, so crisp and true.

"My dearest," the unknown Lucita Almadao started, "It is in great hope that I reach out to you. I am the widow of the General Almadao, an important figure in my country's history. However, after the military takeover and the dismantling of our rightful government, my husband was given to a dishonorable death. To this day I weep every moment I think of the cruelty of his fate."

The storm intensified and the draft from the windows hissed and howled, and the candles in their tarnished candelabra guttered. The prince hurriedly downloaded the letter onto his Blackberry—cracked screen, half-dead battery—because he just couldn't bear the thought of not finishing it that night. The electricity cut off at that very moment, and the prince sighed.

Emilio took the candles to the dining room, further away from the offending window and the drafts, to the comfortable chair where the prince could wrap his feet in a blanket and read on the handheld screen, its light blue and flickering and dead.

"Imagine my horror," the honorable Lucita Almadao wrote, in the words that betrayed the genuine emotions of the one who had suffered deeply and sincerely (the prince had an eye for such things since like knows like), "Imagine the paralyzing terror of one caught up in a dream, unable to wake up, as he was taken to the cobbled courtyard. I remember the white linen of his shirt in the darkness, fluttering like a moth, its wings opening and closing over one sculpted collarbone; I remember the rough soldiers' hands on his sleeves, patches of darkness cut out of the fabric, and the yellow and red of their torches, long sleek reflections on the barrels of their rifles—at least, I think those were rifles.

"I apologize, my dearest one, my unknown friend, for my mind wanders when I think of such matters. It is of course of no concern to you, but I seek your help in freeing his not insignificant fortune from the bank—the Bank of Burkina Faso, to be exact. I seek your help in accessing these funds, since because you're a foreign national with no ties to my husband, the operation may be easier for you. I loathe to think about money at such a time . . . "

The Blackberry finally gave up the ghost, a pale bluish flicker, that dissipated in the yellow candlelight. The prince gave a small wail of disappointment, but soon settled by the window to watch the furious dance of the snowflakes in the cone of the streetlight down below his window. And in his mind, another dance, entirely imaginary, unfolded slowly, like a paper fan in the hands of a young girl: the hands grabbing arms, a shiny sliver of a sharp blade pressed against dark throat . . . the sad fate of the deceased general kept replaying as he remembered the widow's letter, every word heavy with salt and sorrow.

The next morning the electricity was back, even though Emilio, thoughtful and far-sighted as always, had already transferred perishables onto the slowly thawing window ledge, and started drinking the beer before it grew warm. Once the refrigerator started humming again, Emilio returned the unfinished beverage into the security of the manufactured cold, plugged in the recharger for the Blackberry, and turned on the electric stove to make breakfast.

The Prince sat in the warmest corner of the kitchen, the orange upholstering of the corner seat shifting under his bony backside as if ready to detach from its padding, and composed the letter in his mind. He could not let the plea of the unknown but suffering widow Lucita Almadao go unanswered—he had spent a cold and mostly sleepless night under his thin blanket, tossing from one side to the other—not because of the prominent springs in his couch but rather because her words cut to the heart. He was too busy to even dream about the Bank of Burkina Faso.

After breakfast, he dutifully logged into his account. The mailbox full with the usual pleas:

"I am writing in respect of a foreign customer of our Bank who perished along with his next of kin with Korean Air Line, flight number 801 with the whole passengers on 6th of Augustus 1997," wrote one. "The reason for a foreigner in the business is for the fact that the deceased man was a foreigner and it is not authorized by the law guiding our Bank for a citizen of this country to make such claim. This is the reason while the request of you as a foreigner is necessary to apply for the release and transfer of the fund smoothly into your reliable Bank account," insisted another. The words as familiar as the Prince's own; the only difference between these people and himself was that he suspected the truth about the Bank of Burkina Faso.

He started on the letter to Lucita Almadao, the widow of the slain general. "My dear unknown friend," the prince wrote, "your words had reached me albeit perhaps not to the effect you have intended—for I am too looking for a foreign national to obtain access to 11.3M Euros I have deposited in the Bank of Burkina Faso while I was still the rightful ruler of my beautiful Burundi. I now live in exile, in a cold and frozen city, and I look for assistance from a foreign national such as yourself. I promise complete confidentiality . . . "

The prince frowned at the screen. The words came out in a familiar pattern, honed by many months of repetition, but they failed to convey the emotion he felt while reading the widow's epistle. He deleted the paragraph and started again.

"My dear friend," he wrote, "I apologize for deviating from the form, but the very nature of the Bank of Burkina Faso demands that I should be straightforward with you. You may not know it, but you do not have to be a foreign national to access the funds." He stopped and rubbed the bridge of his nose—he could feel the tension building in his sinuses, like it did every time he tried to put into words what he had intuited about the Bank. "You only need to know what the bank is, but I cannot trust this information to electronic words, for they wander and get lost and fall into wrong hands, so I beg for your help, my dearest one in the transfer . . . that is to say, if you were to hint at your whereabouts, perhaps there would be another way." He hit "Send" before the familiar fog settled over his mind and erased the intermittent knowledge of the Bank's secret workings.

It was afternoon when the Prince had decided that there was no point in lounging about, since Lucita Almadao wouldn't answer right away—no one wanted to appear overly eager or gullible. Instead he took a shower, and told Emilio to iron his good shirt. After tying a tie and wrapping himself into a moth-bitten shearling coat that had seen innumerable better days, he headed to the bus stop.

There were two advantages to living in Moscow that the prince cold see: public transportation and access to classical music. Whenever the mood struck, he headed to the center of the city (bus, then subway)—just like there was always a fig in fruit in every jungle, so there was always a theater in Moscow with a concert or an opera about to start. The tickets, like the public transportation, were accessible to the masses thus killing their appeal for the upper class. The prince had ceased to be the member of the latter some years ago, and although he disapproved of the local weather, he waited patiently for the bus that appeared just as the sensation in the prince's toes and ears started to disappear. He hurried inside, and bounced and jostled all the way to the subway station fifteen minutes away. It was an inconvenience living on the outskirts, but the only habitation he and Emilio could afford was a fifth story walkup on the southeast end of the city.

Once he entered the subway station, it was warm and placid, the stray dogs were coming home from the city's center—they took the subway, riding up and down the escalator with the expression of quiet and standoffish dignity, so that they could spend their days begging by the restaurants and robbing tourists of their hotdogs. Now the dogs poured out of the outbound trains with the rivers of ruddy, white, and black fur, as the human passengers stepped carefully around them. The prince smiled as he waited on the platform, surrounded by beige and yellow marbled columns, and wondered if the sheer numbers of stray Moscow dogs gave them the sort of elevated, exuberant intelligence rarely seen in these beasts elsewhere in the world. He wondered if they possessed some sort of a collective mind, and the thought itched again in the corners of his eyes and between his eyebrows, and he rubbed the bridge of his nose. The bank manifested much today.

As soon as he boarded the train, largely empty, the Blackberry in his pocket buzzed, urgent. It took him a moment to tilt the screen away from the overhead lights' glare, and even then he read the name of the message several times, just to make sure that the crack on the screen wasn't deceiving him somehow. The message was from the widow Almadao. The prince's heart pulsed in his fingertips as he tapped the screen and read her stumbling words.

"My dearest one," she wrote, "it is such a surprise to read your message—words of a man who knows both suffering and hope, and I envy you your dignity and humility—I cannot tell how I cried and howled, and threw myself against the walls, how I broke my fingernails on the frozen cobblestone of these streets, on these icy embankments.

"Yes, my dear unknown friend, I am in the same city as you are—and it is getting dark at four PM, and the shadows stretch, long and blue, in the hollows between snowdrifts. There's slush on the roads and sidewalks, and my black shoes have permanent salt marks, like a wrack line.

"None of it matters; only that the fate has brought us to the same city, too peopled and desolate for words, just as it is fate that we can perhaps salvage what we can from the Bank of Burkina Faso—together, if only you would help me."

The prince's eyes misted over, and he brushed the unbidden moisture from his cheekbone with the edge of his hand. He had never met her, and yet as he read her email, he anticipated every word before his eyes had a chance to take it in, and every heartbeat doubled in his chest, as if it became an echo chamber.

"If the fate has brought us together," he wrote back, "perhaps it will let us find each other; perhaps we shall meet among the dust and music and musty odor. Meet me at the House of Music in an hour."

The House of Music, a relatively small building housing a decent orchestra that offered a small but reliably good range of classical music, and was rarely sold out. Today was no exception—the prince paid his admittance, checked in his embarrassing coat, and wandered down the raspberry colored carpet in his thin-soled and soaked shoes toward the lobby and the concession stand.

He recognized her from afar—she was tall, even taller than him, and the saffron frock loosely gathered at her dark shoulders draped as if it was made when her figure was fuller and younger; its tattered hem splayed on the carpet like feathers.

She recognized him too: she smiled and waved as she lifted the glass of lemonade to her lips painted the color of the inside of a hibiscus flower.

The concert started with the obligatory Pachelbel's Canon and Bach's Fugue and Sonata, but they were barely aware of the music, delirious with happiness at having found each other and muddled by the habitual fog that always accompanied any attempt to think about the Bank of Burkina Faso in a logical manner.

Yet, together and with the help of the strings and the organ, undeterred by the bellicose glances of other music lovers, they managed to tell each other what each of them knew.

The problem with the Bank was the inability of anyone who had deposited money there to get it back. Phone calls resulted in requests for foreign nationals, and playing of recorded strange music. And the physical location of the bank remained unknown—Burkina Faso has been scoured from border to border, by millions of those who had no hope now of returning their fortunes or rewarding the long-lost nexts of kin. It was concluded then that it must be present elsewhere in the world, and in all likelihood the bank did not have a permanent area of residence—hence the constant demand for foreign nationals, since if it moved around, everyone was a foreign national. That made sense, even through the muddled thoughts.

The prince had developed a hunch that the bank's existence itself was not a permanent or assured thing. "You see," he told the widow Lucita Almadao, "once I dreamt about that bank, and I saw it in my mind—clear as day. I saw the porticos and the red bricks of its facade, even the tiny cracks in the cement between the bricks. And the next day, I received a letter from someone I knew, who was able to claim his money that night. He never returned my emails where I asked for locations and details, but I'm sure that my dream helped him somehow."

Lucita Almadao clapped her hands once, and caught herself as the lone sound resonated in the air as the orchestra had fallen momentarily silent, and a few faces turned around to look at them. "I dreamt of it too!" she said in a frenzied whisper, more of a hiss. "It was last summer."

"Mine too. And then several times after that."

"And did it happen every time?"

"No, only once."

She tugged her lip thoughtfully. "So your dreaming might be not the only condition. Necessary, but not sufficient."

"I'm not sure it is even necessary. I mean," he had to slap his own hollow cheek slightly to keep his thoughts on track. "I mean that maybe it doesn't have to be me but anyone—it happened to you."

"To us. Do you remember the date of your fateful dream last summer?"

"July 15th."

"Mine too! Maybe what is necessary is that more than one person dreams it."

Applause broke out around them, and they shuffled with the rest of the crowd into the foyer, for the intermission. The prince sweated and palpitated, and felt his forehead and ears grow too warm from the combined excitement of finding her and being able to talk about the bank to someone, in person. Together, it was easier to break the pall it cast over their thoughts.

They bought lemonade and drank it by the window—if one pulled apart the wine-colored velvet of the drapes, one could see the snow that started sifting from the low clouds, flaring like handfuls of beads when it hit the cones of streetlights and disappearing in the darkness. One could also see several stray dogs sitting by the entrance, waiting patiently for the patrons to leave, concession-stand leftovers in hand.

"These dogs scare me," Lucita Alamadao said, looking over the prince's shoulder. "The other day, one of them startled me just as I was buying food from a street vendor, and I dropped it."

"This is how they hunt," the prince said, still looking out the window. "They are like lions, and hotdogs are their prey. We're merely a vehicle. I heard that these dogs are becoming more intelligent. They know how to take the subway."

"I've seen them there."

"I think they might have a single mind among them." Once

again, his sinuses itched and filled with pressure. "Do you think they can dream?"

Lucita Almadao's eyes, reflected in the dark pane of the window, widened. "Dogs?!"

"Why not? If it is us who's dreaming the bank, we cannot enter it. I would dream it for you, but I'm not enough."

"My dearest one," she quoted softly. "I need your assistance. We can write the others."

"And who will want to be the dreamers while everyone else goes to claim their fortunes?"

Outside, the dogs howled with one voice.

It wasn't an easy task, to train the stray dogs to dream. Their collective mind seemed very focused on food and warmth—especially warmth, since the nights had grown bitter. The prince had opened the doors of his walkup to them, despite Emilio's protestations—had no other choice, really. They slept on the floor and by the radiator, under the kitchen chairs, on Emilio's pullout couch. The apartment smelled like warmed fur, and filled with quiet but constant clacking of claws on the parquet.

The prince was at first terrified and then amused when the dogs started paying for their lodgings: they arrived with wallets, sometimes empty, sometimes with money in it. One day, as he was traveling to see the widow Lucita Almadao, he learned how the dogs got the wallets.

As the train slowed down, pulling closer to the station, the prince saw a stray dog hop onto the seat next to a well-dressed man, the sheen of his sharkskin jacket making a lovely contrast with a crisp white shirt and his striped burgundy tie, which looked Italian and expensive. The dog whined and smiled, his thick tail of a German shepherd mix thumping against he vinyl of the seat. The man smiled and petted the dog's head gingerly—who wouldn't, looking at those bright eyes and pink tongue. The train pulled into the station and the doors hissed open, just as the dog thrust his muzzle into the man's jacket, grabbing the wallet from his inner pocket, and bounded onto the platform, just as the stream of incoming passengers hid him from view and prevented the robbery victim from chasing after. The man cursed, and the prince buried his face in the newspaper. That night, a German shepherd mix showed up at his door, with an Italian wallet, moist but otherwise undamaged, in his mouth.

Lucita Almadao stopped by every now and again, to help talk to the dogs and to pet the stray heads, their tongues lolling gratefully and eyes squinting with pleasure. She told them about the Bank of Burkina Faso and her dead husband, breaking the dogs' and the prince's hearts anew. He talked to them too and showed them the emails, the constant stream of pleas by the lost and the banished, the plaintive song playing in a loop, asking again and again for assistance from foreign nationals in their quest to liberate their stolen millions or to reclaim rightful inheritance. The dogs listened, their heads tilted, their ears pricked up. Most of them left in the morning to take the bus and the subway, but came back at night, with wallets and an occasional watch.

It took them almost all the way to New Year, but slowly, slowly, the dogs started dreaming in unison: their legs twitched as if they were running, and their tails wagged in their sleep. When the prince looked out of the window, he occasionally glimpsed a brick or a part of the wall, a segment of a bank vault hovering, disembodied, over the no-mans land of the frozen and snowed over yard. Once, he ran for the apparition but it crumbled, and a piece of dream-wall fell on his shoulder, almost dislocating it.

The dogs were getting better at dreaming as the prince and the widow Lucita Almadao got worse: the two of them barely slept, sustained by the flickering candlelight and Emilio's stern stares, by the sleepless hope that left them ashen in the mornings, desolate in the first gray light falling on the stalagmites of candlewax. The dogs left in the morning, and the widow Almadao sometimes left with them, and sometimes, bowled over by fatigue, she curled up and slept on Emilio's couch, dog hair clinging to her black, cobweb-thin mantilla. The prince dozed off in his chair and waited, waited for the dogs to come back home.

They were ready to give up on the night it actually happened— it was a dead hour after the moon had set but the sun had not yet risen, the hour between wolf and dog, when the prince started to fall asleep. A sharp tug on his sleeve woke him, and he startled, wide-eyed. He thought he was dreaming at first when he saw the brick façade and the golden letters over the double oak doors: **THE BANK OF BURKINA FASO.** The dogs snored in unison, and Lucita Almadao clutched her hands to her chest.

When they ran down the steps, the Bank still stood, not wavering, a solid construction hewn out of stray dogs' dreams. The sun was rising behind it, casting a faint promise of light like a halo around the bank.

"We better hurry," Lucita Almadao said.

"Of course," he answered.

Side by side, they walked toward the bank, their feet leaving long blue depressions in the old snow, shivering in the cold, the knuckles on his left and her right hands almost brushing against each other.

KIKIMORA

The fall of communism came about when I was in the middle of my PhD in astrophysics; the steel jaws of 1990 followed close behind. My hometown, a speck on the forested expanse of Siberia, felt its hungry bite. Even Novosibirsk, where I attended graduate school, careened into the cold, joyless chaos, buckled by that wolf-year. This was when I decided to move to Moscow, trying to escape the grey limbo.

"Looking for an easy life," they called it. I just wanted to be able to support myself; is that asking for too much? But there were no need for astrophysicists, and secretute jobs that were abundant did not appeal to me. I had to fall back on my gymnastic childhood, and started teaching aerobics to the tourists who stayed in Ukraina Hotel. There, through the gym window, I could see the river bend carving off the downtown from the rest of the city. And there I met Anya.

She was a maid with the master's degree in psychology. We ran into each other in the locker room—I was just getting ready for class, and she was cleaning the mirrors. I noticed her because of the way she was looking at me—not sizing up competition, but simply appraising. I introduced myself, and soon we were commiserating on the impossibility of finding a job in one's field.

We laughed at first, and then grew silent, contemplating the world in which an advanced degree was a requirement for a janitorial job. She was younger than I, but still she felt old and outdated in the scary, shifty-eyed world that was springing around us, the world with no past or future but only a slightly soiled present. Then we kissed.

I looked over her shoulder, to make sure that there was no one watching, and I saw a tall, dark-skinned man with deep green hair, who stood in the doorway. I jolted and pushed her away; she gave me a wounded look, and the stranger was gone.

"Marina?" She stared at me, puzzled and annoyed.

"Sorry," I said. " I thought there was someone at the door."

She smiled, and a hidden secret place seemed to have opened in her eyes, letting thorough a warm glow. Like a hearth. Like home. Protected from the cold river wind and uncertainty. "When are you getting off?"

"After 6 pm class. You?"

"At eight. You can wait for me, and come over if you want."

I nodded. "Where do you live?"

"Kozhukhovo."

It was a long trip to the suburbs, but I didn't mind. We held hands on the subway. Anya laughed.

"What?"

"Just funny. If we were men, can you imagine the looks we would've got?"

"Prejudice has its place," I murmured, sinking my face into the faux fur collar of her coat. Even the most opinionated old women did not seem to think that we were anything more than friends. It suited me fine—Anya's wispy hair was brushing against my forehead, and I breathed in the smell of her skin and the still-present aroma of mothballs from her coat. Out of the corner of my eye, half-closed in bliss, I saw the green-haired man again.

He stood holding onto the overhead rail, oblivious to my attention. Everyone in the subway car either ignored or did not notice him. At first, I guessed him for a Chechen, with his dark skin and an old-style Caucasus cloak, with its ostentatious shoulder pads. But no shoulder pads swept up so abruptly and vertically; the shape of the cloak suggested parts no human body had a right to possess. And the dark hue of his skin was imparted by neither sun nor ethnicity—it was the color of tree bark, furrowed by more than age. He swayed with the car, and his dark green hair shimmered and swayed too.

It occurred to me that he was supposed to have a green beard. At first, I could not puzzle out the source of this thought; then I realized that I had seen such a creature before. Deep within the Siberian woods, a forest spirit commonly known as a leshy.

I smiled at the green-haired stranger. The thought that there was something untouched by the present made living tolerable.

His moss-green eyes met mine, and a slow smile cracked the dark wood of his face. That smile made me feel like someone from home came to visit, bringing homemade preserves and letters from long-forgotten relatives.

"What are you looking at?" Anya whispered into my ear.

I knew better than to point at the leshy, and just shrugged. He got off at the next stop, and Anya's hand snuggled under my elbow.

I was glad to find out that even a place so cold and pedestrian as Moscow in November had its own spirits. After all, it used to be a forest once, and apparently its guardian leshy had endured longer than the trees.

Anya nudged me, and withdrew her soft hand from the comforting proximity of my breast. "We're here."

Anya lived with her parents and a grandmother. All of them seemed quite happy to meet me, and fed us supper of stuffed peppers, followed by several liters of tea. It was a warm and homey three-room apartment, replete with a cat and a fish tank. I petted the cat who purred emphatically, and tried to ignore the kitchen-table conversation that centered on politics and inflation, like every conversation did those days. I kept glancing over to the window, where I could see the streetlamps reflected in black river water. I wondered if the granite-encased riverbank was home to rusalki.

The sound of Anya's name brought me back to the kitchen table.

"She's almost twenty-five," her grandmother lamented. "Only in a time like this, how're you supposed to find a man? All the good ones are barely making ends meet, and all the rich ones—" She stopped, her wrinkled face expressing a great desire to spit. "Bandits and thieves."

"I know," I said. "I'm twenty-seven."

Anya's mother nodded sympathetically, and Anya drank her tea to conceal a fit of laughter.

I never told my parents about my sexual proclivities—I didn't want to complicate things; yet, I was mad at Anya. I felt dirty as they invited me to stay the night, promising to lay out an inflatable mattress in Anya's room. They wouldn't be so welcoming if they knew. I just didn't like taking advantage of their naiveté.

Anya kicked me under the table. I caught myself, trying to straighten out my facial expression—I knew that I was giving Anya what my grandmother called a "wolf look." Not pretty on a girl.

We waited until everyone was asleep, and giggled and made love in the dark, hushing each other and giggling more. It was still dark outside, but the quality of the darkness, the way it retreated around the streetlamps in the yard and the edges of the sky suggested that the morning was not far off. I returned to my inflatable mattress, leaving Anya to sigh in her sleep, but felt restless.

I perched on the windowsill. It started to snow, and I watched the fat snowflakes flutter through the cones of light cast by the streetlamps, and disappear into the darkness again. I was not surprised when I saw the leshy standing in one of the light cones, his hair encrusted in a translucent helm of melting snow.

"What do you want?" I whispered.

His answer resounded clear in my ears, as if he were standing next to me. "Come with me, and bring her along."

I glanced at Anya, who smiled in her sleep, the tabby cat curled up on her pillow.

"Yes, her."

"Why?"

"Trees need water to grow."

"What do you need me for?"

"You're a swamp thing, a green kikimora from a Siberian bog, an in-between place that bridges wood and rivers."

I huffed. I read enough children's stories to know that kikimoras were nasty, ugly things. "I'm certainly not a kikimora. Get bent." I slid off the windowsill and lay down, my heart beating against my ribs. I thought of the fairy tales, of everything I knew about leshys. They seemed malevolent more often than not—they could fool you, twist you around, make you lose your way in a forest. Only until now I never believed the stories.

I slept very little that night. My dreams were heavy, suffocating—I had no doubt that it was the leshy's doing. I dreamt of green slime covering my body, of tree bark growing over my skin, of the tree branches sprouting from my arms and legs. Of poisonous mushrooms in my underarms.

The leshy was apparently offended by my rudeness, and did not manifest himself for a while, except in dreams. Still, I tried to make sense of his words—forest and swamp and water, of his need, of how Anya fit into it. If she were the one he wanted, why didn't he show himself to her? Was I just an intermediary, or something greater? I could sense his presence in my dreams, deep and dark, tangled and permeated by the smell of the swamp.

In my waking life, I spent all my free time with Anya, and often could not wait to get out of my class to see her sweet dimpled face, to feel her soft hand in mine. And when she did not show up for work one day, my heart ached with a premonition of disaster. I called her at home, but no one there knew where she was.

I was a mad woman then, torn by grief and remorse, furious with my failure to ward off misfortune. I looked for Anya in every crowd, on every subway station, in the windows of every building I passed. I looked for her on the granite riverbanks, but the river was already encased in sickly green ice.

I looked for her in the ghostly-pale faces of rusalki, souls of drowned girls, their mouths gaping like underwater caves, their long, loose hair streaming and floating around their faces as if lifted by slow current. I found them under the bridge the night of the winter solstice. They did not shiver in their thin garments, and their eyes were remote and starless. They held hands and danced in a circle, their bare feet insensitive to the cold of the stone bank and of ice that encrusted it.

"Have you seen her?" I begged. "Did she drown?"

Their ethereal faces turned one pale cheek, then the other in a slow underwater no. "Not our sister," came their quiet, gurgling voices. "We've seen no girl falling through the ice; we've seen no girl struggling for air; we've seen no girl dragged into black, silent water. We've seen no new sister, and we dance without her."

I was somewhat comforted by their words. "Can you ask others?"

"Drowned puppies and alley cats haven't seen her either."

"Can you ask the leshy?"

They shook their heads in unison, their hair undulating like seaweeds. "Ask him yourself. You're an in-between one, a neither-here-nor-there—" Their voices trailed off, and they returned to their slow dance. They held hands and spun, sometimes on stone, sometimes on ice.

I stood and watched them, deaf and dumb from cold, darkness, and despair. They were long gone, and my feet grew numb, and the stars spilled over the sky like breadcrumbs on a table, when I regained my voice. I howled at the dark river, at the city nestled like an infant in the crook of its frozen elbow. I screamed for the leshy to come out, come out, wherever he was, and to give my Anya back. I knew that the bastard twisted her around, made her lose her way in the dark and the cold, to make me come for her.

No answer came, and I wandered away from the river, toward the boulevards that circled the heart of the city, studded with oversized jewels of frozen ponds, towards Alexandrovsky Garden. The streets were sleek with black ice that reflected the streetlights, as if there were another city hidden in frozen puddles. A façade of a three-story old mansion reflected there too, and its closed doors seemed open in its reflection. After a moment of hesitation, I closed my eyes and stepped into the upside-down maw of the reflected doorway.

For a moment, my foot touched the slippery solid surface of ice, and then broke through, into a faintly fluorescent, moldy air of an underground forest. Long beards of Icelandic moss hung from the rimed branches of dead spruces, and no footsteps resonated on a soft carpet of their fallen needles.

"Leshy," I called. "Give my girl back to me."

The wind rose and moaned and bent the treetops almost to the ground. The frozen whip of my hair lashed my face, and the hoarfrost in the air stung my eyes, narrowing them to rheumy slits.

"Come out, you bastard!"

I had no idea of where I was going in the underground dead forest, screaming into the wind. I never questioned it, but let my guts lead me as long as my legs would carry me. Soon, buckled over by the wind, I sank to my knees in deep moss by a slender birch. It creaked and moaned under the assault of the wind. Yet, its bare branches bent over and around me, forming a protective cocoon, stroking my shoulders.

"Help me," I whispered.

The branches hugged me closer, and I felt rejuvenated and strong, as the dying tree poured the last of its life into me.

"I'm looking for a girl, as fair as your bark, as gentle as your touch. Have you seen her?"

The birch shuddered and stretched its branches against the howling storm, pointing deeper into the forest. I cringed as I heard a sharp crack of snapping wood. I thanked the birch and was on my way, plunging headlong into the solid wall of the wind.

I had no sense of direction, but the leshy was too eager to divert me: as much as he tried to confuse me, to make me lose my way, I kept turning into the wind, until I crossed a clearing and stood on the shore of a lake, its water calm despite the storm. Cattails fringed its shores, their leaves green and erect, their brown heads nodding to me as if in greeting. Yellow water lilies stood still over its mirror-clean surface; I realized how thirsty I was.

I drank on my knees, like an animal, the cool water soothing my cracked, burning lips, its water washing away the sting of the cold. I looked at the surface, waiting for it to calm down. I was expecting to see my face, but instead I saw Anya. The water caressed my fingers, and I recognized her despite her change.

A quiet fell over the world, and I could hear my labored breathing. And then, someone else's.

I turned around.

"So you've found her," the leshy said.

I nodded, and touched my fingers to the lake Anya's surface in reassurance. "I came to take her back."

The leshy smiled, and I noticed how much he'd aged since our last meeting. The bark of his skin seemed diseased, mottled with fungi, and the deep green of his hair was turning lichen-grey. "Take her back, eh? How are you going to accomplish that?"

I scrambled for an answer. If she were dead or unconscious, I would've gathered her into my arms and walked away. Were she turned to stone, I would've broken my back but carried her out. But she was liquid that poured over my fingers, streamed down my face, wetted my lips. "Turn her back to her human form," I said.

He smiled still. "I wish I could do that."

I raised my fist, furious with his smirk. "Don't play with me, or I'll smash your face in; I'll burn your forest, I'll salt the ground—"

He raised his palm. "Quiet, girl. I cannot do what you ask, threaten all you want . . . I am not strong enough." He seemed embarrassed as he uttered the last words.

"Why not?"

"My forest is dying without water. I need you to bring it to the trees."

"And then you'll let us go?"

His steep shoulders slumped. "If that's what you wish, kikimora."

"Don't call me that!"

"I can call you whatever you wish me to, but it won't change what you are." His eyes were black holes, bottomless in the bark of his face; deep dark caverns, home to bats and night birds. "I need a swamp to bring the water to my trees; I need creeks and puddles, moss and bogs."

I sighed. "How do I do that?"

He gave me an apprehensive look, as if worried that I will swing at him again. "I'll help you along. Just be what you are."

And then I was. I unraveled and un-spun, my limbs splaying and elongating. My fingers twined with Anya's, watery and comforting. My skin split, exposing the hummocks of sphagnum moss (were they always there?), and my veins divided and opened, overflowing with blood as clear as Anya's. The tree roots entangled in my toes, I stretched and engulfed, fed and watered, laughed and nurtured. And Anya's hands caressed mine, our lips met, our hearts beat as one. I felt the leshy nearby, getting stronger, feeding on us, melding with us, mud and water, blood and moss, lichen and stone.

I did not know how many days had passed, but the trees came back to life—the spruces had regrown their needles, and the birches stood surrounded by a pale halo of young greenery. The leshy, healthy and exuberant, disengaged himself from the tree roots and my mires, and stood once again in a human form next to Anya's shore. I followed his example and deflated and creaked, putting myself back together. My skin had grown green like my hair, and mushrooms sprouted where my fingers used to be. "Turn her back," I said. I would take care of myself later.

"As you wish."

The water of the lake agitated and formed a pillar, still and shining like glass. Then its surface clouded, as if someone spilled milk into it, and Anya's sweet face looked at me without reproach. She stepped onto the shore of an empty lake basin, her skin clear, her hair long and golden, flowing down her shoulders. My breath caught in my throat, and simultaneously I grew self-conscious and ashamed. She was so pretty and perfect, and I had become a nasty, ugly thing. A swamp kikimora, fit only to frighten travelers and give children nightmares.

The leshy and Anya smiled at me, unfazed.

"I can't go back like this," I said to the leshy. "Can you make me the way I used to be?"

"If that's what you want." He shrugged with pretend indifference, and looked away.

"Anya?"

She shook her head. "I'd rather stay." Her voice lilted and sung, like a creek jumping from stone to stone. "What's back there? What do you miss?"

I stumbled for words. There was nothing there but the cold and the wolf-year, eager to tear out every jugular. Nothing but the shifty-eyed people, quickly dismantling everything that we ever knew, everything that retained a shred of meaning. Nothing but money that no one had but everyone wanted.

"Well?" the leshy said. "Should I turn you into a girl and send you on your way?" A spark danced inside his deep tree hole eyes, as if he already knew what I was going to say.

"I'm not a girl," I said. "I'm a kikimora." I wrapped one arm around Anya's soft waist, and the other around the snags of the leshy's shoulders, becoming a deep morass between a crystal clear lake and a dark forest, an in-between, a bridge between water and land, past and future, now and forever.

MUNASHE AND THE SPIRITS

Oh, how she wailed. The sky shuddered and storm clouds split open at her hoarse, inhuman cries. Munashe cringed at his mother's unarticulated, bare suffering, at her voice rising higher and higher, lunging for heaven. He looked at blood that came out of her throat and curdled on the earthen floors and rank pallet, black and granular like coffee grounds. He listened to the sound of her fingernails biting into the floor, dragging across it with a jerky movement of the dying.

He sat by her, trying not to be annoyed at her eyes, white with fear, swiveling in her hollow-cheeked face. He made nice, and brushed her long hair out of her face, stroked her cheek with filial attention.

"Let me go," she pleaded in staccato gasps.

He tried to make his voice soothing, reassuring, as if talking to a child. "Where would you go, mother? You're too weak to walk, and no village would take you."

"Munashe."

"I can't, mother. You should be grateful that I am staying here with you."

"Please."

He sighed. "You should've thought about that before you went and turned into a lioness."

She gasped and cried some more, and he could not help but laugh. The woman was deluded enough to think that she was still human. She tried to convince him, thrusting her dark, withered arms into his face. "Look at me. I am not a lion, I am your mother." As if he couldn't see the hungry beast looking out of her eyes, the red glow of its pupils burning hotter than embers of the cooking fire. He heard from old men that women went wild, turned into beasts, and there was only one way of turning them back into humans.

He took a charred piece of impala meat from the coals, and offered it to his mother. "Will you eat now?"

She cried. "It is too hot, too black. I can't eat this."

He nodded to himself. She wanted raw meat, of course, like any lion would. He tried to do good by her, taming her with cooked meat, but so far she hadn't taken any. And her time was running short. AIDS was killing her, and if she went as a lion, her afterlife would be bleak—if she would even have an afterlife.

He ate alone, in the retreating light of the fire. The darkness reached for him, spreading its hungry fingers like a wrathful spirit, its bottomless mouth opened wide to swallow him whole. His mother made no other sound but her labored breath, and faint scratching of her fingernails on the floor. Like a beast, she wanted to crawl away, to find a secluded place in the savannah grass, where she would expire alone, lamented by wind, buried by ants, kissed by red dust. Fortunately, she was too weak to do so. He waited for the scratching to stop before he went to sleep, curled on the earthen floor of the grass hut. Far away, hyenas gloated. They knew that a lion would be dead soon.

When Munashe woke up, his mother was dead, her eyes opened wide but blind, her pallet stained with sweat and blood. Munashe grunted his discontent, and hurried toward the doorway of the hut. There, he stopped and clamped his hands over his mouth to hold back a wail of terror that swelled in his chest. Instead of the yellow, undulating expanse of the savannah, punctuated by lopsided umbrellas of acacias, a solid green wall of a forest surrounded him. There were no lions or hyenas, but only colobus monkeys chattering up in the trees.

The monkeys saw him, and wrinkled their faces, baring tiny, needle-sharp teeth that curved inward. "Munashe," they sang in nasty childish voices, "Munashe, mother-killer."

Their taunt, as direct as it was cruel, brought him out of the daze. "No," he yelled back. "It was not my fault. AIDS killed her, not I."

One of the bigger monkeys swung on the bough and leapt from branch to branch, until its face was level with Munashe's. The monkey's breath smelled stale, and its inward-curving teeth glistened like small yellow fishhooks. "Really?" it hissed. "Did you take her to the doctor, did you make sure that she ate well? Did you care for her in her comfortable home, or did you drag her away from people, from help?"

"I was trying to help. She turned into a lion—she wouldn't eat anything but raw meat."

The monkey's eyes gleamed; its terrible mouth opened wide, and the monkey cackled, the sound of its laughter like scratching of dead leaves. The monkey leapt and landed on Munashe's shoulders. Before he could toss off the unwelcome rider, the monkey's hind legs and long tail wrapped around his neck, and the sharp claws of its hands dug into tender cartilage of Munashe's ears. "Run now, donkey boy, mother-killer!"

Munashe twisted and struggled to get out of the monkey's hurtful grip, but it only laughed and tightened the chokehold of its tail, and wrenched his ears until they bled. Exhausted and terrified, Munashe ran, as the monkey steered him by the ears, deeper into the forest.

It was dark and stuffy under the canopy of the tall trees, and thorny lianas snagged the sleeves of his shirt and the trouser legs, ripping them, digging into his skin until he bled. His lungs expanded and fell, but sucking in the humid air was like trying to breathe underwater. His vision darkened and he took a faltering half-step, stumbling on the ropy roots, falling, anticipating the touch of soft ferns that lined the forest floor. A sharp tug on his ear made him cry out and right himself, picking up his step.

"You don't get to rest, mother-killer," the monkey screeched in his ear.

He ran until the air turned purple and then black, and strange noises filled the air. Something hooted, something chuckled, something else whined in a plaintive, undulating voice. Before the darkness swallowed him, he saw a single bright light beckoning him from behind the trees. The monkey made no objections as he directed his torn feet toward the light.

He came across a grass hut nestled between two strangler figs. The light he saw came from a small lantern perched atop the flat roof.

The monkey gave him a quick, vicious smack on the back of his head, and Munashe bent low, and hurried through the blanket-covered doorway.

"I brought him as you asked," the monkey said, and leapt off his shoulders, to take place next to a military-style woodstove that filled the hut with unbearable heat.

In the glow of the embers, he saw a low cot, and an old, fat woman that reclined upon it. Her bare breasts glistened, framing her swollen abdomen, from which a belly button protruded like an upturned thumb. Her bright eyes held Munashe's for a moment. "Well, well," she said. "Looks like Tendai did a good job." She gave the monkey a fond glance, and it hopped and chittered.

"Who are you, lady?" Munashe's cracked and swollen lips moved painfully.

"I am Tapiwa," she said. "You will serve me until your debt is paid."

Munashe was about to protest, to say that it wasn't his fault, but only sighed. Salt of his sweat burned like fire on his cracked lips. He felt certain that no matter what he said, he was already judged and found responsible for his mother's demise. His only hope of returning home was to listen and to obey; perhaps then they would let him go. "How may I serve you?" His gaze wandered involuntarily to her elephantine thighs circled by rims of fat, and to the dark, curly vegetation of her pubic hair.

Tapiwa noticed the direction of his glance, and shook with a booming laugh. "Ah, not that way, boy. I have bad bedsores, and I need someone to take care of them. Tendai and Vimbai are not strong enough."

"I'll do whatever you need me to, lady. But can I have a drink of water?"

Tapiwa nodded. "You may drink and you may rest. Tomorrow morning, you start."

The morning brought feeble light and the smell of dead embers and sweat, as Munashe started on his task. It took him a few tries to roll Tapiwa's bulk to her side. Waves traveled under her skin with every move, and his fingers slipped on her smooth, damp skin. Two monkeys—Tendai and his brother Vimbai—watched from the perch atop the woodstove.

Munashe puffed, but finally Tapiwa was stable on her left side, her left breast flopping to the floor. Munashe looked at her back and gagged—where her skin should have been, there was nothing but an open sore, running from her shoulders to her backside. A white mass shimmered and moved inside the wound, filling it, spilling to the pallet with every breath Tapiwa took. Maggots.

"What are you waiting for, boy?" Tapiwa said. "Clean them up."

Munashe extended his shaking hand to the living carpet of vermin, and a few maggots popped under his touch. Still, he gathered a handful, looking for a place to throw them.

"On the floor, on the floor," Tapiwa said, impatient.

He obeyed.

Tendai and Vimbai left their roost, and gathered the maggots with their long fingers, stuffing them in their mouths.

"You want to help me?" Munashe said.

The monkeys chattered and laughed, and shook their heads, their jaws moving energetically.

And so it went—Munashe scooped out the maggots by the handful, and the monkeys ate them, showing no signs of getting sated. Munashe kept his eyes half-closed, and breathed through his mouth; his mind wandered far away, back to his home village, to the fields worked by women and children, to the smells of manure and upturned soil, to the proud cassava mounds, surrounded by yam and cowpeas.

Munashe missed home every day of his joyless labor. While Tapiwa was not unkind, her wounds grew re-infested every day, and Munashe was starting to suspect that his labor would never be over. And he gave Tapiwa the care he did not give his mother, care he could not give to all the people in his village—hollow-cheeked men that came home from the city one last time, to their patient wives, thin and hard and strong like strips of leather. Tapiwa, the fat spirit—for he was sure that he was in the spirit forest—was all the sick, all those destroyed by the new way of life that he could not heal. Her sores wept for all.

At night, when the woodstove blazed, burning the already hot air of the hut, Munashe crept outside, under the sultry starless canopy of the forest, and prayed to the ancestral spirits to free him. He cried until his eyes ran dry, and rested in a crouch, listening to the night-sounds; there was chittering and chirping, sighing and moaning, wailing and weeping. And grumbling. His muscles tensed as he listened to the approaching roar—could that be a leopard? Twin lights shone through the treetops, and moved closer, like falling stars. Munashe's mouth opened in awe as he realized that the sound and the light issued from a very old, very large Cadillac, painted bubble-gum pink. The Cadillac descended, leaping from branch to branch like a most agile monkey.

The Cadillac gripped a low horizontal branch with its front wheels playfully, swung, and somersaulted, landing in front of Munashe with a flourish.

"Hello, Mr. Cadillac," Munashe said, shaken, but present enough to remember his manners.

"Hoo! What a dim boy!" the voice came from behind the tinted window. The window rolled down, and a smiling skull with red eyes blazing from under an old khaki baseball hat stared at Munashe. "Why would you think that the car was alive, hm?"

"I . . . I don't know, sir."

"It's a spirit car." The car door swung open, letting out a tall skeleton dressed in a tattered tuxedo, with the sleeves and trousers that were too short. The skeletal remains of his neck were wrapped in a dirty red tie. "Now tell me what you need. You didn't call me here for nothing, did you?"

Munashe told the skeleton his story, all the while marveling at the ease of spirit summoning in the spirit forest.

The skeleton listened with an inscrutable expression. "So, you want me to rescue you from your servitude?" he said once Munashe had finished.

Munashe nodded. "Please."

"Maybe. But first, tell me—what did you learn from all this?"

Munashe stumbled for words. "I don't know, sir. Maybe that everyone needs to be taken care of?"

The spirit skeleton nodded. "I suppose they do. What will you trade me for my help?"

"I don't have anything," Munashe said.

The skeleton's eyes flashed. "You have flesh, boy. How much flesh will you give me for my help?"

Munashe closed his eyes, and thought about his mother. How emaciated she was. And still she lingered, grasping onto life with her stick hands. "Take as much as my mother had lost," he offered.

The skeleton's grinning mouth moved close to Munashe's face, breathing out the smell of liquor and stale meat. It drew a great breath, and Munashe felt millions of tiny teeth gnawing on him, moving under his skin, shaving off his flesh pound by pound, yet never spilling any blood or damaging his skin.

When he opened his eyes, the skeleton seemed bigger and fatter—as much as a skeleton can be fat. He nodded to Munashe and got into his car. "Tomorrow night wait here for my uncle. He'll help you."

"Wait!" Munashe waved his arms after the Cadillac as it started its graceful ascent. "What's your name?"

"Fungai," the skeleton answered, and he and the Cadillac were gone, swallowed by the weakly glowing branches.

The next day, Munashe felt weak but almost cheerful as he went about his task. Tendai and Vimbai, the monkey brothers, noticed, and each gave him a vicious smack and an ear-boxing. Even that could not dispel Munashe's good mood, and he grinned through the tears.

"Ah, you're learning," Tapiwa said. The living shroud of maggots that simmered on her back did not seem to inconvenience her in the least.

Munashe looked up. "Learning what?"

She shrugged, sending the maggots spilling over the pallet and the floor, where Tendai and Vimbai made quick work of them. "That there is a point in every pointless task," Tapiwa said.

Munashe was not sure if he agreed. A pang of guilt coursed through his body—taking care of his mother was a pointless task; she would have died anyway. So instead he chose a task he thought he could accomplish—taming the lion back into the human form.

When the night fell, he snuck outside and waited by the giant strangler fig. He wondered if Fungai's uncle also drove a Caddy.

Something tugged on the shreds of his trouser leg, and he looked down. He almost cried out at the sight of a small baby next to him that stood on all fours, its tiny, long-fingered hand clutching the fabric of Munashe's trousers. Worst of all, the baby's face was projected on a large TV screen; instead of a head, the TV perched atop baby's shoulders dwarfing his small, withered body.

Munashe swallowed hard a few times. "Are you Fungai's uncle?"

"Yes," flashed the letters on the TV screen. Then, they were supplanted by a large red question mark that took up the entire screen.

"How can I heal Tapiwa's wound?" Munashe said. "How can I go home?"

"One or the other," the screen said.

"Both, please. I can't leave until she's better."

The baby's face reappeared, smiling. "You could. I could help you leave right now," it said. Apparently, the TV had sound too.

Munashe bated his breath. This was better than he dared to hope. Still, he resented abandoning his hopeless task, no matter how pointless. "Help her first, and then help me leave."

"One or the other," the screen said.

"Then help her. I know I can leave after she's better."

A question mark again.

Munashe sighed. "I don't know for sure, but I think this is how it works."

Fungai's uncle shrugged his tiny baby shoulders, and showed his face again for a moment, before displaying a chart. "Find the kobo tree -> Find the Lady-Who-Lives-Inside -> Ask for a wishing thread -> Ask for her price."

"What's a kobo tree?" Munashe asked, but Fungai's uncle was already crawling away, the mahogany casing of his television head striking tree trunks that stood too close to his path.

The next night, Munashe set out looking for a kobo tree. He wasn't exactly sure what he was supposed to be looking for, but reasoned that it would be easy enough to recognize. His expectations were fulfilled once he saw a majestic blood-red trunk, crowned with blue foliage and peppered with small yellow flowers.

"Lady?" he called. "Lady-Who-Lives-Inside?"

The Lady-Who-Lives-Inside stood before him as soon as he uttered her name. She was a tall young woman, the most human-looking creature he had encountered so far. Munashe thought that she was just like any woman in his village, until he noticed her stomach—or rather, that she did not have one. There was a large round hole in her midsection, where her belly should've been, framed by the arches of her ribs and pelvis, and festooned with red fragments of gore that fringed the empty space, as if her organs were ripped out of her.

"I need a wishing thread," Munashe said. "What is your price?"

The spirit reached inside of the hole and pulled out a thin string of sinew, red and blue and yellow. "For this," she said in a high nasal voice, "I want the same from you."

Munashe nodded and clenched his teeth as the spirit's clawed fingers—ten on each hand—pried apart his skin and muscle, sinew and bone, until a tiny piece of Munashe dangled, dizzying, in front of his face.

"There," the Lady-Who-Lives-Inside said, and gave him her thread. "Touch it to whatever wound you wish to heal, and it will be done."

When Munashe returned to his village, he was barely able to recognize it. A silence hung over the normally noisy settlement, and the tidy houses bore an indistinct yet unmistakable air of neglect. The cassava fields were overgrown by the weeds, and no rows of women with hoes were fighting to reclaim the fields.

He went from home to home, calling the names of his uncles and friends. No one answered, and Munashe wondered if he was gone longer than he thought. He looked inside the empty houses, and found only desolation and dust. And bones.

It took him a while to discover the living inhabitants of the previously small but vibrant village. Several scrawny, mangy dogs emerged from the fields, as if disbelieving that there was a human there. Two children with bloated stomachs and protruding ribs soon followed.

"What happened?" Munashe said. "Where did everyone go?"

"Dead," the older of two children replied. "AIDS, and something else."

"Is anyone else alive?"

The children shook their heads, and looked at him with shiny hungry eyes. "Do you have any food?"

"No," Munashe said. "But I'm sure we can find some."

In one of the abandoned houses he found a hoe. He looked over the fields where the weeds reigned, strangling the cassava plants. With a sigh, he heaved the hoe and brought it down upon the arrogant weeds, mashing them into the ground, working them into the dry yellow soil. Munashe was starting on another hopeless task.

BY THE LITER

My neighbor, businessman Ipatov, was killed a few years ago, back when they still sold beer by the liter. I remember him because he was my first.

I'd just returned from the corner kiosk, my shirt drenched with cold condensation from the flank of a five-liter beer-filled jug I held against my chest. Outside of my apartment building I heard sirens and saw the yellow police cruisers and a white ambulance van with a red cross on its pockmarked side. My neighbor Petro, a middle-aged Ukrainian with heavy brows and a heavier accent, watched the commotion of people and vehicles and dogs from his second-story balcony.

"Petro," I called. "What happened?"

Petro looked down at me. His wifebeater bore a fresh oil stain that made the fabric transparent; his fleshy nipple and the surrounding swirl of black chest hair stood out in naked relief against the oil spot. "Huh," he said. "What happened? Guess three times."

I stopped for a smoke and a rubbernecking as the cops went inside, and the paramedics brought out the gurney with the lifeless body under a white sheet. The wind snagged the edge of the sheet and it fluttered, exposing the bluing face of businessman Ipatov and his naked shoulder, branded with the cruel marks of the electric iron.

"Racketeers," I informed Petro.

He scoffed. "You don't say."

His scorn was justified, I thought as I transferred the jug of beer from one cradling arm to the other and ashed my cigarette with a flick of lower lip. Racketeers overtook cancer, heart disease, and traffic accidents on the list of death causes of common businessmen somewhere in the late eighties; by the early nineties, they had all but run the other ailments off the mortality and morbidity reports. As Russian business grew healthier, so did its practitioners—nary a single one of them died of any diseases.

One of the paramedics, a young lad with a blond and green Mohawk, smiled at me. "Can't go anywhere." He slouched against the gurney and lit up. "Fucking canaries are blocking us in." His gesture indicated the yellow cruisers huddled behind the van. "Assholes. They're still investigating the scene."

The other paramedic, an aging man with a paunch and chronically disapproving eyes, nodded at my beer jug. "Rest it on the gurney, son. Heavy, ain't it?"

I confirmed and set the jug next to the lifeless remains of my once neighbor. I didn't know yet that beer and the recently dead from violence were a dangerous combination.

"Did you know him?" the old paramedic asked, indicating Ipatov's outline under the sheet with a jab of his cigarette.

"Neighbor," I said. "Seen him around."

"His hands were lashed together with that blue electrical tape," the young paramedic said. "The cops said his employees called the police when he didn't show up for a meeting this morning. His wife doesn't even know yet. The cops said, take him to the morgue; his wife won't thank us if we leave this for her to find."

Petro emerged from the front doors, passing by the murder of old ladies on the bench. "Electric iron?" he said as he reached the gurney.

I nodded and squinted up at the stingy May sun. "Getting warm."

"Yeah," said the younger paramedic and licked his lips thirstily. "Who knows how long we'll be stuck here?"

By all rights, I should have been winging my way home, up the stairs to the third story, beer under arm. But the weather was nice, the company seemed all right, and the beer was best drunk with friends or, missing that, acquaintances. "You want any beer?" I said to Petro and the paramedics.

They kicked dirt for a bit but agreed.

"Funny how it is," the older paramedic named Misha said, taking a large swallow out of the jug he held with both hands. "Here's a man, who lived, lived, and then died. May he rest in peace."

His younger fellow, Grisha, took the jug from his mentor. "God giveth," he said and drank hastily, as if worried about the taketh away part.

The old ladies looked at us disapprovingly, and I tried my best to ignore them.

But not Petro. "What are you staring at, hags?" he challenged, and waited for his turn with the jug. "Haven't seen a dead man before?"

The grandmas squawked, indignant, but avoided the altercation.

Yes, the dead man. The telltale signs of the iron torture indicated that the thugs wanted something—probably money. I wondered why Ipatov didn't just give in to their demands. Or it could be a turf war. "Hey Petro, do you remember what sort of business he ran?"

"Money," he said. "All businesses make is money. Did you

notice how they don't manufacture anything anymore? All the food and shit is imported. Even vodka."

"Yeah," I said, and glanced apprehensively at the half-empty jug as it made its way back to me. I would miss it.

The four of us killed the jug, and as its amber contents diminished, Misha's loquacity grew. "You know why a Russian man is driven to drink?" He didn't wait for an answer and gestured expansively. "It's 'cause of all the space. Steppes, tundra, everything. You have all these open horizons and the human soul can't take all that sober."

I could see a weak point or two in this theory but didn't point them out, enchanted by the image of a soul cowering in fear of horizons.

"What do you do?" Grisha asked me.

"I'm an actuary," I told him. "Manage risks."

"He should've hired you," Grisha said, pointing at dead Ipatov.

I shrugged. There was no point in telling them that the risk of death in businessmen was so close to certainty that the only thing I ever recommended was saving enough money for a coffin. They liked them ostentatious. I should probably attend Ipatov's funeral, I thought. This is when the dead man's memories first stirred in me.

Businessman Ipatov led a quiet life for most of his existence—I remembered his grey adolescence as a treasurer for his school chapter of Komsomol, his joyless pursuit of a college degree in one institute of technology or another, his brief courtship and marriage. After that, I could not remember anything.

Not being given to superstition, I arrived to the only logical conclusion—the dead man's soul and/or memory had entered mine, either due to my extended proximity to the gurney or to the consumption of beer that rested against him. If I were a dead soul, I supposed, I too would be drawn to the golden shine of the beer jug, I too would prefer it to the cold eternity of whatever awaited Ipatov as an alternative. Still, I found it disconcerting; sleep had proven elusive that night, as I kept reliving Ipatov's tremulous first masturbatory experiences and his terror of the laws of thermodynamics and physical chemistry.

I went outside and looked at the windows of the façade. As expected, there was light in Petro's, and I walked to the second floor and knocked. He opened quickly, as if he were waiting just behind the door. His eyes were haunted.

"Come in," he said, and led me to the kitchen. My mother always said that the kitchen is the heart of every home; Petro's apartment's heart was clogged with crap that spilled into the swelling pericardium of his one-room efficiency. "Sorry for the mess."

"It's all right," I said. "I live alone too."

I sat at the kitchen table. A few overfed cockroaches sauntered toward the wainscoting, still decent enough to feign fear of humans.

"Do you hear him too?" Petro asked.

I nodded. "Remember rather."

Petro sighed. "He screams and screams and screams. Can't sleep at all."

"You remember his last days?"

"Yeah," Petro said. "Everything from when he first started the business until . . . "

So if I got his youth and Petro—his business career, it meant that Ipatov's generic Soviet childhood and the working life in whatever state enterprise he was assigned after receiving his degree was sloshing inside the two paramedics.

Petro also had the gold, the death. "Why did they kill him?" I asked.

"Money." Petro heaved a sigh. "Wouldn't pay up protection."

"Oh."

Petro hesitated for a while, but finally said, "Did you know he was Jewish?"

"No. Does it matter?"

Petro huffed. "You got me all wrong, Anatoly. I'm not one of those nationalists, okay? I'm not the one of those 'drown Muscovites in Jewish blood' types. But this torture . . . did you notice that they burned Kabbalic symbols into him? He knew what they were, 'cause he was a Jew."

I perked up. "What symbols?"

"A triangle, for the trinity of Sephiroth. And circles inside of it. I think this is what held his soul here."

"That's the tip of the iron," I said. "And those little holes in it. It's just a coincidence."

"So? The symbol's still holy, no matter how it was made." Petro tilted his head to the shoulder, as if listening. "What's Kether?"

"No clue," I said. "Ask Ipatov."

"I can't. I only remember for him. And he forgot what Kether is."

Petro made tea and we drank; the cockroaches, hearing sugar, crowded in the corners, their antennae undulating eagerly. I contemplated the electric irons and their built-in alchemic and magical powers. I wondered how many more souls hung about, trapped by the thugs' unwitting alchemy. Judging from the newspapers and the latest mortality reports, lots. That gave me an idea.

The problem with Ipatov's memories was that they were much like my own. His adolescence was similar to mine, and remembering it just didn't satisfy my longing for worthwhile experiences. Ipatov's shortcoming was shared by many of our contemporaries—we all remembered the same signifiers of childhood: summer camps and songs praising youthful and heroic drummers, we all treasured a rare trip south, replete with a pebbled beach and a mind-boggling abundance of peaches. Standardized, trivial lives, their monotony only broken by an occasional memory of a grandfather—those were rare. We all viewed the change of regime with joyful trepidation; some were later disappointed, some were not.

I learned all that as I started visiting the scenes of body removals, sometimes tipped off by Grisha, who took as much pleasure in the soul consumption as I did, and sometimes by the police, who would tell you anything if you offered to supplement their dwindling state wages. Like where the dead bodies were, and how to call a specific ambulance if one wanted. They also didn't mind letting Grisha dawdle, and they didn't mind us drinking great golden jugs of beer after we let them sit next to the Kabbalic symbols burned into dead businessmen's flesh. Beer never failed to lure the dead souls.

Far as memories went, it was hit and miss. Most blended inauspiciously with my own, grey and generic, difficult to separate from each other. But there were rare splashes I lived for—the memories of a tropical island and feathery palms, the glitter of New York on a rare pre-perestroika trip abroad, an exotic hobby of orchid collecting, a fresh memory of love so consuming that even torture could not distract from the thoughts of the beloved.

Grisha and I compared memories over the phone. We prided ourselves in our acquisitions; we both grew very fond of a young Chechen who enjoyed flowers and Persian rugs and had an abiding fascination with high-breasted women. We snickered over a paunchy, middle-aged guy who believed himself a reincarnation of Gautama Buddha, the belief especially ironic considering that he had fallen in the shootout between two organizations, which quarreled over the protection money from three stores by Borovitskaya. After he was shot and unconscious, his enemies captured him and meted out their slow electric revenge.

"Sad," Grisha observed. "He could've went to Valhalla had he been slain in battle."

It's the tidbits like that that made me lust after Grisha's soul. But according to the mortality reports, paramedics tended to die of alcoholism often co-morbid with traffic accidents, and not of the homegrown Kabbala of the bandits.

One of our later finds, a neckless thug with the requisite burgundy jacket, brought Ipatov to the forefront of my mind. He seemed much like the rest, with a piquant difference—his father was a mid-caliber apparatchick back in the days, as Grisha, who received the entirety of his youth, told me. I got the good part: his adult life. He was the one who killed Ipatov.

He remembered Ipatov as a small man who would not pay what he owed—a peculiarity that filled the thug with perplexed bitterness. Through his memory, I saw Ipatov's face as it was in his last moments—his white spasming lips and the shirt torn to expose his shoulders and chest. "Just take me from here," he pleaded in a hoarse voice thick with a suppressed scream. "Just don't let Lilya see me like this."

The thug flicked away the butt he smoked down to the filter, and burned his iron magic into poor Ipatov, workmanlike as always. He wondered vaguely whether Lilya was Ipatov's wife, and thought that he too used to date a girl named Lilya when he was a vocation school student.

The thug had trained to be a car mechanic, but then things changed; he fell into being a thug like many others—ex-cops, Afghan vets, who had no other employment options. I marveled at his conviction that what he did was justice: people who owed money should pay it back, and the thug was there to enforce the law in the law-enforcement vacuum. Ipatov's agony was thug's justice, and I enjoyed the juxtaposition of the two memories, enclosing them like pearls with the soft generic mantle of my own.

Our collecting days came to an end when they stopped selling beer by the liter. The cans just didn't have the same appeal to the souls, and who could blame them? Could a fat man wiping his balding, apoplectic head with a handkerchief and gracing cans of Danish beer compare to the thick amber and sensual droplets of condensed moisture on the cold glass? No, my friends, he could not. The souls remained behind, fearful, trapped behind the charred alchemy of the electric irons, and Grisha and I had to content ourselves with what we had.

Now, even the electric irons are going out of fashion, Grisha tells me. We still see each other and reminisce; he often tells me about Ipatov's childhood, of how he once threw up on the bus during the field trip and all the other kids made fun of him for weeks. I tell him of Ipatov's crush on the Komsomol secretary, and of his loathing of thermodynamics. Of course, we have other, much more interesting lives and memories, but Ipatov gets precedence. He was our first, and that ought to count for something.

A PLAY FOR A BOY
AND SOCK PUPPETS

ACT I

SCENE I

(*Sock drawer. In the drawer, there is a SOCK PUPPET—a grey cotton sock with red and blue stripes and black button eyes. The SOCK PUPPET speaks in a soft halting voice.*)

I stare at the ceiling from my drawer, feeling empty and happy. If I squint, the crystals of the popcorn relief above me catch moonlight and sparkle, transformed into tiny stars right before my eyes. I have hours until the morning comes and steals my solitude.

I work with autistic children. They are a difficult bunch, rocking back and forth, spitting, flapping their hands, screaming silently, screaming aloud, banging their heads on the desks, going rigid, going limp, biting. One of them bit me, right above my left button eye, and I needed stitches. Nine of them, in bright red woolen yarn. I'm happy They did not remove my eye and make me a pirate, but the scar hurts, especially before rain.

The morning comes, and brings the rain and shutting of the doors, car honking outside, hurried footsteps, and an infernal whine of the food processor. I count days, hoping despite knowledge that it might be Saturday and I won't have to go. The illusion is shattered when They walk in, pick me up, and shove me in a duffel bag with the others.

The others: there is the clown, the man, the woman, the naïve child, the dog, and the cat. I'm the autistic sock puppet, and to stay in character I do not talk to the others, block out their chattering with swaying in rhythm with the bag and muttering "November" over and over. I think of how strange it is, to have your personality just assigned to you. I think that I would've liked to have some say in the matter.

SCENE II

(The interior of a clinical building. It is filled with people, mostly parents and children entering. The BOY is hidden among the others, but announces himself by periodic loud screeching. The SOCK PUPPET narrates.)

We arrive at Behavioral Therapy. The children are arriving too—they are brought over in cars and SUVs, and file in, some voluntarily, most not. Their parents or guardians drag them by their hands, as the children hiss and fight. Many are wearing little helmets—so bright, in red and yellow and blue, as if the colors can make it better. I want to go home.

Instead, I feel Them enter me, fill me, put words in my mouth. I play an autistic child named Elija, and the others show me how to do things. The children watch, some puzzled, some indifferent. I teach them skills. I teach them empathy. I pretend to eat Goldfish crackers that They give me, and some of the children perk up. The children like crackers, apparently.

After the show is over, the children have their own work to do, and it is my turn to watch. I watch them sort buttons. The teachers say that it is a useful, real-life skill, and that they can use it for future employment. The parents smile and nod, no doubt imagining their offspring sorting through rows and rows of buttons for money, for the rest of their lives. Parents leave, still smiling. They'll be back later.

One of the children starts screaming, aaaaaaaaaaaaaa, and does not stop even when the teacher holds him down so he cannot move. His hands flail, and another teacher grabs his wrists and presses them against the desktop. Too hard, I think. She is pressing too hard.

The kid is subdued, and the rest carry on with their sorting. Whoever is done first gets two Goldfish crackers. The rest get one. The little fake fish smile eerily.

The child who threw a tantrum earlier does not sort. "Darren, you won't get a cracker if you don't sort," one of the teachers says. The kid looks back from under his helmet striped like a watermelon, and crosses his arms on his chest. He just wants to be left alone, and for once I know exactly how someone else feels. He does not get a cracker. They call him "recalcitrant."

ACT II
SCENE I

(*Sock drawer. All of the sock puppets are present. There is a view of the window, and it is grey and raining outside.*)

On the weekend, we do not go to see the children, They do not drive us to the small building of red brick with blue awning, do not make us spout the wrong words.

The others decide to take this opportunity to practice. They love practicing.

"Come on, Elija," says the woman. She likes to pretend to be my mother. "Let's work on not hurting the cat."

I look at the cat—he is striped red and white, and his green eyes are made of shiny stones. I wish I had eyes like that. I do not want to hurt him.

"Come on," the woman says.

"Aaaaaaaaaaaaaaaaaaaaaaaa," I scream. "Aaaaaaaaaa."

She backs off for a bit, but then she remembers what they say about not giving in to the tantrums.

"Now, Elija," she says. "Stop it."

I flail more, aaaaaaaaa, the frayed elastic beating against the roof of our drawer. I bang my head on the wood until my eyes are ready to pop off.

They leave me alone. I calm down and think of the kid, Darren. I wonder if they leave him alone on weekends. I want to see him now, and speak to him in my own words. I want to tell him that "recalcitrant" means "good."

The others are caught up in their rehearsal. The dog plays a family friend, and the man and the woman explain what "autism" means. The cat is trying to eat the naive child, but only chews on his painted-on face with its soft woolen mouth impotently. The clown laughs.

I cannot take it anymore, and rock and slither my way to the opening of the drawer, where a single sunray and dancing motes penetrate the darkness. I struggle my way outside and fall to the ground, narrowly avoiding the knob. I would hate to get my stitches caught on it.

"Where're you going?" the dog says after me, belatedly. I ignore him.

I crawl under the door into the hallway, and look both ways, as They tell everyone to do. I reach the front door undetected, and squeeze through the mail slot.

SCENE II.

(*The street, freshly washed by the rain; most of the stage depicts a wet pavement, with several large puddles. The buildings on the background are out-of-focus and not quite real. The SOCK PUPPET is in the center, lying in one of the puddles.*)

It is early, and the streets are mostly empty. I crawl along, trying not to think that I have no idea of how I would find Darren. I concentrate on staying undetected, and freeze every time someone goes by, but they don't seem to notice an old sock lying on the ground, the black buttons of its eyes shiny, blank.

Two joggers jog by, and one of them stops to look at me. "Hey look," he says. "It's a sock. Now we know what happens to the missing left socks, eh? They run away."

His friend laughs and does not stop, so the jogger leaves me be and takes after his friend. I sigh with relief and crawl along, slowly, imperceptibly, inching my way toward the brick house.

ACT III
SCENE I

(*No change from the previous stage design. It appears that the SOCK PUPPET did not move at all.*)

I'm so exhausted I fall asleep in a puddle, and drift off, soothed by the slow saturation of my every fiber with dirty rainwater. I do not dream. I wake up in motion, and realize that I'm being carried off by a dog—a real one, with hot pungent breath and warm mouth.

"Rex, put that down!"

The dog growls a bit, and chews me hastily, guiltily, dribbling spit and tearing out one of my stitches before spitting me out and running to join its owner. I wince in pain as I feel the old gash beginning to reopen.

I slither across the road, not caring about thick rubber tires that run me over again and again, flattening me, sapping my desire to find Darren. What will I say to him? How will I find him? I concentrate on crossing the road. I give up on looking both ways.

On the other side, I lie panting for a bit, and look around. I glimpse the small brick building, its doors concealed by a corrugated sheet of metal. I try to remember the direction from which the kids usually come. I make up my mind and crawl toward the narrow slit of the horizon, as the setting sun bleeds all over it.

I hear chittering, and I turn to see a squirrel, its barbaric incisors bared, its eyes glistening. I try to shoo it away and rock, aaaaa, and twist and flail. Undeterred, the beast starts picking on my elastic, and I feel myself unraveling. I bang my head on the pavement, but the squirrel picks me up in its small hands (thank God it's not putting them inside of me), then its mouth, and runs up the tree, as I flap along. The nature was stupid when she created socks—we have no defense mechanisms whatsoever. I hang limply and whisper "November" to calm myself down.

SCENE II.

(The interior of a tree hole. Light penetrates in slants from somewhere high above the stage. The SOCK PUPPET, torn and wet, is on the bottom of it.)

The squirrel carries me to its nest in a deep treehole, and I worry that it will continue the horrid unraveling it has started below until all of me is gone. I wonder if a ball of yarn has a soul, but I doubt it. When I cease to exist, so will my spirit.

The squirrel nestles into the hole, and lays me on the bottom of it. I play dead until morning. When my captor is gone, I open one eye, carefully, and look around, to discover bits of moss and paper, but no other captives. With that, I make my escape. The squirrel runs out and back in, and out again, and I make very little progress, trying to worm my way up the vertical wooden wall. I watch my stitches and unraveled threads, making sure they do not get caught on splinters and jagged edges of the hole.

The squirrel passes me as I reach the opening in the trunk. I freeze, but the obtuse beast pays me no attention, its small mind apparently preoccupied with the wafer end of an ice-cream cone it clutches in its teeth. It passes me on its way inside.

SCENE III

(Playground in the park. There is a large tree, and the SOCK PUPPET is hanging out of the hole in the tree. The BOY is off-stage, but his shrill cries betray his presence.)

I peek out of the hole, and forget about my trailing threads and open gash. I stare at the town, washed by the first September rains into muted pearly purity, spreading below me. I whimper at the bigness of it, but I cannot deny its beauty. I peer with my button eyes, and everything stands out in startling clarity. I see dogs and kids running around, and realize that the squirrel dragged me to the park filled with children and their parents. I look for a watermelon-striped helmet. I cling to the rough bark of the tree, high above everything, and wait.

I decide to call for Darren, and I wail, aaaaaaaa, and my gash hurts, and my threads are sore and unraveled. I scream my inarticulate suffering, hoping that he would hear me, until I grow hoarse.

And then I hear him, aaaaaaa, screaming back at me. For me. Green and black stripes come into my view, and I see Darren running, I see Darren chased by the woman who usually brings him to Behavioral Therapy. "Darren, honey," she calls. "Come back. Mommy will give you a cracker."

The kid does not want a cracker and he runs straight for my tree, a fresh gash in his forehead glistening red, like mine. It takes persistence to hurt oneself while wearing a helmet. He tilts his pale face toward the sky, and his mouth opens expectantly.

I jump. I sail through the air and plummet, alternately, until his hands snatch me out of the air. His hands hold me, carefully, and do not try to enter me. I cling to him, grateful.

"Elija," he says.

The woman is gaining on us, and I hurry to tell him. "Don't let their hands touch you," I whisper fiercely. "Don't let them speak for you."

He nods that he understands, and hugs me close. I drape over his shoulder and he runs. The woman recedes behind us, panting, her hands on her knees. We leave behind the park and its trees and horrible squirrels, we splash through every puddle we can find. I look at the sky, empty, happy. I hope that there is a place without intrusive hands, where one can scream and flail and speak his own words.

(Both the BOY and the SOCK PUPPET exit stage left.)
CURTAIN

THE TASTE OF WHEAT

Dominique came from solid peasant stock, not frequently given to fancy; still, in the privacy of the thick bones of her skull, she dreamt of an Asian gentleman who insisted on being called Buddha, and small dogs with sharp white teeth.

The heavy sleep descended unannounced, smothering her with dreams in the middle of dinner with her family, or in the wheat fields while she was threshing. Any blink could turn into a jumble of images and voices, and then someone would shake her shoulder and say, "Dominique, wake up."

Sometimes the dreams stopped before she was forcefully pulled away from them, and then she would hear what they said. "What is wrong with her?" and "You'd never think looking at that girl." Then she blushed, and let the world in shyly, through the slightest opening of her lashes. The sun was fuzzy in their frame, and the faces—soft, undefined, kind. Then she would get up, smoothing down her skirt around her wide hips.

"You seem so healthy—milk and blood," people said. They kept the second part of their comments silent, but Dominique knew what it was. She was defective, and no man would take a wife with falling sickness, no matter how well-fed and ruddy-cheeked. Her family thought that it ought to bother her, but it did not. She only shrugged and went about her business, ready to be assaulted by dreams with every step she took.

She worked in the fields with the rest of her compatriots, from the time when the sun rose to the sunset. But at midday she left the merry din of people laughing and talking, children squealing, oxen lowing, and went home to tend to her grandfather. He was too feeble to venture into the fields, and she took it upon herself to make sure that he was fed and attended to.

The old man looked at her with his colorless rheumy eyes that had seen so many harvests come and go, and she almost wept with pity. He was the only person she had ever known who understood what it was like to inhabit a body ready to betray him at any moment.

"Don't worry, grandpa," Dominique said, blinking hard to cool her suddenly hot eyes. "Maybe some day you'll be born as a butterfly, alive for just a day, your life short and painless and beautiful." She spoke in a hushed voice; even though she knew that her parents and siblings were in the fields, she worried about being overheard. Sometimes (more often as the time wore on) she intentionally garbled her words, so that only her grandfather could understand. She rather liked appearing as a large, mumbling thing, half-witted from her fits.

She fed her grandfather, pushing an awkward spoon between his gums, pink like those of an infant. His skin seemed simultaneously translucent and tough, like the wings of a dragonfly, with quartz veins intersecting under its pale, downy surface. His hooded eyelids stood like funeral mounds over his dead eyes, the coarse salt of his eyebrows casting a deep shadow over them.

"Grandpa," Dominique said, "you are so good, you deserve to be a butterfly." She thought for a bit, the wooden spoon in her red idle hand dripping its grey gruel. "They say being a dog is pretty good, but I'm not so sure—all you get is yelling and kicking. Unless, of course, you are Buddha's dog. Perhaps a bird . . . the kind nobody hassles. Like a hawk; just promise you'll stay away from the chicken coops, or people will throw stones at you. Promise me."

Grandpa nodded, in agreement or in encroaching sleep, she couldn't tell. She wondered if her grandfather was afflicted by the same visions as her, if he too dreamt of the stocky Asian gentleman and his dogs, adorable and vicious. Before she could decide one way or another, they all stood around her, and she lay on the earthen floor of a dark cavern. The dogs snarled, showing their needle teeth.

"What we think, we become," Buddha said, with his habitual feeble smile.

Dominique sat up, despite the snarling dogs, and nodded.

"Be grateful you didn't die today," he said.

The dogs growled deep in their throats but settled down.

Buddha shifted on his feet, with a look of consternation showing on his moonlike face. "Words have the power to both destroy and heal. When words are both true and kind, they can change our world."

The dogs barked and leapt, and Dominique woke up with a start.

She collected herself off the floor, smoothing her skirt and blushing. "Sorry, Grandpa," she said.

The old man did not answer. His body pitched forward in his chair, and a thin streak of gruel hung off the corner of his lips. With a sinking heart, Dominique realized that he was dead, dead on her watch, dead because the dreams stole her attention away from him. She fell to her knees, grabbing the cold hands with blueing fingernails, and keened.

Her wails brought people from the fields. They came running

and hushed when they saw the dead man. After a few seconds of respectful silence, they talked about the funeral arrangements, while Dominique still keened, her cries hanging over the thatched rooftops of the village like tiny birds of prey.

They buried Dominique's grandfather two days later. The frost came early that year, and the ground grew hard. The diggers' hoes struck the dirt with a dull thump-thump-thump. The diggers sweated as Dominique's family clustered about shivering, drawing their warm clothes tighter around them.

Dominique never looked at the diggers, and let her gaze wander over the bare fields and the grey hills that lined the horizon. She searched for her grandfather, and worried that she would not recognize him in his new form. Was he a leaf blowing in the wind, a tiny calf that followed its mother on rubbery, slick legs, a sparrow perched on the roof? Life of all persuasions teemed about her, and Dominique despaired to find him. "I'm so sorry, Grandpa," she whispered into the cutting wind as it singed her lips.

After the funeral, Dominique walked home among the neighbors and relatives who filled her house with their heat and loud voices. She made sure that everyone's mugs were filled with mulled wine, and that everyone had plenty of cracked wheat and raisins. It was for her grandfather. Buddha's words buzzed in her ears like flies tormenting dogs on hot summer afternoons, "To be idle is a short road to death and to be diligent is a way of life." Dominique did not want to die—not until she found out what happened to her grandfather.

Then it occurred to her that the nights were growing longer and colder, and many woodland creatures must be feeling hungry and alone. Quietly, she picked up the bowl with wheat and raisins and stepped outside. No one noticed either her presence or departure, just like they didn't notice their own breathing.

The wind whipped her hair in her face, as she peered into the freezing darkness, her eyes watering in the cold. She thought about the moles that burrowed through the ground, and the little field mice that skittered across its surface on nervous light feet, of the weasels that eyed the chicken coops when no one was watching, and the shrews that stalked millipedes. There were too many to feed, to many to search through. How could even Buddha hope to recognize one soul among the multitude?

She set the bowl a few steps away from the porch and tightened her shawl around her shoulders, shivering, listening to the quiet life that teemed about her. She was too large, she realized, too lumbering to ever hope find her grandfather. She needed to be smaller. And she needed a better sense of smell.

She thought of the tales the old women told around the fire, about the mice who decided to become human, and crawled into the pregnant women's wombs, to gnaw at the growing child and to displace it; they grew within the women, shed their tails and claws, and were born as human children. One could only recognize them by the restlessly chewing teeth and the dark liquid eyes. Surely there must be a way for a woman to become a mouse.

The winters were always long, with nothing to do but tell stories. Dominique withdrew more, and gave herself to her sleeping fits with zeal, like a soldier throwing himself onto the bristling pikes to aid the cavalry charge. Dominique tried to aid Buddha's visit, so he would answer her questions.

One day, he appeared. His dogs were subdued and teary-eyed, shivering and sneezing in small staccato bursts. The winter was not kind to them.

"Are your dogs all right?" Dominique asked.

Buddha looked up, into the dripping ceiling of his cave. "A dog is not considered a good dog because he is a good barker."

"I cannot find my grandfather," Dominique said, the fear of waking up lending her voice urgency.

"All things appear and disappear because of the concurrence of causes and conditions," Buddha replied.

"I have to find him though," she said. "I think I need to become a mouse, or another small creature, so I can search better."

"He who experiences the unity of life sees his own Self in all beings, and all beings in his own Self, and looks on everything with an impartial eye."

"Just tell me," she begged. "Without riddles."

Buddha finally turned his empty eyes to her. "People create distinctions out of their own minds and then believe them to be true. You are no different than a mouse; you just think you are."

Before Dominique could thank him, the walls of the cave melted around her, and she came awake on the floor of the barn, in the warmth of steaming, sleepy breath of sheep and chickens. It was clear to her now—she created the world with her thoughts, and she could alter it just as easily. At this moment of enlightenment, Dominique's clothes fell on the floor, and a small brown mouse skittered away.

Soon, the little mouse discovered that her new mind could not hold as much thoughts as the human one, and it worked hard to hold onto its single obsession: find an old man who was now something else. But first, she needed to eat.

Dominique the mouse remembered that the granary was close to the barn, and hurried there, her little brain clearly picturing the earthen jugs overflowing with golden grain. She made it there safely, avoiding the prowling cats and the eyes of the humans, and ate her fill of crunching, nourishing wheat. After that, she was ready to go.

She let her nose lead her—it twitched toward the wind, sorting through many smells, some comforting, some exciting. She noticed the smell that mixed familiarity with strangeness, fear with solace, and decided to follow it.

The fields lay barren, and the mouse squeaked in terror as it ran between the frozen furrows of the fallow field, vulnerable in the open ground with no cover. Her little heart pumped, and her feet flew, barely touching the ground, until the dry grass of the pasture offered her its comfort. She dared to stop and catch her breath, and realized that the smell grew stronger.

She found an entrance to an underground burrow, and followed the long and winding tunnel. White hoarfrost covered its walls, and the anemic roots extended between earthen clumps, as if reaching for her. The mouse shivered with fear and cold, but kept on its way until she saw the pale light, and heard soft, high-pitched singing echoing off the white burrow walls. Dominique the mouse entered the large area in the end of the tunnel, and stopped in confusion.

The candles cast the silhouettes of the gathered field mice, making them huge and humped. The mice were serving the Mass. Their voices rose in solemn squeaks, and their shadows swayed in a meditative dance, rendering the walls of the cave a living tapestry of black, twisting darkness and white frost, glistening in the candlelight. The mice prayed for sustenance.

Dominique stayed in the back of the crowd, too shy to come forth and ask her questions. Even her desires grew clouded, and for a while she could not remember why she was there. Snatches of thoughts and images floated before her dark beady mouse eyes: a jug of grain, the thick arm of her father clutching across his wife's pregnant stomach as they slept, a stretching neck of a new chick. An old man with the eyelids like funeral mounds.

The mice stopped their chanting, and lined up to partake of the Eucharist. The mouse who was a priest by all appearances held up a thimble Dominique recognized as her own, lost some time ago, and let all the mice sip from it. Dominique joined the line. Several altar voles helped with the ceremony, distributing grains of wheat and helping the feeble with the sacrament.

Dominique shuffled along, and waited for her turn. No one seemed to notice that she didn't quite belong there, and the vole shoved a sliver of grain into her mouth. She chewed thoughtfully, as her eyes sought to meet the gaze of the priest.

Finally he turned to her, his work completed. "What do you want, daughter?"

Dominique found that she could communicate with the mouse priest easily. "I'm looking for an old man." She stopped and wrinkled her face, trying to remember. "He died, and become someone else. I have to find him."

The mouse priest moved his sagging jowls with a thunderous sigh. "We dreamed of the others coming into our midst, and we prayed for signs . . . none came."

"But I smelled him here!"

The priest turned away, mournful. "It was God you smelled."

Dominique sighed and followed the mice, who filed out of the main chamber into a complex system of burrows. She found a tunnel that led upward, and enticed her with the smell she sought.

The snow had fallen while she was underground, and she sputtered and shivered as the white powder engulfed her, its freezing particles penetrating between hairs of her coat. She half-struggled, half-swam to the surface.

Buddha was outside with his dogs, running weightlessly across the moonlit snow. His dogs preceded him, their noses close to the ground. They followed a chain of danger-scented footprints. A fox, Dominique guessed, mere moments before seeing the fox.

It looked black in the moonlight, and it dove into the snow, coming up, and diving again. It seemed puzzling at first, but then Dominique heard muffled squeaks, pleas, and cries of pain. The fox was hunting mice, too busy to notice that Buddha's dogs were stalking it.

The fox sniffed the air, and turned its narrow muzzle toward Dominique. Her heart froze in terror, and her feet screamed at her that it is time to run, run as fast as possible. But she remained perched on two hind legs, looking the fox straight in the eye. "Have you seen my grandfather?" she asked the fox.

The fox stopped and tilted its head to the shoulder.

"He's not a mouse," Dominique explained. "At least, I don't think so. He died and was born as someone else."

"Ask the mice," the fox suggested, yawning. Its teeth gleamed in the moonlight. "They would know—they get everywhere."

"I tried. But they are only praying, and—"

The dogs she had forgotten about pounced. The fox shrieked, trying to shake two small dogs that latched onto the scruff of its neck.

"All things die," Buddha commented.

The pale petals of the stars came out and the moon tilted west. Dominique alternated between burrowing under the snow and running on the surface. She followed the trail of the fox who ate so many of her brethren.

Dominique did not need to sleep; her dream fits were but a distant memory. She wondered if all mice were sleepless, and realized that she had never seen a sleeping mouse. She also wondered whether they spurned Buddha because he only came to those who slept.

As she contemplated, she realized that the smell that was urging her on was growing weaker. She turned her snout back, and caught it again—back where the fox full of mice was being rent to pieces by Buddha's dogs.

The old mouse told her that it was smell of God, and she turned back to the mouse burrow, to the church. To her horror, she found the burrow desecrated, dug up, and the surviving mice huddled in the ruined passages.

The old mouse priest was among them. He shook and cried. When he saw Dominique, he hissed. "It was all your fault; you brought the fox to our church."

Dominique shrugged, unsure if she was able to take on a burden of another responsibility. The smell of her dead grandfather was overpowering around her, emanating from all the mice, and especially the old priest. Even her own breath carried the scent of him. "You told me that was the smell of God," Dominique told the priest. "But where is it coming from?"

The priest still wept. "His flesh was made grain, and this is what we take as our Eucharist. The flesh of God."

Dominique remembered the taste of the grain sliver on her tongue, and squeaked with frustration. Why did she think an old man would come back as a mouse or a bird? What better destiny was there than to be wheat?

She remembered the golden expanse of the ripe ears of wheat, the singing of women, the even thumping of the threshers. She thought of her grandfather, when he could still leave the house, walking behind the reapers, picking up stray ears fallen to the ground, smelling them, chewing their milky softness with his toothless mouth. And then, she missed home.

She comforted the mice the best she could, telling them of Buddha and his protective dogs, but she never told them that the flesh of the grain was her grandfather's, that he came back to her in the taste of wheat and the communion of mice.

She spent the night and the next day digging new burrows, and collecting what grain was left in the field, so her mouse brethren could have shelter and the Eucharist. But her heart called for her to go home, until she could resist the urge no longer.

Dominique was tired. Her small feet screamed with pain as she crawled back into the village. She wanted to be human again. She remembered vaguely the words of a round gentleman, punctuated by sharp barking sneezes of his small needle-teethed monsters. But she could not recall their meaning, she could not remember how she became a mouse, her feeble memory overpowered by the taste of wheat.

The only recourse left to her was to do what all mice did in a situation like that. She skittered along the row of straw-thatched houses, listening, looking. A sharp, salty smell attracted her attention, and she circled a small house, its doorway decorated with wilting, frosting garlands of wheat and oak boughs. Newlyweds.

She found a narrow slit between two planks by the door, and squeezed inside. It was warm and the house was filled with smoke from the dying embers in the woodstove. Two people lay in the bed, asleep, naked.

Dominique's nose twitched as the smell grew stronger, and she followed it up onto the bed, light on her feet, scampering across the folds of the sheepskin covers.

The sleeping woman shuddered but didn't wake up as the tiny mouse claws ran along her thigh.

The smell was overwhelming now, and the mouse closed her eyes, and squeezed into a narrow, moist passage that smelled of sea. The woman moaned then, and the soft walls that surrounded Dominique shuddered.

She reached a widening of the burrow, and entered a warm, unoccupied cave. There, she curled into a fetal ball, tucking her long tail between her legs. Soon, her tail would fuse with the walls of her fleshy cave, and she would become a small person, with black liquid eyes and restless jaws of a mouse.

CHERRYSTONE AND SHARDS OF ICE

I sat with my face in my hands; not due to inebriation, which was greater than what my finances allowed, but less than what I wanted it to be. My distress was caused by a combination of events that involved the crooked militia, a slick merchant, and a deceitful woman. As a result, my financial and moral state left much to be desired; so I drank on credit.

Just as the world was starting to soften around the edges, a shadow fell across the stained tablecloth of the restaurant table. I did not look up. While I was not a man to avoid the inevitable, I still did not relish the sight of my doom's portents. I wanted to see neither goons, nor the ungrateful bitches.

"Excuse me," said a male voice directly above and far, far from my bowed head. "Messer Lonagan?"

The address was polite enough to make me raise my gaze. Two thugs in the uniforms of the Areti clan grinned at me with as much sincere joy as a shark that spotted a flounder.

"Yes," I said, too smart and too experienced to lie. "What can I do for you?"

"Venerable Mistress Areti desires to see you."

I sighed and took another sip of my wine. "I'd rather stay where I am. I had the most wretched day, and surely the Venerable Mistress can find someone better qualified than I." Not that I liked turning down a paycheck, but Areti's gold to a businessman was like a millstone to a swimmer.

One of the thugs grabbed my right wrist, pressing it against

222

the table where it rested. The other goon opened his jacket, extracting a pistol with a heavy handle, flipped it in his hand with a rehearsed motion, and brought it down across my fingers—lightly, but with enough force to give me an idea of how much it would hurt when he did it in earnest. His eyes glinted with a malicious promise.

"Please don't break my hand." I felt tired rather than scared. "I need it."

"Will you come then?"

What was a man to do? I followed them out of the restaurant, into the streets filled with silvery mist highlighted by an occasional hazy sphere of a gas lamp. On our way, we took a shortcut and skimmed along the edge of the deaders' town, where ghostly dead man's birches shone through the droplets of moisture in the air, their branches studded with tiny green flickers, the condensation weeping silently down their trunks.

We walked across a wooden bridge that creaked and resonated under our feet. I smelled something musty, and a moment later spotted a dead beggar, who sat in the middle of the bridge, reclining by the guardrail. His eyes bulged out of his swollen dark face, and his thick purple tongue protruded where his lower jaw used to be, but was now gone, lost forever. He would not walk around for long, and seemed to know it—his white eyes were turned upwards, greeting the stars as they sprinkled across the darkened sky.

"Filthy rat," said one of my guides. "He probably died a beggar."

"Likely," I agreed, and couldn't look away.

The other guide spat, propelling a gob of saliva and phlegm that landed with a satisfying smack onto the beggar's left eye.

"I can't believe it. They are everywhere nowadays—their part of town just keeps on spreading."

"That doesn't require a great deal of faith, to believe that," I said. "The dead will always outnumber the living."

"How's that?"

"You live, you die. Everyone who's now alive will end up in the deaders' town. Even you, so be nice to them."

The guards huffed, but their gazes slid off the beggar and turned downward, to the slats under our feet. One could live in this place and be carefree only if he did not think of his inevitable demise, the inexplicable one-way traffic. I couldn't ignore this silent but constant shuffling from one side of the town to the other; I couldn't forget that the deader city swelled with every passing year, encroaching onto the town of the living. Soon, the alivers' town would be but a fleck in the sea of rotting flesh. I was never carefree.

I shook my head and stepped off the bridge onto the quartz pavement, where the gaslights were installed with regularity, and the trees emitted no deathly glow, but cast deep, cool shadows, soft as crushed silk. A light perfume of jasmine scented the night, and soft singing came from nearby—the sort of thing the alivers enjoy.

The Areti manor squatted squarely on the hillside, its windows shuttered, but a soft glow of lamplight seeped around the edges, beckoning. The three of us entered the hallway. Darkness pooled in the rounded recesses of the walls, and my soft-soled shoes seemed too loud. There didn't seem to be any people here, just echoes. There were no doors either—just curtains that billowed in the entryways, blown about by the dusty winds that skipped around the manor, unchallenged.

"In here," one of the goons said, and pulled open a curtain decorated with a beaded dragon. Its eyes glinted in the firelight that reached from within.

I entered a vast hall drenched in shadows. "Venerable Mistress?"

"Right this way, Lonagan." She reclined on a chaise made of solid oak, and still it creaked under her weight. The fireplace cast a semicircle of orange light, and I stepped closer.

Her face was oval and pretty, with large doe eyes and a prim, full-lipped mouth. Her long auburn hair curled and cascaded, descending onto her shoulders and chest, playing like waterfalls across the vast terrain that was her body. She was a landscape, not a woman—hills and valleys of flesh stretched before me in every direction, barely contained on the gigantic chaise. Only her face and hands seemed human.

I bowed. "What can I do for you, Venerable Mistress Areti?"

She smiled, and for a moment I forgot about her distended body, and looked into her ink-blue, almost black eyes. "I hear that you can find things."

I inclined my head. "That is indeed the case. What would you like me to find?"

Her smile grew colder, tighter. "I thought you could figure that out."

"No," I said with rising irritation. "I'm not a magician. I'm just a thorough man."

She undulated with laughter, sending slow, hypnotic waves through her flesh. "All right then. I lost a gemstone—or rather, it was stolen from me. By the deaders."

"Are you sure?" The deaders were not known for crime—that was the province of the still-living.

225

"Oh, quite sure. You see, they are recent deaders, and I fear that my men were somehow responsible for their transition."

It still sounded strange to me, but I nodded. Who was I to judge? Perhaps they had the stone on them while they transitioned; perhaps their passions were slower to die than was common. "What is this stone like?"

"It's a cherrystone." She lifted a delicate, fine hand, and spread her index finger and thumb half an inch apart. "Small, pink. You'll know it when you see it."

I was certain of that. Even though I've never held anything as valuable as a cherrystone in my hands, I heard enough about them and their powers to know how rare they were. Especially pink ones—chances were, it was the only one in town.

"What about those who took it?"

She shrugged. "Ask my guardsmen for a description."

"Do you know their names?"

"I would imagine they've shed their names by now, so they would be useless to you."

So it was longer than a week since they were dead. Yet, I couldn't imagine why she would wait a week to start looking for her cherrystone. The only conclusion that made sense was the one that didn't make sense—that they were dead while committing the theft.

"Be discreet," she said, just as I was about to leave. "You understand how precarious my situation is."

"Of course, Venerable Mistress. I won't say a word."

I left the crackling of the fire and the oaken chaise behind, and walked along the corridor, back to the entrance. This place did not fill me with trepidation any longer—the air of lonely neglect made me feel sorry for her, despite the Areti's bloody reputation.

I liked to think that my sympathy was not contaminated by the promise of a paycheck.

One had to be careful in the deaders' town, and I watched my step, even though I had connections there. The inhabitants were not violent by nature, but protective of what little lives they had. I prepared myself for the stench by putting a generous dollop of wintergreen ointment under my nose, and stowed the can in my pocket. Abiding the old habits, I waited for the nightfall, to sneak in under the cover of darkness.

The moment my foot touched the soft moss that grew through the cracks in wooden pavements, I realized that I was foolish—deaders did not sleep, and night made no difference. I heard the ice merchants calling in high voices, and the scraping of their trunks full of green translucent chunks of ice as they pulled them by the ropes.

I kept close to the buildings, and hid my face in the collar of my jacket. A few passersby did not seem to notice me, as they shambled along. Jas, the deader I was going to see, lived well away from the border of the alivers; it wasn't the first time that I visited him, but the gravity of my task made me feel ill at ease.

I saw his house, recognizable because of the brick-red shutters, and sped up my steps. The houses seemed superfluous—if it wasn't for the need to contain the cold, the deaders could've just as easily lived outside, shambled along whatever streets, forests or valleys they chose. But they kept to the town, nestled inside in the protective cocoon of ice, trying to slow their decay. Couldn't say I blamed them.

I passed a white house, with a small courtyard and a garden in front of it, and paused. One did not see decorations in these parts too often. And I also saw a young girl in the yard. Unaware that anyone was watching, she hummed to herself, and practiced her dance steps. She must've died just recently—her skin was pale but whole, and her downy hair blew about her thin face as she twirled with her arms raised. I didn't know exactly what happens after death, but I noticed that it affected coordination; the girl stumbled, and almost fell over. Stubbornly, she steadied herself, and started on sidesteps.

She noticed me watching, and gasped. In her fright, she bolted away, running straight into a gatepost. It would've been comical if the impact wasn't so great—it threw her backwards, and she landed on her rump.

I swung the gates open, and helped her up. "I'm so sorry," I said. "I didn't mean to scare you. I just stopped to watch—you dance very prettily."

She sniffed. "Do I have a bruise?"

I nodded. An angry purple spot was spreading across her white forehead.

She gave a little cry and whimpered. Dead didn't weep, but there was a phlegmy rattle deep in her chest.

"I'm sorry," I said. "It's just a bruise."

Her mouth curled downwards. "You don't understand. It'll never heal."

I knew that she was right, and felt wretched. I didn't mean to shorten her time, I didn't want to speed up her decay.

She finally looked at me. "It's not your fault. It was an accident."

I nodded. "Thank you."

"You're an aliver. What are you doing here?"

"I came to see your neighbor," I said. "The one who lives in that house."

"I know him. I think. A tall young man, right?"

"Yes, that's the one. I guess I'd best be going."

"Why do you want to see him?" I was certain now that she hadn't been among the dead for long—she asked too many questions. The deaders were usually more reserved, less curious.

Of course I wasn't going to tell her the exact truth; but I wasn't going to lie either, not after I hurt her. "He's my brother," I said. "Used to be, I mean."

Her mouth opened in awe. "And you still see him?"

"Why not?"

"No one else does."

She was right, of course. I opened the gate, all the while feeling her curious stare at the back of my neck. Before I stepped into the street, I turned to face her again. "I know. The alivers prefer not to think about the folks here. And I can't stop thinking about them . . . you."

I knocked on the dingy, peeling door of the house with red shutters. It gave under my knuckles, and I stepped inside. My teeth started chattering as soon as I crossed the threshold.

"It's you," Jas said.

"It's me. How are you?"

He sat slouching on the floor, his back propped against an ice chest. It was half-full of dirty water and pellucid ice shards. He had changed little since last I saw him—perhaps a bit more decay darkening the skin around his eyes and on his temples, perhaps more sinking around his mouth; but he was still in good shape—as good as one can expect after ten years of death. "All right, I suppose. You?"

"Same." I sat by the door, the warmest spot of this one-room house. "Want me to fetch an ice merchant for you?"

"Nah. What do you want?"

I gave a laugh that sounded unconvincing even to me. "Do I need a reason to see you?"

He coughed, and it sounded like something came loose in his chest with a sickening tear of wet tissue. "Nah. But you usually have one. I'm not as dull as you think."

"I don't think you're dull. You're right; I do have a question. I'm looking for two deaders—new ones. One is tall and dark, has only one hand. The other is medium height, light hair, no beard. Young."

The ruin that was my brother nodded. "I know them. Still, it wouldn't kill you to come and just visit."

"I didn't think you wanted me to. Every time I come you act like you don't want me here."

"I don't want. I can't; I'd like to, but I can't. And I forget a lot, y'know?" His tongue turned awkwardly in his mouth, scraping against blackened teeth. "When you come, you remind me. And I don't want to forget. So please come. To remind me."

"Jas . . ."

"Lemme finish. Other deaders, they don't remember squat. Who they were, and they tell me, they tell, 'How do you know you even have a brother? Who can know such a thing? You can't remember about the alivers.' But I do, because of you. I'm lucky—everyone else, they're alone. But not me, not me."

"All right, Jas." My voice shook a bit, but I didn't think he'd noticed. "I'll come more often. But now I need to know about those men."

"Why?"

I hesitated; not that I mistrusted Jas, but the deaders had loyalty to their own kind, not to the alivers—even if they were kin. "They might know something that is of interest to me."

Jas shook his head. "You're still dealing in secrets. Dangerous trade."

"I know. I almost had my hand broken the other day."

Jas sat up. "Like the man you're looking for."

I felt a chill, and it didn't come from the icebox. "I thought his hand was missing."

"They broke it first, then cut it off, then slit his throat." Jas spoke with relish. I noticed it before; the deaders seemed to enjoy the details of death.

"Who?"

Jas shrugged. "The Areti goons, who else? I sure hope they don't want anything from you; they and the deaders have been fighting for no one remembers how long."

"You know why?"

He nodded. "Every deader knows. It's about a curse, and a cherrystone."

"Areti's cherrystone?"

His lungs whistled a bit—the sound that signified laughter. "Is that what she'd been telling you? No, that's ours. It's our curse, see, and we're keeping it, Areti or not." Jas stood. "C'mon. There's someone I want you to meet."

I stepped toward the door, but Jas shook his head. "It's too warm out. We'll go the other way."

He creaked and groaned, but bent down enough to touch the earthen floor. He groped around in the dirt.

"Can I give you a hand?"

"Sure." He pointed out a bronze ring mounted on a wooden trapdoor, hidden under a layer of dirt. I never noticed that it was there.

I pulled on the ring, and as the dust and grime cloud

settled, I saw a rickety ladder leading downwards. "Where does it go?"

"To other houses . . . everywhere. It's nicer to travel underground, cooler."

That explained the scant traffic on the surface. I let Jas descend, and followed him. It wasn't nearly as dark as I had expected—strange fluorescent creatures darted to and fro among the weakly glowing walls of the tunnel, and sick, gangly dead man's birches illuminated the way with their dead light.

There were ladders everywhere, and the deaders too—the underground seemed a much more animated place than the surface. I mimicked Jas' shambling gait, eager not to attract attention. "Should I even be here?" I asked Jas.

He stopped and mulled it over for a moment. "Don't see why not. You'll move here, sooner or later. As long as you don't hurt the deaders, you're all right."

I was moved that he never even considered the possibility of my betrayal; then again, perhaps it was one of the deaders' limitations. Just as they forgot their relatives, so perhaps they lost their understanding of the ways of the living.

He led me deeper into the labyrinth. The passersby grew less frequent, and the light—weaker. I could not discern the direction, but guessed that we were close to the river once I noticed drops of moisture seeping along the support beams through the earthen walls.

He stopped and looked around, as if getting his bearings. Then, he sat down on the earthen floor.

"What now?"

"Now we wait," he said.

We didn't wait for long. I did suspect before that the deaders could communicate with each other through some unfathomable means. Soon, four deaders showed up, then three more. All of the newcomers sat down on the floor and remained quiet, as more of them kept arriving.

There were all kinds of them there—young and old, and even one child. Some were dead long enough to lose most of their skin and flesh—at least two hundred years; others were quite fresh. Even the girl I met earlier showed up; I noticed with a pang of guilt that the purple bruise on her forehead was spreading. Despite my repeated application of the wintergreen ointment, the air grew putrid with their smell, and my heart was uneasy. There I was, underground, surrounded by a throng of deaders. If they turned on me, I would never be able to fight through them—or find my way back to the surface. The trust I attributed to Jas was actually mine.

Underground, I had lost the sense of time, and only knew that it was passing—slowly, like water weeping from the walls. The sounds of soft, dry voices of the deaders mingled with the dripping of water; while the monotony of it was somewhat lulling, the content was certainly not.

I learned that the cherrystone in question was cursed. A traveling warlock passed through our town, many years ago. When the Areti came to the warlock, demanding that he lend his talent to them, they were met with a refusal. They sent their thugs to make him pay for their humiliation, but the thugs were never heard from again. The warlock was nonetheless angry with the Areti. Before he left, he hid the cherrystone somewhere in town, and told them that as long as the cursed stone was within the town walls, our dead would walk the land.

When his prediction came true, the Areti looked for it. They looked everywhere—on the bottom of the river, under every rock, even in the catacombs under the deaders' town. After a few years they stopped looking—old legends are easy to forget. The cherrystone was left be, until the present Mistress of the Areti clan realized her mortality. The search for the cherrystone had become an obsession, and she sent her goons and hirelings to look for it. It took her awhile, but she had learned that it was in deaders' town.

"Why does she want it?" I said.

"To end the curse," said one of the oldest deaders.

I nodded. I could understand that desire, and yet I wasn't sure why the Areti were so concerned about it.

"It's their family's curse, or so they see it. It's the matter of honor for them," said the child. "They don't care what will happen to us. They only know that they don't want to become us."

There was no good way to ask this question, but I asked anyway. "Do you . . . do you like being like this?"

They whistled and chortled, their laughter akin to scratching of nails.

"You'll see when you're in my shoes," Jas said. "It's more life, even though you might not see it as such. See, I don't relish being what I am, but I still prefer it to lying still in the ground, being eaten by worms."

"Do you know where that cherrystone is?"

The crowd grew silent, and I felt their eyes on me, judging, weighing. "'Course we do," Jas said. "That's the first thing you learn as a deader—it's important, see. And we tell it to each other every day, so that we don't forget—about the Areti, about their snooping goons . . ."

The appearance of two more deaders interrupted him. One was tall and dark, one-handed. The other, a teenager, seemed young enough to be his son, but his light hair belied this conclusion. His nostrils were torn open, and a slow trickle of pus trekked across his pale lips and down his chin.

"You came to kill us," the youngster said.

Once again, I grew aware of the precariousness of my situation, and protested my innocence with as much sincerity as I could muster.

"The Areti sent you," his companion said. "Just like they sent us."

I shrugged. "So? I find things; I never killed anyone."

Jas' heavy hand lay on my shoulder. I could feel through my jacket how cold and clammy it was. "He wouldn't do something like that," he said to the gathering. "He knows better."

I nodded. "I do. Only others don't. You think people across the river would listen to me? Or to you, for that matter. Far as everyone's concerned, if the stone is gone, so much the better. The Areti won't leave you alone. Not with the present Mistress."

Everyone nodded in agreement.

"She won't stop," the bruised girl said. "Not until she's one of us." She gave me a meaningful look. "Will you help us?"

"Whoa," I said. "You're not asking me to kill her, are you?"

They murmured that it wouldn't be a bad idea, and after all, it wouldn't be all bad for her. The deaders' town was a nice place.

"I'm not a murderer," I said. "But I think I can help you. The stone needs to stay in town, right? Doesn't matter where?"

"No," Jas said. "But she won't stop looking."

"I think I know a good place for it," I said. "Just give me the stone, and don't worry about a thing. She'll never find it."

Their silence was unnatural—not even a sound of breathing broke it. Dozens of dead eyes looked at me, expressionless, weighing my proposal in their oozing, ruined skulls. I asked a lot of them—to put their very existence into the hands of an aliver, a being as alien to them as they were to me.

If I were in his shoes, I doubt I would've done what Jas had done: he pointed at the girl with the purple bruise. "Give it to him," he said.

The girl stepped back, away from me, and I reached out, afraid that she would stumble and fall again. She remained on her feet—I supposed she was getting a hang of her new limitations. "Why do you think he'll help us?" she asked Jas, but her hand was already reaching for her chest.

"He's my brother," Jas said.

Her fingers pushed away a flimsy shawl that cradled her slender shoulders, and I gasped at the sight of a deep wound, left by a dagger. That was what killed her—an angry father, a jealous husband, a sullen stranger. She reached deep into the wound, pulling out a small round object, covered with congealed gore. I tried not to flinch as the bloodied cherrystone lay in my palm.

"Be careful with it," the one-handed man told me. "It's a powerful thing."

"What can it do?" I said, rolling it on my palm gingerly. It left a trail, but didn't seem very powerful.

"Whatever it has to do," Jas said.

The sight of the moonlit Areti manor greeted me from afar. It was deep night, and not a window shone in the darkness. The bulk of the building sat immobile but sinister, as a stone gargoyle ready to come to life and rip out the heart of the next victim. I heaved a sigh and slowed my steps; no doubt, the manor would be guarded, and I was disinclined to reveal my presence just yet. Fortunately, in my line of business I had learned a thing or two about surreptitious visits.

I avoided the front door, where the two goons of my recent acquaintance sat on the steps, trading monosyllabic talk. My soft-soled shoes made no sound on the grass as I edged around the corner and along the wall, looking for a different point of entry. There was a backdoor, as I had expected, latched shut from the inside. Worse, the door was cased in iron, and a slightest manipulation would surely reverberate through the building.

In the pale moonlight, I let my fingers run along the edges of the door, looking for a gap. The door was quite well fitted, and I procured a short knife with thin blade from my pocket, and forced it between the door and the wall that surrounded it, trying to feel the latch inside. The scraping of metal against metal tore the still air. I jerked my hand away, and fell into a crouch by the wall. I waited for a long while, but nobody appeared.

I explored the perimeter of the manor again, in hopes of finding a ground level window or another door. None were forthcoming, and I returned to the back entrance guarded by iron. I wondered if the cherrystone could be of use, and took it out of my pocket. It glowed softly, and I touched it to the door. Nothing happened.

"Come on," I whispered to it. "Do you want to be found and destroyed?"

The stone did not answer.

I felt foolish, carrying on a conversation with an inanimate object, but persisted. I sat down, my back against the cold wall, cradling the stone's tiny light in my open palms. "See," I told it, "it's like this. I could just give you up, take my money, and go home. But it's bigger than me or her or even you . . . "

My voice caught in my throat as my own words reached me. There was no doubt that the Areti would kill me—break my fingers, cut off my hand, perhaps rip my nostrils open, just like they did to the dead boy. But I also realized that it would be better to die now and have a place to go than eke out another few years and succumb to the black nothingness to which people from other places went. We lived with the deaders for so long that we saw them as a nuisance; we didn't realize how lucky we were to have them—to become them. And this stone made it all possible. I closed my hand around it, protecting it, protecting all of us.

The stone grew warmer in my hand, and soon it burned it. It shone brighter too, and narrow white beams of light squeezed between my fingers—my fist looked like a star. When I touched it to the door, the metal sang, barely audible, and the door swung open. I entered the dark dusty hallway, my way illuminated by the cherrystone.

I followed it to the dark recesses of the sleeping manor, to the kitchen. There, a massive brick stove towered against the far wall. The light beams cut through the stone as if it was butter, forming a long, narrow tunnel behind the stove, just spacious enough to let my hand through.

I released the cherrystone, and let it roll into its new hiding place. As it cooled and darkened, what was left of its power sealed the passage, returning it to the normal appearance of the brickwork of the stove and stone of the walls.

As quietly as I entered, I left. I crossed the river as the sun was rising above the rooftops. I listened to the crowing of roosters and to the first banging of shutters, inhaled the sweet aroma of baking bread, basked in the first sunrays alighting on my shoulders. I was heading back to my favorite restaurant, where I intended to drink until the Areti thugs found me.

I thought about what would be my last trip to the deaders' town—how I would shamble along, until I arrived to Jas' house. I would have to tell him right away that I was his brother, before I forget and lose the tentative connection between us, and ask him to remind me. Then I would settle next to the ice chest, and we would talk, in loopy, halting sentences. And we would remind each other every day, so that we don't forget, keeping the memory of our shared blood alive.

SEAS OF THE WORLD

Jillian sits on the windowsill, and looks outside, where the first snowflakes flutter in the pale glow of streetlights. It is cold; her breath leaves white patina of fog on the black plastic of the phone receiver. She imagines the phone ringing in Rick's dark apartment. The answering machine does not come on—he never had one—and she counts the rings. Seven. Eight. Anything to keep her mind from wandering. She can spend all night listening to the receiver. Fourteen. She imagines Rick's bare feet padding across the cold ceramic tiles of the kitchen floor, his hand tugging up the pajama bottoms riding low on his waist. Last she saw him, he looked like he'd lost weight.

"Hello?" His voice breaks through the twenty-first ring, hoarse. "Jill?"

"Yeah. Did I wake you?" It is a stupid question—it is 4 am, of course he was sleeping soundly in this dead hour. She feels a small pang of guilt at denying him oblivion.

"Yes." He never lies, not even in the small reflexive way when he's woken up. "Are you all right?"

"I guess," she says. And then she is crying, weeping into the receiver, a part of her mind worrying if it is possible to cause a short by crying into an electrical appliance.

"I'll come over."

"No need to . . . I'm all right."

"I'd like to come over. If you don't mind."

"I don't."

The phone is silent again, and she sits on the windowsill, trying to keep her mind away from the horribly missing piece of her existence. She thinks of the ways Rick annoys her.

She thinks of their meeting in court. The divorce proceedings were over with, and there was just the question of custody. Jillian bit her lip all the way to the courthouse, and spilled her coffee down the front of her white shirt as soon as she got there. She despised herself for this, especially once she saw Rick in his immaculate suit. Not an expensive one, but the man made any clothes look good. He owned them, while she couldn't reach a truce with hers. Her clothes betrayed her by getting dirty or twisted, just like her hair tended to get in her face, and the makeup smeared itself at inopportune moments. How she hated Rick then, how she feared him! Any judge in his right mind would take one look at them and decide that she was a pitiful mess, while Rick was together, a fit parent. Able of providing good care to a child. Reliable.

She mopped up the coffee stain the best she could, and stood before the judge brimming with desperation. She stammered out her reasons why Derryl should stay with her—she loved him so much!—and fell quiet, turning an uneasy gaze to Rick. He didn't look back, the pale clarity of his eyes for the judge only. He didn't argue that Jillian should have custody, he just wanted visitations and vacation time. She hated him for being more generous than she.

The dead receiver in her hand comes to life. "If you require assistance from the operator . . . " She puts it back on the cradle, startled, upset that the delicate silence of the night and the snow was spoiled by this mechanical voice. She cringes and thinks of Rick, willfully, like it is some sort of an exercise. Thinking of Rick keeps her together until the doorbell rings.

She hugs him as he comes in, and cringes at how prominent his ribs are, how gaunt his face looks. He didn't get a chance to shave, but even the scruff looks proper on him. Like he meant it.

"I missed you," he says. Looks at her face, searching for clues. Always searching for an indication of how she feels.

"I missed you too," she says, and forces a smile. "Don't worry, I'm not going to ask for sex."

He breathes relief and adds, "I didn't say you are."

"But you thought it."

He doesn't deny.

"Want anything? Coffee, tea?"

"Coffee," he says. "Please." He sits at the kitchen table, his large pale hands lying passively palms-down on either side of his empty cup. She hugs her shoulders and waits for the coffee to percolate.

"I'm sorry I woke you," she says.

"It's all right." He looks at his hands. "I'm the one who is sorry. It was my fault that—"

"No," she interrupts. "I don't want to talk about that." It's enough to know that he's feeling what she's feeling.

He takes the cue. "How's work?"

"I haven't been in a while." She looks at the snowflakes dancing outside the window. It will get light soon. "Don't go tomorrow . . . I mean, today. Stay here. Call in sick."

"Okay," he says, always obedient.

When they first met, his obedience shocked her. She found him on the beach ten summers back. It was late, and the beach was deserted; she enjoyed her solitary walks, almost dissolving in the darkness and the relentless pounding of the surf. She screamed when she stepped on something that seemed alive; it turned out to be the hand of a man lying in the sand.

"I'm sorry," he said. "I didn't mean to startle you."

She squinted as he sat up. In the pale moonlight, he seemed lost.

"It's okay," she said. It was difficult to tell what he looked like in that light. "I must be going."

He followed her; she should've been scared, but she wasn't. He followed her not like a prowler but like a lost puppy. He spoke quietly, and she strained, trying to hear his words above the surf. "Caspian," he said.

"Is it your name?" she asked. "Caspian?"

"Yes," he said, his eyes wide and dark.

They reached the boardwalk and strolled along the fronts of rickety wooden shops.

"What's your first name?" she said, just to say something.

His gaze cast about wildly. "Rick," he finally said. She followed the direction of his gaze to the sign of the Rick's Bait and Surfing Supplies. She pretended not to notice.

He sips his coffee, his face turning pink in the hot steam. He whispers under his breath, and she strains to hear. He takes a deep breath. "Aral," he whispers. "Azov, Black, Red, Arabian, Laccidive, Andaman, Yellow, Dead."

"Dead," she repeats, and starts crying again.

"It's my fault," he says. "I shouldn't have told him."

She cries too hard to answer, to react, and he resumes his litany. A nervous habit he has, naming all the seas in the world.

"Philippine, Sulu, Koro, Java, Halmahera, Mindanao, Savu, Sunda, Arafura, Celebs, Molucca, Bismark, Coral, Solomon, Tasman, Bohol, Visayan, Camotes, Bali, Sibuyan, Flores, Timor, Banda, Ceram."

It calms her a bit, like it calms him. "It's not your fault," she says. "It's nobody's fault."

"I shouldn't have told him."

"Told him what?"

He swallows hard. "About me. About him. The way we are."

She stares at him. She thinks he might be finally cracking, feeling the loss more than he shows. She feels selfish for forcing him to always be reliable, to make her feel better. "You want to tell me?" she says.

"Caribbean, North, Irish, Hebrides, Celtic, Baltic, Bothian, Scotia, Labrador, Sargasso, Balearic, Ligurian, Tyrrhenian, Ionian, Adriatic, Aegean, Marmara, Thracian—" His eyes are distant, glazed over. Dark. "These are my seas. His seas."

It is always like this. Ice and water, jagged black cracks like stationary lightnings running across the floes. The taste of fish, tightly clenched nostrils, lungs expanded like bellows. The shadows of other seals, floating in a graceful arc, their flippers trailing behind them like twin tales of a comet.

Rick does not know if it's a dream or a memory; neither does he care. He tells Derryl of the slow falls and rapid ascends, of the green depth of water. Of the migration routes, of the ecstasy he felt as the water turned from icy to balmy, with every mile south. Of the coral reefs where water ran clear as tears, of the fishes as bright as they were poisonous, of the quick darting of dolphins overhead, of their staccato laughter superimposed over the short, sharp barks of the seals.

Derryl listens, wide-eyed, as the two of them walk on the beach. "How did you become a person?" he asks when Rick stops talking.

Rick shrugs. "I just stopped being a seal." He talks about the Sargasso Sea and its streaming grasses, undulating underwater like mermaid's hair, and of the fat eels that come to this sea from all over the world. He talks about following the stream of eels from the Black Sea all the way to Sargasso, of the Aegean and Marmara, Ionian and Adriatic, of Greeks and Scythians, the deeds of men forever branded into the ancestral memory of the seals.

Derryl looks at him with warm brown eyes. "I want to be a seal too," he says.

Rick is listening to the surf. "Then you'd have to stop being a person," he says, distractedly.

It is light outside when Jillian looks out of the window again. The world is dressed in a shroud, a shroud her son never had. A shroud for a boy who did not want to be a person.

"It was an accident," she says.

He shakes his head, vehement now that he found the courage to tell her.

She sighs. "It doesn't matter, Rick. It doesn't matter why or how." She makes more coffee and they drink it, silently, as the snow is falling outside.

Jillian thinks of the Arctic seas and the ice—so thick—that opens suddenly wide to reveal black water underneath. She thinks of the smooth seals turning cartwheels in the black depths, oblivious to cold and wind whipping the land half to death.

"Laptev," Rick whispers, "White, Barents, Beaufort, Chuckchi, Lincoln, Kara."

Jillian thinks of the black seals perched atop white floes, of their sharp barks that tear the frozen air like tissue paper. She wonders, beyond hope, if Derryl got his wish.

Rick calls work, telling them that he won't be in. Then he settles by the table again, his hands palms down on the stained surface.

"Tell me about seals," Jillian says.

END OF WHITE

Coronet Kovalevsky had never expected to find that land was finite. It seemed so abundant to him when he was younger, something you could never possibly run out of—or run off of—that the very suggestion seemed ludicrous. Yet there he was in the summer of 1919, teetering on the precipice of the Crimean peninsula, with very little idea of what to do after Wrangel's inevitable defeat and his own presumed tumble into the Black Sea. He had decided that he would not join the Bolsheviks—not so much out of any deeply held belief but rather because of his inherent disposition to avoid any large amounts of soul-overhauling work. He appeared committed and idealistic from the outside, even though inside he knew it was mere laziness and ennui.

So he lingered with the rest of his regiment in the small Crimean town (more of a village, if one was to be honest) named N., close to the shore, away from the invading Red armies and the dry, fragrant steppes that smelled like thyme and sun. At first, the officers kept to themselves, spending their days playing cards in the town's single tavern, and waiting for the news from the front. The evacuations of Murmansk and Arkhangelsk had already started, and the British hospital near N. promised the same opportunities for salvation, if the things didn't go the way Wrangel wanted them to. They waited for the fighting, for some way to end this interminable standoff. Kovalevsky hoped that his demise would be quick and, if not glorious, then at least non-embarrassing.

But the days were warm, the house he stayed in had white curtains on its tiny windows, cut like embrasures in thick clay walls—walls that retained pleasant coolness long into the afternoon heat. A split-rail fence half-heartedly guarded long rows of young sunflowers and poppies, with more mundane potatoes and beets hidden behind them, and a couple of chickens scratched in the dust of the yard. It was not unpleasant, if overly rustic.

The owner of the clay-walled, thickly-whitewashed house was one Marya Nikolavna, a small and disappearing kind of woman who seemed neither overjoyed nor appalled to have an officer quartering in her house; but nonetheless she frequently brought him homemade kvas and ripe watermelons, their dark green skins warm from the sun and their centers cold as well water, red and crumbling with sugar. She did not complain when Olesya started to come by.

Oh, Kovalevsky could tell that there was gypsy blood in Olesya—there was wildness about her, in the way the whites of her eyes flashed in the dusk of his room, the way her pitch-black braid snaked down her back, its tip swinging hypnotic as she walked. It took him a while, however, to recognize that it wasn't just the wild gypsy fire that smoldered hot and low in her blood, it was something else entirely that made her what she was.

It was a cloudy, suffocating kind of day in July, when everything—man, beast, and plant—hunkered close to the ground and waited for the relief of a thunderstorm. Unease charged the air with its sour taste, and Kovalevsky, feeling especially indisposed to getting out of bed that day, watched Olesya pad on her cat-soft feet across the wide floorboards, her half-slip like a giant gardenia flower, her breasts, dark against the paler skin stretched over her breastbone, lolling heavily. She opened the curtains to peer outside, the curtain of her messy black hair falling over half her back. Her profile turned, silver against the cloudy darkened glass. "It's going to rain," she said, just as the first leaden drops thrummed against the glass and the roof, formed dark little craters in the dust, pummeled the cabbage leaves like bullets.

And just as if the spell of heavy, lazy air was lifted, Olesya straightened and bounded out the door, shrieking in jubilation.

Kovalevsky, roused from his languid repose by the sound as well as the breaking heat, sat up on the bed, just in time to see Olesya running across the yard. He cringed, imagining her running through the village like that, half naked—not something he would put beyond her—as she disappeared from view. She soon reappeared, fists full of greenery, and came running inside, her wet feet slapping the floor and the black strands of her hair plastered to her skin, snaking around her shoulders like tattoos.

"What's this?" Kovalevsky asked, nodding at the tangled stems in her fist beaded with raindrops.

"This is for you," she said as she tossed a few poppies, their capsules still green and rubbery, at his bed. "And this"—she held up dark, broad leaves and hairy stems of some weed he didn't know—"this is for me."

She found his pen knife on the bed table and drew crisscrossing lines on the green poppy capsules, until they beaded with white latex. Kovalevsky watched, fascinated—the drops of rain, the drops of white poppy blood . . . it made sense then when Olesya drew the blade along the pad of her left thumb, mirroring the beaded trail in red. And in this cut, she mashed a dark green leaf, closing her eyes. She then wadded up the rest of the leaves and stuck them behind her cheek, like a squirrel. She tossed the pearled poppy capsules at Kovalevsky. "Here."

He wasn't naïve, of course—he just didn't feel any particular need for additional intoxicants. But under Olesya's suddenly wide gaze, her pupils like twin wells, he drew the first capsule into his mouth and swallowed, undeterred by its grassy yet bitter taste.

His sleep was heavy, undoubtedly aided by the monotone of the rain outside and by the drug in his blood. He dreamed of waves and of Olesya, of her bottomless eyes. He dreamed of her wrapping his head in her white underskirts so that he became blind, mute, and deaf, and his mouth filled with suffocating muslin. He woke up, coughing, just as the moon looked into his room through the opened curtains and opened window. Olesya was gone—of course she was, why wouldn't she be? Yet, he was uneasy, as he stared at the black sky and the silver moon. He imagined it reflecting in the sea, just out of sight, in parallel white slats of a moon road. It was so bright, the large fuzzy stars in its proximity faded into afterimages of themselves.

The opium still clouded his senses and his mind, and he lolled on the border between sleep and wakefulness, his mouth dry and his eyelids heavy, when fluttering of curtains attracted his attention. He peered into the darkness and managed to convince himself that it was just the wind, a trick of light, but just as he started to drift off, a spot in the darkness resolved into an outline of a very large and very black cat, who sat on the floor by the foot of his bed, its green eyes staring.

Now, the cats as such were not an unusual occurrence—like any place that grew crops, the village was besotted by mice, and cats were both common and communal, traveling from one barn to the next yard, from a hay loft of one neighbor to the kitchen of another. They were welcomed everywhere, and their diet of mice was often supplemented by milk and meat scraps (but never eggs: no one wanted the cats to learn to like eggs and start stealing them from under hens). Yet, this cat seemed particularly audacious, as it sat and stared at Kovalevsky. He stared back until his eyelids fluttered and gave out, and he felt himself sinking into his drugged sleep again; through the oppressive fog, he felt the cat jump up on the bed and he was surprised by its heft—the bed gave and moaned as the beast, soft-pawed, kneaded and fussed and finally curled next to his thigh.

The next morning came with no traces of the strange cat's presence—or Olesya's, for that matter. Kovalevsky felt rested, and decided to visit the only drinking establishment the village possessed—indicated only by a faded and yet unusually detailed sign depicting a black goat with what seemed to be too many limbs, a fancy often found in rustic artists. The tavern was located in the same building as N.'s only hotel; it was a wide, low room housing a series of rough tables and serving simple but filling fare—borscht and dumplings swimming in butter and sour cream, then black bread and pickled beets and herring. This is where most of the officers spent their days—at least, those who had not been lucky enough to take up with one of the local sirens.

To his surprise, the tavern was quiet; the owner, a well-fed and heavily mustachioed Ukrainian named Patsjuk, lounged at the table nearest to the kitchen.

Kovalevsky asked for tea and bread and butter, and settled at the wide table by the window. The grain of the rough wooden slats was warm under his fingertips, a tiny topographic map, and he closed his eyes, feeling the ridge, willing them to resemble the terrain they had covered. There was just so much of it—on foot and horseback, on the train, sleeping in the thin straw, next to the peasants and lost children crawling with typhoid lice. The railroads and the regular roads (highways, dirt paths, streets) went up and down and up again, wound along and across rivers, through the mountains, through forests—and his fingers twitched as he tried to remember every turn and every elevation, until Patsjuk brought him his tea and warm bread, peasant butter (melted and solidified again into yellow grainy slabs) piled on the saucer like stationary waves.

"Where's everyone?" Kovalevsky asked. His tea smelled of the same heavy greenery that tainted Olesya's breath last night, and he wondered about where she went—to what Sabbath.

Patsjuk shrugged and leered. "Wouldn't know. Your Colonel was by the other day, but he's just about the only one who even comes anymore. I suspect the rest discovered the moonshiners, or some other nonsense abomination." He spat.

Kovalevsky nodded—Colonel Menshov was just the type to keep to the straight and narrow, away from any shady liquor, very much the same way as the rest of the regiment were likely to do the exact opposite. Kovalevsky could only assume that he hadn't heard anything of the matter due to his recent discovery of novelty intoxicants, of which Olesya was not the least.

One needed intoxicants at the times like these—at the times when one's army was all but squeezed between the pounding waves and the impossible, unturnable tide of of the Reds, and the matters of being compressed like that (and where would one go under such circumstances) seemed impossible to ponder, and

Kovalevsky tried his best to let his gaze slide along the ridges and the valleys of the yellow butter, to distract his uneasy mind from things that would make it more uneasy. To his good luck, an outside distraction soon presented itself.

Colonel Menshov walked into the dining room, in a less leisurely step than the circumstances warranted—in fact, he downright trotted in, in an anxious small gait of a man too disturbed to care about outward appearances. "Kovalevsky!" he cried, his face turning red with anguish. "There's no one left!"

"So I heard," Kovalevsky said. He slid down the long, grainy wooden bench to offer Menshov a seat. "Patsjuk here says they fell in with the moonshiners."

"Or Petliura got them," Patsjuk offered from his place behind the counter unhelpfully.

"What Petliura?" Menshov, who just sat down, bolted again, wild-eyed, his head swiveling about as if he expected to see the offender here, in the tavern.

"He's joking, I think," said Kovalevsky. "Symon Petliura is nowhere near these parts."

"In any case, it's just you and me." Menshov waved at Patsjuk. "If you have any of that moonshine you've mentioned, bring me a shot of your strongest."

Kovalevsky decided not to comment, and waited until Menshov tossed back his drink, shuddered, swore, and heaved a sigh so tremulous that the ends of his gray mustache blew about. "What happened?" he said then.

"Darkness," Menshov said. "Not to mention, everyone except you is missing."

"They'll come back."

"I'm not so sure." Menshov gestured for Patsjuk to hurry with another drink. "Demons and dark forces are in this place, you hear? It's crawling with the unclean ones."

Kovalevsky looked at Patsjuk, who busied himself pouring a murky drink from a large glass bottle, and appeared to be doing everything in his power to avoid eye contact. Kovalevsky guessed that he probably played not a small part in straying Menshov off the straight and narrow.

"What led you to that conclusion?" Kovalesky asked.

"Cats," Menshov said, and waved his arms excitedly. "Haven't you seen them? Giant black cats that walk on hind legs? These are no cats but witches."

Kovalevsky felt a chill creeping up his spine, squeezing past the collar of his shirt and exploding in a constellation of shivers and raised hairs across the back of his head. He remembered the nightmare weight of the cat, and Olesya's smolder stare, her hands as she cut the poppies, how they bled their white juice . . . He shook his head. "There was a cat in your house?"

"Last night." Menshov slumped in his seat. "The awful creature attacked me as I slept—I woke and was quick enough to grab my inscribed saber. I always have it by my bed."

"Naturally," Kovalevsky said.

"The cat—and it was large, as large as a youth of ten or so—swiped at my face, and I swung my saber at its paw. It howled and ran out through the window, and its paw . . . it stayed on the floor. God help me, it's still there, I didn't have the bravery to toss it or to even touch it. Come with me, I'll show you, and you'll see that this is a thing not of this world—that it has no right to be at all."

Kovalevsky followed, reluctant and fearful of the possibility that Menshov was neither drunk nor addled. The fact that he even entertained the thought showed to him how unhinged he had become—then again, months of retreat and the trains crawling with lice would do it to a man. He wondered as he walked down the dusty street, large sunflowers nodding behind each split rail fence, if the shock of the revolution and the war had made them (everything) vulnerable—cracked them like pottery, so even if they appeared whole at the casual glance, in reality they were cobwebbed with hairline fissures, waiting only for a slightest shove, a lightest tap, to become undone and to tumble down in an avalanche of useless shards.

Menshov stopped in front of a fence like every other, the wood knotted and bleached by the sun, desiccated and rough, and pushed the gate open. It swung inward with a long plaintive squeal, and Kovalevsky cringed. Only then did he become aware of how silent the village had become—even in the noon heat, one was used to hearing squawking of chickens and an occasional bark of a languid dog.

"You hear it too?" Menshov said. "I mean, don't hear it."

"Where's everyone? Everything?"

There was no answer, and one wasn't needed—or even possible. The house stood small and still, its whitewashed walls clear and bright against the cornflower-blue of the sky, the straw thatched roof golden in the sunlight. Kovalevsky knew it was cool and dry inside, dark and quiet like a secret forest pool, and yet it took Menshov's pleading stare to persuade him to step over the threshold into the quiet deep darkness, the dirt floor soft under his boots.

He followed Menshov to the small bedroom, vertiginously like Kovalevsky's own—square window, clean narrow bed covered with a multicolored quilt,—his heart hammering at his throat. He felt his blood flow away from his face, leaving it cold and numb, even before he saw the grotesque paw, a few drops and smudges of blood around it like torn carnations. But the paw itself pulled his attention—it was black and already shriveling, its toes an inky splash around the rosette of curving, sharp talons, translucent like mother-of-pearl. If it was a cat's paw, it used to belong to one very large and misshapen cat.

"My God," Kovalevsky managed, even as he thought that with matters like these, faith, despite being the only protection, was no protection at all. His mind raced, as he imagined over and over— despite willing himself to stop with such foolish speculation—he imagined Olesya leaving his house that morning, the stump of her human arm dripping with red through cheesecloth wrapped around it, cradled against her lolling breast.

"Unclean forces are at work," Menshov said. "And we are lost, lost."

Kovalevsky couldn't bring himself to disagree. He fought the Red and the Black armies, and he wasn't particularly afraid of them—but with a single glance at the terrible paw, curling on the floor in all its unnatural plainness, resignation took hold, and he was ready to embrace whatever was coming, as long as it was quick and granted him oblivion.

He tried to look away, but the thing pulled at his glance as if it was a string caught in its monstrous talons, and the more he looked, the more he imagined the battle that took place here: in his mind's eye, he saw the old man, the hilt of the saber clutched in both hands as if he became momentarily a child instead of a seasoned warrior, his naked chest hairless and hollow, backing into the corner. And he saw the beast—the paw expanded in his mind, giving flesh and image to the creature to which it was attached. It was a catlike thing, but with a long muzzle, and tufted ears and chin. It stood on its stiff hind legs, unnaturally straight, without the awkward slumping and crouching usually exhibited by the four-legged beasts, its long paws hanging limply by its sides for just a second, before snatching up and swiping at Menshov.

Kovalevsky always had vivid imagination, but this seemed more than mere fancy—it was as if the detached paw had the power to reach inside his eyeballs somehow and turn them to hidden places, making him see—see as Menshov staggered back, the saber now swinging blindly. He propped his left hand against the bedpost, gaining a semblance of control, just as the monster reached its deformed paw and swept across Menshov's bare shoulder, drawing a string of blood beads across it.

The old man hissed in pain and parried, just as the creature stepped away, hissing back in its low throbbing manner. With every passing second, Kovalevsky's mind imagined the creature with greater and greater clarity, just as the still-sane part of him realized that the longer he stared at the accursed paw, the closer he moved to summoning the creature itself.

He clapped his hand over his eyes, twisting away blindly. Whatever strange power had hold of him deserved the name Menshov gave it—it was unclean and ancient, too old for remembering and cursed long before the days of Cain.

Menshov's mind was apparently on a similar track. "If we die here," he said, quietly, "there's no way for us but the hellfire."

"Would there be another way for us otherwise?"

Menshov stared, perturbed. "We've kept our oath to the Emperor. We fought for the crown, and we fought with honor."

"That's what I mean." Kovalevsky forced his gaze away from the paw and turned around, as little as he liked having it behind his back. "Come now, let's see who else can we find. And as soon as we do, we best leave—if they let us, if we can."

They searched for hours—but no matter how many doors they knocked on, only empty shaded coolness greeted them, as if every house in the village had been gutted, hollowed of all human presence, and left as an empty decoration to await a new set of actors. And the more they saw of it, the more convinced Kovalevsky grew that the buildings must've been like that— empty, flat—before they'd moved in. Where were the villagers? And, most importantly, where was Olesya? Was she just a vision, a sweet nightmare created from his loneliness and fear, aided by the soothing latex of the poppies in the yard and Patsjuk's dark green tea?

"Was it always like this?" Menshov said when the two of them finally stopped, silent and sweating. "Do you remember what this place was like when we first got here?"

Kovalevsky shook his head, then nodded. "I think it was . . . normal. A normal village."

He remembered the bustling in the streets, the peasants and the noisy geese, bleating of goats, the clouds of dust under the hooves of the White Army's horses when they rode in. Did they ride in or did they walk? If they rode, where were the horses— gone, swept away with everything else?

And then he remembered—a memory opened in his mind like a fissure—he remembered the view of the village and how quiet it was, and how he said to a man walking next to him (they must've been on foot, not horseback) that it was strange that there was no smoke coming from the chimneys. And then they walked into the village, and there was bustle and voices and chimneys spewed fat white smoke, and he'd forgotten all about it. "Maybe not so normal," he said. "I remember not seeing any smoke when we first approached."

Menshov nodded, his gray mustache shaking. "I remember that too! See, it was like an illusion, a night terror."

"The whole town?" Kovalevsky stopped in his tracks, his mind struggling to embrace the enormity of the deception—this whole time, this whole village . . . It couldn't be. "What about Patsjuk and his tavern? We were just there. Is it still . . . ?"

"Let's find out."

As they walked back, the dusty street under their feet growing more insubstantial with every passing moment, Kovalevsky thought that perhaps this all was the result of this running out of land—running out of the world. After all, if there was no place left for the White Army, wouldn't it be possible that some of them simply ran and tripped into some nightmare limbo? It seemed likely, even.

The tavern stood flat and still, and it seemed more like a painting than an actual building—it thinned about the edges, and wavered, like hot air over a heated steppe. Illusion, unclean forces.

Patsjuk sat on the steps, and seemed real enough—made fatter, more substantial by the fact that Olesya perched next to him, her round shoulder, warm and solid under her linen shirt, resting comfortably against the tavern's owner's. Both her hands were intact, and Kovalevsky breathed a sigh of relief, even if he wasn't sure why.

She grinned when she saw Kovalevsky. "There you are," she said. "See, you took my medicine, took my poison, and now you're lost. The loving goat-mother will absorb you, make you whole again."

Menshov grasped Kovalevsky's shoulder, leaned into him with all his weight. "Why?" he said.

A pointless question, of course, Kovalevsky thought. There were never any whys or explanations—there was only the shortage of land. By then, the ground around them heaved, and the dead rose, upright, the nails of their hands still rooting them to the opened graves, their eyes closed and lips tortured. The streets and the houses twisted, and the whole world became a vortex of jerking movement, everything in it writhing and groaning—and only the tavern remained still in the center of it.

Kovalevsky's hand, led by a memory of the time when he cared enough to keep himself alive, moved of its own volition, like a severed lizard's tail, and slid down his leg and into his boot, grasping for the horn handle of the knife he always had on him. He hadn't remembered it, but his body had, and jerked the knife out, assuming a defensive, ridiculous posture. He swiped at the air in front of him, not even trying for Patsjuk's belly, then turned around and ran.

His boots sunk into the road as if it were molasses, but he struggled on, as the air buzzed around him and soon resolved into bleating of what seemed like a thousand goats. Transparent dead hands grasped at him, and the black thing, more goat than a cat now, tried to claw its away out of his skull. Kovalevsky screamed and struggled against the wave of ancient voices, but inhuman force turned him back, back, to face the horrors he tried to run from.

So this is how it is, Kovalevsky thought, just as Olesya's face stretched into a muzzle, and her lower jaw hinged open, unnaturally wide. Without standing up, she extended her neck at Menshov. The old man grasped at his belt, uselessly, looking for his saber, even as Olesya's mouth wrapped around his head.

On the edge of his hearing, Kovalevsky heard whinnying of the horses off in the distance, and the uncertain, false tinny voice of a bugle. The Red Armies were entering the town of N.; he wondered briefly if the same fate awaited them—but probably not, since they were not the ones rejected by the world itself.

Kovalevsky closed his eyes then, not to see, and resigned himself to the fact that his run was over, and at the very least there would be relief from the sickening crunch that resonated deep in his spine, from the corpses and their long fingernails that dragged on the ground with barely audible whisper, and from the tinny bugle that was closing on him from every direction.

A HANDSOME FELLOW

1.

When people starve, their eyes become large and luminous, enough so as to invite comparisons with visages of saints on the icons. Which makes sense, since the saints were traditionally ascetic—anorexic even. I forever remember those golden-light eyes, softly unfocused, radiant, otherworldly, so sharply contrasting with frost-bitten fingers and red, peeling skin on wind-burned cheeks.

This is how it went: Svetlana, aged twenty-four and still unmarried despite her beauty, now heightened by hunger, woke up before dawn (which wasn't all that early in Leningrad, in December), and went to check on her mother. The children, Yasha and Vanya, slept in a separate room—a surprising luxury after most of the neighbors of their communal apartment had died. So did Svetlana's father—a large, strong man. People like that were built for peace, for hard work and big rations; it's the small and frail that could last on one hundred grams of adulterated bread a day. His death meant even less food for everyone else—Svetlana was the only one now who worked at the factory and received rations. The only other survivor in their apartment was a young kindergarten teacher Lyuda, all alone in her room adjacent to the communal kitchen fallen into disuse.

Mother was still alive, and she weakly gestured to Svetlana—her hand a scrap of parchment in the dark—to go pick through her jewelry box. They were clever with things they had—most of the rings and nylons were already traded on the black market, for sugar lumps for the children and for extra bread. Sunflower oil and broth from unknown sources were a rare luxury. They avoided meat because of the stories of cannibals who dug up the newly buried bodies and attacked the weak and those who walked alone in the dark—and this is why Svetlana always carried her father's pistol, with a single shot in it.

Svetlana picked through the box. There were pieces left in it, but who knew how long the blockade would last? They should pace themselves, she thought, and picked up a single brooch—a pink cameo with carved white border, like seafoam made stone. "It's grandma Anna's," mother said. Svetlana could detect no expression in her voice—no argument, no affirmation.

"Don't wake the children," Svetlana said. "Let them sleep while I'm gone. When they sleep, they're not hungry, not cold." That day, she didn't have to work her factory shift, and the best pickings at the market were in the morning.

"They sleep longer every day." Mother sighed. "My boys."

Big strong boys, one nine, one twelve, with bodies that would soon be too large to live. "We should evacuate them. They send children out every day. And you could go too."

"Where?"

"Anywhere better than here."

"But the bombardments."

"They'll die here for sure." She bit her tongue—no mother wants to hear these words; then again, no sister wants to say them. "You know it's true."

"There's still time."

The Road of Life was all ice—thick white Ladoga ice, sturdy ice of an unmoving lake. It would hold until at least March. "I'm going, mama."

"Don't be long."

2.

Svetlana wraps her head in a thick grey woolen shawl and wraps her body in an old, oily shearling—her dead father's—and walks down the six flights of stairs (one per floor, third floor is lucky). The cameo brooch is hidden in her mitten and she toggles it on her fingertips, the golden tip of the pin prickling ever so slightly.

The streets shine ghostly white in the dusk, and she watches her felt boots, making sure that they don't step on ice slicks— treacherous pools of darkness in the soft powdery white. She is so focused on avoiding ice, not falling, not breaking her fragile bones, not being caught helpless by the roving gangs of cannibals, that she doesn't notice when someone starts walking along with her, step in step, the smooth swing of his long legs shadowing the uncertain stumble of hers. He smells of earth (its fat, musty aroma was so out of place in the frozen starving city, the stone embankments strangling the black Neva and the sluicing green ice in it in its slow embrace), and she starts thinking of summer without noticing the reason for her thoughts.

Svetlana looks up, finally, as the sun rises and she turns into one of the side streets. A familiar route to the out-of-the-way, the hidden. Wide spaces between old manor houses, narrow streets. She follows the Fontanka embankment for a bit, and then turns again, into Grafskiy Pereulok. Women in thick aprons and boots, clapping their hands in the cold and stomping their feet, speaking in quick hushed half-whispers, "Come here, come here, handsome, potatoes fresh from the fields of out the city, buy a potato for your girl."

Only then Svetlana notices the man who is walking next to her, even though the smell of him is so deep in her nostrils it makes her sneeze. His face is just as out of place as his smell—full and red-cheeked, bright-eyed, healthy. So handsome, so untouched—like a wax sculpture under museum glass. Lips so red.

"How much for potatoes?" she asks the woman.

"What have you got?" The woman draws away a thick covering of canvas off the top of a wooden crate, exposing a few small tubers, malaised and bruised with frost. They would be so sickly sweet in a pot, cooked over their metal stove. More floorboards will have to be peeled off that night—the boys can help with that. And maybe then she could go to the roof with other girls from the neighborhood, to watch out for incendiary bombs. Their building has been lucky so far, but they always have buckets of sand with them to extinguish the foul things should one fall. She stares at the potatoes and lets her thoughts roll leisurely, to distract her from the handsome man standing so close to her, as if he knows her—but how could one know something so alien?

Satisfied with the sight of the potatoes, Svetlana shows the woman her treasure—the cameo brooch left to her mother by grandma Anna.

She nods, and scoops the measly tubers into a newspaper cone; it takes Svetlana all her willpower not to gnaw on them as soon as the newspaper rustles in her mittens.

"Do you mind if I walk with you?" the handsome man says, somewhat belatedly.

She hesitates for a moment—of course, it would be safer with him, unless he decided to hit her and take her potatoes away. She shifts her weight so that the pistol in the shearling pocket rests against her jutting hip. "I don't mind," she finally says. "You can walk where you please."

And back they go, as the dusk slowly lifts and the snow sparkles weakly, as if touched by malaise. They pass two dead bodies, lying by the curb—faces up, eyes closed—and Svetlana wonders if they died like this, side by side, slowly keeling backward, or if someone put them there, pushed them aside to let the traffic through. They pass a small girl carrying half a loaf of bread, clearly visible in its messy newspaper nest— rations for an entire family, looks like, and Svetlana worries that someone would take the bread away from the girl, little as she is and unaware that carrying such treasures openly is dangerous. She stops and waits for the girl to catch up to her, and the man waits too.

The little girl eyes them with suspicion.

"Let me walk you home," Svetlana says. "Do you live far?"

The girl motions east, to the rising sun. "Ulitsa Marata," she says. "Not far."

Svetlana turns to face the man. "Are you coming with us?"

He nods, wordlessly, one corner of his mouth curling shyly but happily.

She wonders if her asking somehow negated her aloof demeanor, rendered it a pretense. Still, she has to take the girl home, even though the two boys wait for the potatoes, all the way back by Neva's embankment.

She follows the girl in silence, and the man follows her—a hierarchy of silent guardians, each watching over the smaller and the weaker one.

"You smell funny," the girl says, spinning around and pinning the man with her stare.

"Can't be helped," he says, smiling shyly still. "You can't help it if your teeth are crooked, can you?"

The girl frowns, clamps her lips shut, and stays quiet until they arrive to a three-storied brick building. "It's just me and grandma now," she says. "Would you like to come in?"

"Some other time," Svetlana says. "I have to take care of my brothers, but maybe I'll bring them by one day, so you can play together."

"Tomorrow?" Light grey eyes up, expectant. Impatient, but how could one not be? It would be foolish to plan ahead for more than a day.

"Tomorrow," Svetlana says.

"I'm Valya," the girl calls out of the cavernous mouth of the entry way, disappearing from view.

"Svetlana," Svetlana calls back.

"Ilya," the man next to her echoes.

3.

Things one needs to extinguish incendiary bombs: buckets of sand, blankets, mittens, several giggling girls. They drag the heavy buckets with effort, heaving them with all the might of their thin shoulders, the shoulder blades and the collarbones straining like twigs under the weight of encasing ice. Their legs wobble in the boot shafts too big for them, like pestles in mortars. And still they laugh and gossip, and stare at the sky.

It's blackout, and from the roof one can see nothing but blackness. I imagine it sometimes, through Svetlana's eyes, straining in this absolute void. Human eyes are made to see, and panic sets in when they can't, and still they strain, trying to reach through the infinite distance of blackness into some pinprick of light. It is so dark here, like under ground. I imagine it would be like this, there.

Ilya shows up, unbidden and silent, and the girls titter more and then silence, after they notice how he follows Svetlana, how he's always helping her with her bucket even though she tells him not to. How both of them avoid accidentally touching their hands together.

He shows up every night they keep watch on the roof ever since. Svetlana doesn't know how he knows—he just appears and sits by her when they rest, or helps with the buckets. They have enough sand up there to extinguish a hellfire, Svetlana thinks, if there was such a thing—but she's a materialist, and knows that there isn't.

He also comes by in the mornings when she goes out to wait in a breadline or to work at the factory, or to take the boys to visit Valya, the girl they walked home on the day of their first meeting. He never goes in with them though, but waits outside, through the cold, through the wind.

Valya's grandmother, Olga Petrovna, is old enough to die soon even without the hunger. She often cries that she's not strong enough to refuse her portion entirely, even though she only eats half and gives the rest to her granddaughter, and to Svetlana's brothers when they happen along. Sometimes she gives Svetlana jewelry to take to the black market. "Get some bread. Don't bring it here though," she says, "or we'll eat it all up. Take it to the hospital across the river. They need it."

Svetlana does as she is told, and Ilya follows, asking for nothing but mute solidarity. He refuses food when offered, but doesn't seem to suffer as much as Olga Petrovna does.

Olga Petrovna has stories and theories. She tells Svetlana that there's food in the city, only Zhdanov and other party officials keep it to themselves; she says that there's grain in Vavilov's

Institute, the Genofond scientists keep all kinds of wheat and rice and every grain known to man. She also doesn't think cannibals are really cannibals. "You're young," she tells Svetlana. "You don't even know who upyri are."

"I know," Svetlana whispers, eyes downcast. The very word, *Upyr*, makes her skin crawl, materialism notwithstanding. There was never a Russian child not scared half to death by the stories of those dead who rose from their graves and ate the living.

"You just remember," Olga Petrovna says, "if they ever come for you, all you have to do is to call them for what they are. 'Upyr,' you must say, and he'll turn into a man—for a little bit, at least."

Svetlana smiles, imagining herself confronting a gang of cannibals with words. "Men are still men. They're still dangerous."

"But if they're human, they won't try to eat you."

Svetlana shrugs, not convinced. With hunger like that, why wouldn't they try to eat anything alive and made of meat?

4.

In her mind, Svetlana never recognized her relationship with Ilya as courtship. It was only when Yasha and Vanya, re-energized by playing at Valya's quiet, cavernous apartment, as barren of floorboards as any other, and by her grandmother's stories and slivers of bread she fed them throughout (children ate from her hands, opening their mouths wide and stretching their thin necks, like baby birds) started teasing. "Bride and groom," they started in a whisper and then, growing bolder, in a singsong, when Ilya and Svetlana walked side by side behind them, heading home to mother. "Bride and groom."

Svetlana blushed and looked at her boots, the slicks of ice, the river swelling up leaden and white up ahead, and at the boy's shaven heads, blue under their hats—anywhere but Ilya's steady gaze and his hale earth smell.

Ilya murmured under his breath, as embarrassed as she felt. She couldn't quite make out the words, but thought that he said "Heart" or "My heart," and her stomach felt warm and tight.

When they reached her house, she looked up at him, into his sparkling eyes. "You can come in, if you wish."

She told the boys to be quiet or she'd box their ears if they breathed a word to mother, probably asleep in her room. The boys tittered, and she twisted Yasha's ear harder than she meant—that quieted them right down. Ilya waited patiently as she herded the boys to kiss their sleeping mother (her breath so shallow) and then to their own room.

She was not on the air-raid duty that night, and she motioned for Ilya to follow her into her room; he instead remained standing as if stuck to the spot, until she whispered fiercely, "What are you waiting for? Come on."

She didn't light the candle and undressed in the dark. She could feel Ilya's solid presence, smell him as she unbraided her hair. She slipped under the covers and soon he followed, the mattress shifting under his weight, his body dense like iron. They lay side by side, their arms barely touching, until Svetlana fell asleep.

In the morning, he was gone.

5.

In the morning, she also discovered that her mother was up unusually early—a fat lardy candle burned in the communal kitchen, and mother, wrapped into two shawls over her nightgown, coat, and boots, her bare venous legs ghostly white in the dusk, sighed and pulled the folding kitchen table to the center. Svetlana's heart sank.

"The neighbor's dead," mother said. "Something awful happened."

Svetlana raised an eyebrow—dead was normal. "Awful?"

"The door was ajar this morning," mother said. "Someone must've broken in. Yasha heard her whimpering and woke me, but when I got there, she already bled out. People are turning savage."

On numb feet, Svetlana hurried down the hall, to the usually closed Lyuda's door. Thoughts buzzed in her head, without taking shape but content with general notions—cannibals, someone killed her, wonder if Ilya's all right.

The woman lay in her bed, and one could think her sleeping if it wasn't for the wide gash in her neck, an extra mouth, blooming in a red obscene flower across her neck. The mattress was soaked with dark blood, but they could probably still sell it, or give it to someone who needs a bed, even if blood-soaked.

The edges of the wound were torn and raw, and there were definitive toothmarks. Svetlana tried to imagine a serrated knife that would leave a cut like that, but the mind rejected the possibility. She folded a doily from the bed table into a dense white rectangle, and stuffed it into the wound, and watched the doily turn slowly pink.

6.

It is important for a city in crisis, no matter how terrible, to maintain elements of normalcy, something people can anchor their sanity to. This is why there's still theater and musical concerts, and this is why when Ilya invites her to see a play, Svetlana accepts. She insists that the boys should come too, and Ilya buys them tickets to see *Les Miserables*—Gavroche is being played by a middle-aged woman, but otherwise the play is fine, and the boys seem to enjoy themselves. Both have been subdued lately and laugh little. They don't even tease when Ilya comes home with them again.

This time, Svetlana is asleep—a sick heavy nightmare sleep—before her head even touches the pillow.

And as I tell you this, I know that you're wondering the same thing that I and my brother, although still too young at nine, wondered about: why didn't she have any suspicions? I have my own theory. I do think that some facts are merely too terrible to consider. Love complicates everything further.

She has nightmares about Ilya leaning over her, his chest pressing on top of hers like a tombstone, stilling her heart, stealing her breath, "My heart," he says. "I hold you in my hands. For the sake of your brothers . . . "

Mother is dead next morning.

7.

Svetlana decided now that she was the head of the household, the boys would have to go. She bundled up Yasha and Vanya—or rather, Vanya, my brother, and me, and gave us all the food she managed to scavenge in these past days. She gave us our clothes, wrapped in blankets, and we stood in the hallway like two tiny transients. "They will be taking more children out this morning," she told us as we walked side by side with her. "Or maybe the next. You must go though, while the ice is still strong. We'll go by Valya's house, see if Olga Petrovna would send her out too."

All the while, her gaze cast about, looking for Ilya, but he failed to show up that day. Who can tell why.

None of us mentioned the dead kindergarten teacher and our mother, lying side by side on the kitchen table, with their windpipes torn out and gnawed raw.

Olga Petrovna, superstitious as she was (Svetlana said to the children that it was because she was from a village, not city-born like us), crossed herself. "When you take them to be buried," she said, "don't take them out of the door—go through a wall or a window. And don't carry the bodies along the roads."

Svetlana sighed. "We live on the third floor, we can't just toss them out of the window. And it's silly anyway."

"Not when an upyr takes a life. Do you want your mother to become one of the cursed? Do you want the devil to take her?"

"There's no such thing as upyr," Svetlana said, and paced back and forth across the cold corridor while the children waited, huddled, by the entryway. "Or devil, for that matter."

"Who gnawed them then?"

"Cannibals broke in."

"And left the bodies?"

"Someone startled them." Svetlana froze to the spot. "I think it was my friend who did—he . . . "

Olga Petrovna didn't need to hear the rest. "Dear child!" she cried. "Daughter! You brought a stranger home? Do you even know what he is?"

"Just a young man," Svetlana said. "A handsome fellow. In any case, I only came to ask if Valya would like to come with us. I want to send the boys out, by the Road of Life. I know there are bombs, but at least they have a chance of getting out."

Olga Petrovna nodded slowly. "Better than them dying here, of hunger or worse." She gave Svetlana a piercing look. "Listen to me, daughter, and if there's anything you'd do, do this one thing: find out where your handsome fellow goes when you're not with him."

"How'd I do that?"

"By cunning." Olga Petrovna hobbled into the darkened cave of her living room, and returned momentarily with a ball of uneven black yarn. "Next time you see him, you tie that string to the hem of his coat. And then you follow along. I'll go get Valya ready now."

Svetlana took the children to the rallying point, where they waited for hours in a long, silent throng of children, old people, a few pregnant women. It was almost dark when the crowd started to move and the engines revved up ahead. Svetlana hugged the boys and cried over them and made them promise to be good and to write and, after the war is over, to find her. Just as she kissed the boys tearfully goodbye, a woman—short, squat, in military boots and a man's jacket—walked up to her.

"We're taking the smallest ones today," and motioned at Yasha (me). "Bring him back next week—they promise more trucks then. Today we have no space for him now, just the little ones."

"Please," Svetlana clutched her hands to her chest. "He's just one boy."

The woman nodded. "And there's no place for him. Do you know how many we turned away today? We're taking the small ones though." Her large mittened hands swallowed Vanya's and Valya's, and the three of them were gone.

Svetlana and Yasha returned home.

The girls from the neighborhood—the same ones that were on air-raid duty with Svetlana—helped her dress the two dead women and to cover up the gashes on their throats. They took them on a sled and carted them to the site of the nearest common grave, near Nekropol. The earth was too hard to dig, and they left them with the rest of the bodies awaiting burial, alone in the dark.

Only two of them in the large communal apartment now, and barely any wood. They sat together under the covers, their breath white mist, shimmering in the darkness like anti-materialist ghosts. They sleep with their arms around each other, secretly grateful for a warm body to hold.

8.

Many children died while evacuating. Many survived, and were placed into orphanages around the country. Most went to school at their new places of residence, and lied about where they were from and what their fathers died of (a living father was a rare treasure, and yet a potential embarrassment—he better be a war hero.) Most of the fathers died in the war, best if it happened in Germany or in the Stalingrad battle. Having a father who died in the siege is a liability, and this is why most of the siege kids lie—having a father who starved to death is only a step above a father who was executed for being the enemy of the people. On the playground, every father is a war hero. Some kids are lucky enough to have fathers and brothers who are war heroes, and they never fail to mention the fact. I hope that Vanya learned the correct lies quickly.

9.

The next morning, Svetlana tells Yasha to sleep and not to open the door to anyone, and leaves for the factory. She is not sure if it's her shift or if the factory is even open, but she goes anyway. She is relieved and terrified to discover Ilya waiting just outside.

"Where are your brothers?" he asks.

"Gone. Evacuated, the boys and Valya." (She is hoping that Yasha is not looking out of the window, like he often does—seeing her coming and going. She is too afraid to look herself and betray him.) "I have to be at the factory."

"I'll walk you," he says.

She wraps her arm under his, gingerly, and they walk arm in arm, step in step, in silence. The sun is out and the river sparkles, and all the while her fingers are working, working, to wind the ragged black thread Olga Petrovna gave her through the buttonhole of his sleeve.

He doesn't seem to notice as they walk, or even as he kisses her goodbye, his mouth moist and cold, lips liver-colored, pressed against hers for one suffocating moment, and then he is gone—walking away toward the embankment, the left bank. He never even noticed that the factory gates were closed.

She waits for the black thread to unravel and lets it slack as he disappears from view. Then, she follows him. They walk again, step in step, separated by a length of black woolen thread. It hangs like silk of a monstrous spiderweb, like a curving meridian line—she imagines it as a thick jagged crack in white ice, running across lake Ladoga, separating her from the evacuated and the saved, a thick woolen thread, fuzzy and itchy, that connects her to him without ever touching. Cleaved, in both senses of the word, along the embankment.

He leaves the embankment near the Admiralty, and goes west. West and west and west, crossing streets and bridges, and Svetlana is so busy keeping the thread in her hand not too taut, not too slack, that she doesn't even notice the names of streets and rivers—Moika, Fontanka, all the same.

She doesn't know this place, and the thread is no longer pulling or unraveling. She is looking at a low metal fence. "What is this?" she asks herself, but a passerby mistakes her bewilderment for curiosity.

"Volkovskoe Lutheran Cemetery," he says, and wraps his wind-chapped face in the wide collar of his thickly padded canvas coat. "Only they're not burying anyone—the ground's frozen solid."

"I know," Svetlana whispers, and follows the thread, along the fence, through the ornate grate. Her feet are numb and her fingers tingle as if it's a live wire, not a woolen thread she's holding. She follows it, unyielding and fateful like the needle of the compass, until the thread snakes across already frozen clumps of dirt, strewn about as if thrown by hooves and paws, and disappears under a tombstone, empty of any names save for a lone star in its left upper corner.

10.

Svetlana did not remember her way back home. Even the hunger retreated, giving place to profound, impossible resignation. It was the second time that year that her world tumbled upside down, and everything that she knew was right was proven to be otherwise: first, it was her secret, unexamined belief that she would be all right that came to an abrupt end in August; now it was . . . she refused to name it even in her mind, no matter how the imagined Olga Petrovna tried to claw through her thoughts, through the erected mental wall of distracting thoughts and resonant determination to *not think about that, you mustn't think about that, you mustn't think that word, you mustn't.*

"Call it by its name," Olga Petrovna insisted, her face clear in Svetlana's mind despite her decisively squinted shut eyes. "It will destroy him."

No, not destroy. Make him human.

"And then what?" Svetlana wondered aloud. No one ever seemed to know the answer, it seemed—once you made those creatures human, you killed them, the wisdom went. Otherwise, you couldn't touch them. But could you let them live?

"I'm hungry," Yasha said the moment she got home. "Can I go where Vanya went? They say there's food there."

"Soon," she promised. "Come now, we'll sleep and the time will go by faster. Before you know it, you'll be in some village in Ukraine, and it'll be warm, and they will have fresh milk in clay jars, and plums and apples and cherries you can pick off the tree."

"And bread and butter," Yasha sighed.

11.

Human arms are a thin thing, especially the arms of a girl starved half to death—such a trifling thing, such an easy barrier to bypass. It didn't matter how much Svetlana hugged Yasha to her in her sleep—just to keep him, until next day, next week, when maybe they would have a place for a larger boy who would soon be large enough for labor, for digging graves in frozen cemeteries and for hauling buckets of sand onto the roofs.

She woke up because the heavy suffocating presence on her chest and the emptiness of her arms, the sticky trace of something cold on her fingers, and a loud, wet chewing. *Soup and dumplings,* she thought in her fogged-up mind, *bread and butter and treacle,* before she heard cartilage and a long whistle of a windpipe suddenly too wide for breath.

It was so dark that even with her eyes wide she couldn't see—but she shut them again, and covered her face with her sticky hands, and screamed, "Upyr, upyr, leave him be!" as loud as she could. In the dark, she flailed, looking for something to hold onto, but there was only darkness seeping between her fingers.

12.

It takes one a while to get used to talking about oneself in third person. I am Yasha, and yet not entirely. I sleep in the Volkovskoe Lutheran Cemetery, even though we're not Lutherans or even German. I wish Ilya was here with me, to explain things, to tell me why I was always so cold and why my own sister wouldn't look at me, wouldn't call me by my name.

That night, he didn't eat me up like he did my mother—he left just enough of a soul glimmer that I woke up under the pile of frozen bodies and clawed my way to the surface. Even though people were hollow-eyed and starving, many wanted to take in an orphan, so I survived without him.

I only learned what happened to him a few days later, when there was an air raid. What that old bat, Olga Petrovna, said about upyr becoming human for a while was true. What she didn't know was that once human, the upyr would seek death—he would go to the roof of some apartment building and wait for the German bombs among the giggling, gossiping girls and the buckets of sand. He would die a hero's death, he would cover an incendiary bomb with his own body and save everyone, and the newspaper would write about him. People would know his name.

And so I wait by my sister's door and beg her, I beg her for the word and a shot from my father's pistol, so that Vanya could finally have a hero for a brother.

PUBLICATION HISTORY

"A Short Encyclopedia of Lunar Seas" © 2008 by Ekaterina Sedia. Originally published in *The Endicott Studio Journal of Mythic Arts*, August 2008.

"Citizen Komarova Finds Love" © 2009 by Ekaterina Sedia. Originally published in *Exotic Gothic 3* (ed. Danel Olson), Ash-Tree Press, 2009.

"Tin Cans" © 2010 by Ekaterina Sedia. Originally published in *Haunted Legends* (eds. Ellen Datlow and Nick Mamatas), Tor, 2010.

"One, Two, Three" © 2009 by Ekaterina Sedia. Originally published in *Hatter Bones* (ed. Jeremy Needle), Evil Nerd Empire, 2009.

"You Dream" © 2010 by Ekaterina Sedia. Originally published in *Dark Faith* (eds. Maurice Broaddus and Jerry Gordon), Apex Publications, 2010.

"Zombie Lenin" © 2007 by Ekaterina Sedia. Originally published in *Fantasy* (ed. Sean Wallace), Prime Books, 2007.

"Ebb and Flow" © 2009 by Ekaterina Sedia. Originally published in *Japanese Dreams* (ed. Sean Wallace), Lethe Press, 2009.

ABOUT THE AUTHOR

Ekaterina Sedia resides in the Pinelands of New Jersey. Her critically-acclaimed novels, *The Secret History of Moscow*, *The Alchemy of Stone*, *The House of Discarded Dreams*, and *Heart of Iron*, were published by Prime Books. Her short stories have sold to *Analog*, *Baen's Universe*, *Subterranean* and *Clarkesworld*, as well as numerous anthologies, including *Haunted Legends* and *Magic in the Mirrorstone*. She is also the editor of *Paper Cities*, *Running with the Pack*, *Bewere the Night*, and *Wilful Impropriety*. Visit her at www.ekaterinasedia.com.